AF279003

The Commander's Daughter
By Colin Moerdyke

Universum Publishing

Published in 2018 by Universum Publishing Ltd.
A Universum Group Company.

Copyright ©2018 Colin Moerdyke

Cover art and illustrations by Eric Williams and Colin Moerdyke
Typesetting by vava.lv
©2018 Universum Publishing Ltd

All rights reserved.
No part of this publication may be reproduced, stored in a retrieval system, or
transmitted in any form or by any means, electronic, mechanical, photocopying,
recording or otherwise, without the prior permission of the copyright owner

ISBN 978-0-9954541-1-8 (paperback)
Second Edition.

To my brother

2018

Shadows come at night
Night is when you close your eyes
And fly up-up-up away home
To the land of the shadows…

Harvie sits on the floor, cross-legged, the cold metal side of her gun pressed to her cheek. It's soothing. She must have a fever, and if they are still alive by the end of the night she should ask Curly Paw for a pill from the medikit they stole last week.

Bone to bone, dust to dust…

Stinky throws a smoke grenade. Blue mist curls up, turning the rays of light sifting through the metal grid above the ducts into a semi-transparent web. Somehow this gives her an illusory feeling of safety, as if the lines are solid.

Packsta does what packsta must…

Growler gets up and walks around, checking their ammo for the last time. He doesn't check hers. Instead, he drops: "Take down as many as you can, then drop the guns and run. Hide. If they find you – cry."

Packsta comes, packsta goes…

"Good hunting, Packsta," she says.

Growler will die tonight; she knows it. He's getting too old, almost sixteen. He'll keep killing until the little ones are safe. The Litter always protects its young. She's a pup, not yet twelve. She must live.

Litter runs, Litter growls…

In the blue mist she can only see the silhouettes of her mates: heads, sometimes shoulders, or a hand passing a gun. No sobs, no whispers – only the humming, the singing of "The Death Chant."

Water drops, air howls…

She moves the power output slider into the "max" position. If the Litter has to kill, it kills.

Anywhere, nowhere, all in one, one in all.

* * *

Harvie pulled an octagun from under her pillow and checked the time on the target tracking display. 04:18. The handle under her palm smelt of warm sweat and semi-absorbed mediskin that encased the thumb she'd broken in last week's training. She must have slept the whole night with her hand on the gun. Only yesterday she'd sworn to Jen Takura that she'd kicked the habit for good, and would move her gun to the locked weapons cabinet. "Not bloody likely," Jen had said. Duh.

Harvie wiped the gun with the corner of her bed sheet and inspected it as she always did. She took out the battery charger and put it back to reset the gun to default, just in case she had messed it up in her sleep. She'd never done that before, but who knew? The dream, even though she'd had it many times, didn't feel like usual. It had left her with a tangle in her stomach, anticipation for a menace much greater than the one from which she had awakened.

Like many times before, she'd dreamed of the last night she'd spent with her Litter pack, and the first night at the headquarters of the Unian Security Forces. That night Harvie had come down with a fever that nearly killed her; it kept her in bed for almost two months. The USF doctor said Harvie had contracted it living rough in the tunnels, but she knew better. Why live when she no longer had to fight to stay alive?

All in one, one in all…

Yet she'd lived. Four long years had passed since then, and she was still alive, and no longer eleven.

Packstas believed "The Shadow Chant" chased away bad dreams like this one. Harvie wasn't so certain. But today she might give it a try. She closed her eyes and whispered the chant words, scanning through the patchwork of images in her head, hoping they'd fade for good.

Shadows are watching over you
Whisper, whisper, calling
Stretch their hands to take you away
To the land of the shadows…

She sat up and pressed the side of the barrel to her cheek, just like she had in the dream. The cold metal felt soothing, helping her break free from the memory that had left a tense feeling in her chest and limbs, as if her combat exosuit had malfunctioned and shrunk in, crushing her trapped body. Yet all she wore were silk pyjama shorts with a matching top the Takuras had given her for her fifteenth birthday. Jen called the colour "steel grey" and said it matched Harvie's eyes. Harvie couldn't care less, but natural silk fabric and her skin turned out to be a perfect match too.

It was the first time Harvie had slept in something that didn't feel like sandpaper. Ever since, she'd fallen into the habit of wearing it every night, for almost a year now.

Ten months and twenty-nine days to be precise. She'd leave the outfit tossed onto the floor every morning before changing into her sim tracksuit, and later find it again in her drawer, clean and neatly folded, begging for her to make one last effort of the day and not pass out on top of her bed in her tracksuit, soaked in sweat and sometimes blood. Most mornings she didn't even remember how she'd managed to put it on, but she'd wake up wearing it. The handle of the gun under her pillow would feel cold and dry, meaning she'd slept through another night without dreaming.

04:20. Harvie stood up. Her bed melted, becoming one with the varistate floor. Her bedding and her pillow sunk into a milky pool that hardened and turned the colour of brushed steel, the same as the room's walls and the ceiling. Harvie liked her room this way – no fake VR windows or interiors, no pretending this room was something other than what it was: a varistate-filled residential cell inside a space station's module.

A place to unload, leaving everything else outside. Just a few concealed cabinets to keep her private octagon collections and a few trinkets like a book of fairy tales that Kato Takura had read to her while she was recovering from the fever.

She put her palm to the wall to open a hidden drawer. It tingled for a second while performing a bio-identity scan and then a hole opened. Harvie put her gun inside, and reached deeper. Here it was. She pulled the doll out: a palm-sized girl with silvery white hair, wearing an orange kimono. *"Konnichiwa Harubi-sama,"* she whispered and bowed. *"Nemui desu, ne?"*

The doll's facial features had worn off with time, and it did indeed look dozy. "What have you been up to?"

Harubi didn't answer. The doll never said a word, not once in the past twelve years. It simply followed her, from her mother's funeral, to the cabin on her dad's ship. To the rescue pod that took her away from the exploding *Ranger*. To the Litter lair on an orbital station, once abandoned and then reclaimed by USF. Then back into the hands of the same person who had given it to her in the first place – General Kato Takura, once her father's loyal friend and ally. His wife, Jen, had given the doll a good wash, almost restoring Harubi to her old glory.

Harvie stroked the doll's hair and put it back. Let it enjoy the rest it deserved, in a tiny dark wall alcove, guarding Harvie's collection of custom-made firearms. She closed the drawer.

Crossing the room, now completely void of any furniture, she took off her pyjamas and stepped into the shower. A see-through splash screen blocked it from the rest of the room. She closed her eyes and pressed her palms against black marble tiles. They were the real thing, not haptic varistate, even though nobody but her could tell the difference. Rivulets of hot water streamed down her hair and shoulders, soothing, clearing her mind.

Four years ago showering used to be a torture: water rasped her skin, burned her scalp. Harvie could feel every drop and what was worse, she could hear every drop and together they sounded like a stampeding army of spider-like tankbots marching through service tunnels, every sound magnified by the emptiness. She'd fight for her life with whoever happened to be in charge of her grooming. "It's like washing a cat," Jen would say, spraying mediskin over fresh scratches. After a while nobody else would even try to get close.

Now water still hurt, but it was a good pain; the kind that reminded her that she was still alive when she felt void, formless like blank varistate. "Good" pain gave form to her body. It defined its boundaries and put it firmly under her control: every nerve and muscle, every square millimetre of her ghostly-white skin. Feeling alive was to feel whole, and that wholeness often eluded her, making her wonder whether she had in fact perished with the rest of the Litter and become a Shadow, whatever that meant.

With her eyes still closed, Harvie turned the shower off. Water drops rolled off her hair onto the black stone tiles with a rhythmic sound. She turned on the air dryer and ran her fingers through her hair, wondering whether it might be time to cut it; once again it had grown into an unruly ashen mop. Ponytails didn't work; the hairbands hurt with "bad" pain: annoying, distracting. She'd rather have her hair shorter, but for some reason Jen Takura would never let her cut it above shoulder-length or change its natural ash-blonde colour. And one never should question the advice of the principal of the USF Cadet Programme. Not if they wanted to graduate.

Harvie wanted it badly, to put an end to all of it: The gruelling study to maintain the top 10 per cent grade average at school in addition to her cadet training; the bone-breaking PT. And the worst of it: four years of Jen Takura.

"We could adopt her," Jen had said once, tucking her in bed. Harvie had just been discharged from the hospital, no stronger than a rag doll, spending her days in half-sleep not much different from a coma. Jen spoke Japanese, not yet aware that Harvie could understand every word. "But she'll never adopt us." She was right about that. Jen was right about many things, even though Harvie hated to admit it.

By now Harvie should have had enough of General Takura's wife, a skinny redhead always dressed in blue denim overalls as if ready for a full day's work at a ranch; of her voice, low, deep and forceful, with a broad Kansas accent and a certain coarseness that came with a lot of shouting at teenage girls with octaguns. Four years of putting up with Jen's dry sarcasm: her sharp remarks, always painful, always hitting the target. Always a "bad pain" at first. But somehow it felt better after a while. Connected. Whatever that meant.

Four years as a USF cadet. Technically, Harvie should be able to graduate this year in the rank of USF Junior Officer. But then technically she shouldn't be on the programme at all. Most people had to be at least sixteen to enrol. Even today she was still a few weeks short. General Takura might have had enough clout to put an eleven-year-old on the training programme, but it would take a unanimous agreement of the whole Unian Board to promote an underage cadet to a USF officer. Not bloody likely. Her perks were already above a cadet's level and she'd done a dozen field assignments she shouldn't technically have been cleared for. Technicalities were never her forte, from the moment she was born in the medical cabin of a battleship.

Harvie returned to her room and opened a concealed wardrobe cabinet. The Supplies had already delivered a fresh change of clothes for the week – a pack of disposable undies, three workout suits, two sets of military-style uniforms. She changed into a combat track workout suit and picked a sim weapon, a custom-made precise replica of a closed-space combat octagun, without the octalon charge battery. Another cadet would never have been allowed to keep even a toy of this weapon in her room, let alone the real thing under her pillow. Certainly not a girl who screamed at night and pulled the weapon out with her eyes closed, gasping for air, aiming at enemies only she could see.

But whenever Harvie pulled the gun out, the screaming would stop. Just like Jen Takura had predicted.

No, Jen hadn't said that, not exactly. It was Harvie's second week at USF, and she still had the fever and she screamed every night until a nurse would come and sedate her, but then Kato Takura came and stopped the drugs, and brought along his wife to deal with the rest. "Just give her a damn gun," Jen had said, and when another voice muttered something indistinct, she snapped. "I don't give a horse shit if she kills someone. We don't run a boarding school here. If they let her kill them, it's their problem."

4:28. Harvie put a sweatband on to keep her hair in place, put her sim octagun and a couple of water bottles into a beaten-up backpack with the USF logo. Two track runs before breakfast, then maybe two more to make sure her sim rating stayed well into the four digits. Last time she let it slip into the hundreds, Jen suggested in front of the whole assembly to add a comfort blanket and a dummy to Harvie's "toy collection." None of the cadets smirked or chuckled. Instead her classmates went out of their way to express their deepest sympathies.

That same night, Harvie found under her door a pile of chewed-up teddy bears, empty milk bottles and boxed pacifiers with bows made of flashing pink ribbons. Not a small feat in a space station located a few thousand miles away from the nearest infant. Someone had even procured a pack of reusable nappies and put one on a stuffed toy pup with stitched crosses in place of eyes. A note pinned to its chest read: *Litter always protects the young. All in one, one in all.*

Jen might've been a horse whisperer, but nobody tames a wild horse to give it an easy ride.

These memories were toxic; they could eat Harvie's brain up like maggots, if she let them crawl inside her head. She rubbed the back of her neck, running once again through her mental check of the plan for the day. Two sim tracks, medium level for an easy rating boost, breakfast, then about an hour of schoolwork, then another track – this time a real thing, the highest complexity level – lunch, four more study hours while her body recovered, martial arts class, bloody homework again, quick dinner if she had time. She had to find time; Jen would take penalty points off her rating for each missed meal. Triple points if it happened two days in a row. That Harvie accepted without a grudge. She knew she could go days without food, not even noticing she was hungry until it knocked her off her feet. Taking care of her body had never been Harvie's particular strength.

The combat sim track, unmanned at this hour, smelled of stale sweat and wet rubber. A dim security light cast long shadows across the empty industrial warehouse-sized floor covered with worn-out mats, hosed overnight with water. Harvie stepped into the freshly repainted yellow circle and waited for the sim console to boot up and scan her biosig. In a moment two projection screens appeared at her face level, one with the picture of Harvie's head and torso, another one with her record sheet. Nine hundred and ninety-eight. Still a good 200 points higher than any of the cadets in her training group, but it didn't matter. Fifteen hundred, said Jen, or you won't graduate. If Harvie wanted to stay on the same terms as others she could, but then she wouldn't be out of the programme till she turned eighteen. If Harvie wanted any more exceptions for herself, her performance had to stay exceptional.

She selected the medium level, as she had planned, but then hesitated. Perhaps it was time to up the game. Her school term results were coming in and she knew she had done a lame job on her Japanese essay. Anything less than 90 per cent and she'd earn ten more penalty points off her score, plus a point for every per cent less than ninety. Kato Takura had thrown that into the deal for her. His wife had always been relaxed about academics. For Jen Takura, manners mattered, not grades.

Harvie moved the mission difficulty level to "medium high," then after another second's hesitation, to "high." She'd done that level before, many times. No reason to go easy on herself now. An amber system message alert blinked at the bottom of her record sheet. Harvie dismissed it; it was just a reminder that this was not her recommended setting for a morning workout. She could ignore the amber ones. The reds were the ones to worry about. Three red alerts in a row, and the sim mission would abort and its score would reset to zero. It had happened to her before.

She confirmed her choice and scanned through the mission specs. *Setting: Nearspace, small urban station.* She had to get to the third floor of a busy shopping mall, locate a pebble parked on the roof, get inside and start the engine. *Time to complete: 5 minutes. Number of enemy's forces: unknown. Weapons: unknown. Undercover or not: unknown.*

Difficult? Harvie shrugged. On a good day she could pack three of these into a 30-minute workout, with short breaks in between. She chose a lighter sim gun and put it on a sling under her black hoodie. Open carry in a civil setting would earn her a red alert straight away.

Just as she always did before launching the sim, she inhaled, taking in the vast emptiness of the training room and its silence filled with barely audible hums and rattles. Then she pressed "Start."

2

The sim room came to life. The walls bulged and bent, exploding with a myriad of glistening metal cylinders – varistate core bots – that joined together into metal platforms, scaffoldings, and partitions. Three or four floors? It was too quick to notice for sure. A stucco facade, brightly lit with neon signs and projected adverts, covered the interiors before Harvie could get a good look. Never mind. It would be cheating anyway.

Another cheat trick would be to linger in the yellow circle for a few more seconds. The mission timer wouldn't start until she stepped out, but she hated doing that even with nobody around to notice. She hadn't made it this far by cutting corners. She adjusted the hoodie to make sure once again that the gun sling was not visible, and stepped through the mall's doors.

A whirlwind of noises, smells, lights and sounds assaulted her straight away: Sensory distractions, her weak spot. Harvie could lose up to thirty precious seconds just trying to tune them out. She paid no attention to the security guard at the door – very unlikely a threat – and headed straight into the crowd of virtual shoppers.

Not so virtual, it turned out, when a twenty-something man on a hoverscooter bumped into her shoulder. While most of the shoppers were simple 3D projections to create a feel of a busy marketplace, there always were a few android-like ones, with a varistate core. She had no way of knowing which was which from a distance.

"Hey you, watch it!" the man shouted. A few shoppers turned their heads. The security guard at the door moved towards her. If he tried to talk to her, she would lose precious time. Now making it to the top in five minutes didn't seem as easy as before.

"Sorry," Harvie said, forcing out a smile. The sim would register all her verbal responses and make the dummies act accordingly. The man with a hoverscooter muttered something and sped away. Harvie glanced back. The security guard at the door paced nonchalantly past a sweet shop. All seemed fine, but something didn't feel right. No time to think about it now; she'd tackle the problems as they appeared.

Harvie spotted an escalator at the end of the hall and dashed towards the rainbow-coloured array of stepping stones that slowly drifted upwards. She walked briskly, dodging the shoppers, trying to keep her pace natural so she didn't trigger any "suspect behaviour" responses from the sim. The closer she got to the stairs, the more she could sense the nauseating smell of fried bananas from an ice-cream parlour reeking of burnt palm oil and some other concoctions of unknown origin. *C'mon,* she thought. *It never smells that bad in real life, this sim is so rigged!*

As if the system could read her thoughts, the smell only intensified and then a loud, off-tune singing burst from the loudspeakers: *"Happy birthday to youuuuuuu, happy birthday, dear Xin Li, happy birthday to..."*

Block it. Harvie stopped and closed her eyes for a second. Roof. Get to the roof. A toddler ran into her path, chasing a vintage toy police car, flashing lights, sirens and all. He tripped over her foot, fell, and began wailing. More looks from the shoppers. Harvie gently picked the boy up and smiled. Manners. Blend in.

About a minute was already gone, Harvie reckoned as she walked up the escalator's steps, and she hadn't yet left the ground floor. Her blending-in strategy wasn't quite working out. She looked up. A man stood on the opposite descending stairway, staring at her. Definitely the same man she'd bumped into at the entrance, minus the hoverscooter, plus a baseball cap. Harvie steeled inside. The sim never used the same face models without a reason. Yet the man was going down, away from her – why? A few seconds later their bodies became level. The man pulled out a gun and shot at her, close range.

Harvie ducked before her mind consciously registered the gun. A woman next to her yelped and clutched her bulging stomach, eyes wide with a primal fear of a mother about to lose an unborn child. A system message flashed at Harvie's eye level: *Red Alert. Civilian Casualty.* The escalator froze and a few people above Harvie dashed to help the woman. Someone grabbed Harvie's arm and yelled into her ear: "Are you okay, kid?"

Screw manners. Harvie pushed the shopper to the side and ran up the stairs, elbowing the dummies. "Miss, miss!" someone yelled at her back. "Can anyone stop her?" The upstairs' security guard blocked her way. Likely a civilian, unarmed. *Can't shoot him, but* – Harvie pulled her gun out. "Let me go," she ordered. The guard slowly raised his arms and stepped back. Tunnels, now. At least she wouldn't amass any more collateral damage in there.

Harvie ran towards the back door of a lingerie boutique, knocking over a couple of hangers. She pushed through a barricade of boxes and cleared the access to a small door marked "Authorised personnel only." Which one of the shops had access to service tunnels was a hunch, based on her firsthand knowledge of the space station's hidden underbelly. Litter's nighttime raids on the shops had kept packstas fed and clothed; and the experience proved priceless in the sims.

She shot twice a couple of inches below the digital lock. A faint whiff of smoke curled from the hole. Harvie put her fingers inside and pulled out a bunch of wires. *Red, blue, purple on the top – pop! – Here goes the lock. Do it quick, do it right and packstas gonna eat tonight.* What Litter chants lacked in verse quality, they made up for in practical mnemonics.

Sneaking into the familiar world of dimmed lights, hushed sounds and steady, predictable smells of unmanned infrastructure had always been a relief. But this time Harvie felt an uneasy knot in her stomach as she climbed the steel ladder inside the water pipeline duct. A soft but persistent background hum didn't quite belong in the place and she couldn't work out its origin. If something felt wrong in a sim, there was always a reason – unless, of course, it was just another sensory distraction.

She had to get into an air duct; they always led to the roof – the legacy of mainland architecture. Some things were only too predictable in their lack of practical sense in Nearspace. Like roof ventilation ducts. The breathing air mix always came from downlevel, gravity-wise. The sims followed the design to a tee, stupidity and all.

Speaking of stupidity – a chilling realisation hit Harvie: she hadn't blocked the tunnel access door behind her. A rookie mistake. A medium-level sim would let it slide, but not this one. She stopped for a moment and listened to any human or bot movements inside the ducts. The distracting hum grew louder, but finally she could place it: firefighting pumps refilling sprinkler tanks. Nothing to worry about.

Less than a minute left. She might just make it, but there was no way she could do another two sims like this one in a row. The dream had drained too much of her strength this morning; she was sloppy, unfocused. Maybe things would get better after breakfast. Harvie pulled a heavy grid off the air duct, climbed inside, and swore. Instead of the roof it ended at the side of the building, on the third-floor level.

Harvie looked down. A fall from this height would be cushioned by the training room mats, but the sim would pronounce her dead and abort the mission, with a zero score. She was sure she might be somewhere around a thirty-five to forty mark, could easily walk away with fifty points to her record. Worth trying. She aimed at the narrow walkway that ran along the wall about two metres below the duct and prepared to jump.

A flash of light blinded her. *Amber alert. Firearm damage. Severity: medium low.* Gunshot wounds were the most unreal thing in the sim, hurting nothing but one's score and ego. But too much virtual damage meant a death call from the sim. A cadet with three death calls in a row would lose a good fifty points off her score. Jen called it the "You only live twice penalty."

No more time to lose. Harvie jumped. She knew she wouldn't make it before she landed; she'd put too much force into it and overshot. She went down two floors and crashed onto the roof of a glass-covered passage connecting two build-ings. A sharp burst of pain pierced her leg. Broken? *Red alert. Severe physical damage.*

"Shut up, you!" Harvie's anger swelled up. It was just a damn leg, couldn't possibly be more than amber. The man in the baseball cap appeared in the air duct. If he shot her, she'd be out.

She got him first. The man groaned and hurled down, im-paling himself on a pebble navigation antenna, which protrud-ed from the roof of the passage. The spike came out of his back, glistening with dark red. Death in the sim always looked gory, even gorier than in real life.

"Thirty seconds to mission time-out."

Harvie stood up and limped towards the fire escape stair-way that led to the roof. She could still make it. Putting most of her weight onto her good leg, she rushed up the spiral stairs, up one floor, then another one. The gate at the top was locked. Harvie hurled over the banister and reached the roof edge.

"Ten seconds."

She pulled and grabbed the ledge. A burst of water hit her in the face. Fire sprinklers. In an instant the ledge became too slippery to hang onto.

"Seven."

She let go of the banister and pulled up.

"Six."

Harvie's knees slammed into the wall and the pain in her damaged leg took her off guard. The ledge slid under her fin-gers. She fell down, crashed again into the passageway's roof, bounced off and slammed flat onto the mats that were, when falling from this height, not much softer than solid concrete.

In the last few moments of consciousness, Harvie watched the shopping centre and its patrons decompose all the way to a varistate skeleton that crumbled and retreated into the walls, back into its neutral state. The room was once again void and silent, with the exception of a prostrate body on the floor.

The bright spotlights under the ceiling smudged into a single shining halo and then dimmed, and Harvie no longer felt any pain.

3

She can't move, can't see. The fabric sack on her head smells of chemical dye. Harvie wonders what the point of it is. Maybe they want to scare her, but she's not afraid of the dark. She thinks of the time she floated in the rescue pod for two weeks, alone. Then she thinks of Dad.

"I want you to be strong," he said before he sealed the pod. She wasn't afraid. She's not afraid now, either. She's strong, just as he wanted, even though her pack lost the fight. She assumes they have lost, but she can't remember any of it.

The smell becomes too much to bear. It's not just the sack; her hair, her sweat smells too, and there is a dull metal taste on her tongue. She coughs. It's not a dye, she realises, fighting the urge to vomit. And there was no fight. Gas bots, that's what they used: tinier than ants, fast, deadly; very hard to acquire; expensive; illegal.

Someone comes in, lifts the sack and puts an airmask on her face. The smell subsides. They give her some water. She drinks. They take her to a toilet. She complies, even though it's awkward in the long cocoon-shirt. A woman with a raspy, harsh voice assists her. Her hands are rough and smell of cigarettes.

When they walk back, Harvie asks about the rest of the Litter.

The woman says nothing.

Bone to bone…

Harvie doesn't sleep. She lies on her side, the back of her head against the vibrating wall, listening to the low, steady hum of the ship's engines. The faces of packstas come to her; she lets them go, one by one, singing the chant words in her head as they disappear into the darkness. The sense of loss is palpable.

All in one, one in all…

She tries to remember the day they found her in the abandoned cargo dock, after she almost ran out of food and water. The man Dad sent for her hadn't come. She later saw Growler boasting a Ranger badge, but she never asked him about it. Growler doesn't like questions. *Didn't* like…

After a while she falls asleep and misses the arrival and docking. She wakes up to two voices above her, speaking Japanese. Both have accents. One is Nearspace urban, with dragging, soft vowels; the other one is distinct mainland Japanese: harsh and short.

"This is the girl who taught the Litter how to use firearms. She is quite a legend, this kid!" The Nearspacer chuckles. "It took us six months to track the gang that's been hiding her. We've got two little rascals, pressed them a bit, you know. Until one of them cracked."

Rage swells up inside her. It takes some real pain to make a packsta talk.

"That's too much information, Lesavre, both on your sources and your methods."

"I've lost twenty-three of my people to these skunks, Major General."

"As I've said, too much information. But thanks for your effort. We will take it onwards from here."

The sack on her head comes off. She blinks, getting used to the light. A middle-aged Asian man stares into her face. She stares back, scanning his every feature. She knows him. She frowns and squints, trying to remember.

A doll. A doll dressed in orange, silvery hair, white round head, about the size of her palm. He handed it to her, and she said…

"*Konnichiwa, Takura-san.*"

She remembers.

"You know who I am?" He looks startled; it reassures her.

"Yes." She answers in English. Images float into her mind. "You're Major General Kato Takura, from USF. You visited Commander Flemming's ship four years ago. You two talked about displacing the Legion from the quadrant between the Saudade and Helios stations. You brought a Japanese doll, a girl in an orange kimono. I didn't like it. I said dolls are stupid."

The man gapes at her, aghast.

"You are… Denise?" He gasps. "Deni, Rod's little girl?"

She pulls her chin up. "My name is Harvie Flemming. There's no Denise." She squirms, but the shirt is wrapped tight around her chest. "Now, can you tell your people to take this thing off?"

"But, of course! I had no idea… I thought you died, with your father!" He shakes his head and mutters while the other men release her. "*Rodo-san-no onnonoko… Deni – sumimasen! … Harvie-sama –* "

"*Onnonoko ja nai!*" she snaps, squeezing her free hand into a fist. "I'm not a girl. I'm a Ranger."

"Hai, Harvie-sama." The man's face is quiet, respectful. He bows, his back straight, arms pressed to his sides. The woman with the harsh voice is there too. She moves closer and leans over. Her face suddenly becomes older, and unkempt red hair disappears into a tight knot at the back of her head. She no longer reeks of cigarettes, but there is another smell that makes Harvie inhale sharply as if short of oxygen.

"What's gotten into your head, Flemming?" the woman says.

***

Harvie focused her eyes. Jen Takura sat in the revolving chair next to her hospital bed. The disturbing smell came from a regenigel mixer in the room that Harvie knew all too well. A short and plump, dark-skinned doctor nodded to her like an old friend. Now it all came together: Harvie had passed out in the sim room, been rushed to the medics, and Jen had come to visit her in person. She wouldn't miss an opportunity to give Harvie a third-degree scolding.

The wisest strategy would be to keep her mouth shut and take it. Not that Harvie had much to say. Not that she could say anything even if she wanted to. Her throat felt numb, the same as her limbs.

Jen sighed, pulled up the diagnostic screen, and zoomed in on a scan of a skull with a couple of dislodged vertebrae underneath. A trace in red indicated the place where they should have been.

"A few more millimetres and you'd be quadriplegic," she said.

Which means I'm not, Harvie thought. The first good news this morning.

"Fortunately, we put them back in their place." The doctor

smiled. "Please make sure they stay there. Your legs were a mess too. Six fractures."

Harvie looked at her toes and tried to wriggle them. They didn't respond.

"Will I walk?" she whispered, straining to speak.

"When the gel sets," the woman replied. "In," she checked her watch, "about three hours, but take it easy at first. And if all goes well, in two weeks I may clear you to resume regular training."

"Two weeks?" Harvie sat up.

"Aren't you happy?" Jen said with mock excitement. "The wonders of medical science!"

Harvie's head spun. Two weeks – she'd miss the cut-off for this year's graduation. Another year shooting dummies in the sim room while cramming for her school tests. She'd rather be quadriplegic.

"You've rigged it," she said, feeling the tears swell up. She blinked hard. Jen wouldn't see her crying, forget it. "You've rigged the sim so it's impossible to beat."

"That's what every cadet says when I boot their ass off the programme." Jen leaned back in the chair. "The sim learns from your mistakes, Harvie. It knows when you're not ready, and you should listen to it, if you don't want to listen to me."

Here it comes. Harvie cringed.

"How many times have I told you?" Jen took her limp wrist. "You're an extraordinary human machine, Harvie, but you are not," Jen squeezed her hand as she stressed each syllable, "*inde-structible*. And your super senses can work against you."

"I'm not going to become any different." Harvie turned her head towards the doctor. "You told me that, Dr Sabira, didn't you?"

"That's not what I told you." Sabira shook her head. "I did say that all your senses are askew, and that's for life, but I didn't say you can't learn to control them."

"Yeah, by the time I'm senile," Harvie whispered.

Jen apparently heard her. "The way you're going, senility will be the least likely problem for you. You'll be very lucky to survive puberty."

Harvie tensed her jaws. "I thought I'd been doing just fine. Until you and General Takura killed off my pack." She bit her tongue. She'd never shared with Jen or Kato the things she overheard on the night of her capture. For the whole of her first year at USF she'd even managed to keep it secret that she understood conversational Japanese without trouble, until she accidentally snapped at Himiko, a new Kamakura-born cadet who enjoyed making snide remarks behind Harvie's back in her native tongue.

Jen's face darkened. "That's not true and you know it."

Too late to back off. She might as well get it off her chest once and for all. It didn't seem she had much more to lose. "I know he hired the people who did it."

Jen lifted her eyebrows. "How…? Never mind. Yes, he did hire Lesavre. Do you want to know why?"

"To get me. Isn't that obvious?"

"Yes, to get you. Before the Legion cleaned the station of all 'tunnel rats.'"

Harvie knew at least this part was true, about the cleansing. The Legion always did that after a takeover. Hobos, Litter – they wanted none of it in their stations. In fact, that was what made the Legion so popular with some. Humanism never had much public appeal in Nearspace.

"Yes, Lesavre killed off your pack, but on the Legion's orders, not ours. General Takura did pay him a handsome bounty, though. To save just one little girl."

"And now I'm supposed to be forever grateful. For being locked up in your gladiator cage."

"I'm glad you know about gladiators." Jen made a wry smile. "Looks like Kato's efforts to educate you are paying off."

"*Vitam regit fortuna, non sapientia.*" Harvie couldn't help but quote back Jen's favorite saying.

"Yes, life is ruled by fortune, not wisdom." Jen nodded. "But in your case, a little bit of wisdom won't hurt either. To make sure you don't run out of fortune. Why do you want to get out so badly anyway? Your routine won't be much different after you graduate."

Harvie looked away. Why? To start with, she'd never asked to come here.

"There are people out there who killed my parents. I want them all dead."

"How do you know they aren't dead already?"

"Last time I checked the Legion was still alive and kicking."

"The Legion." Jen frowned. "Sure." She stood up. "Actually, there is another reason I came to see you. One of the senior USF officers is looking for a mission partner. I want you to do a try-out."

Harvie widened her eyes. "I'm being assigned to a live mission?"

"You are having a try-out, that's all. I'm not talking about an assignment yet. It's up to Captain Gulescu to decide whether he wants you."

"Paul Gulescu?" Harvie's heart sank. The man who used to call her Mowgli. The one she kicked in the shin and tried to bite in her first martial arts lesson. The one who said he'd rather teach a cheetah to ice skate.

"Yes, your old friend." Harvie could see in Jen's eyes how much the woman enjoyed her mental anguish. "So, as soon as you can move, report to my office. We have some preps to do."

***

Jen departed, leaving Harvie at the mercy of Dr Sabira, who winked at her like an accomplice.

"They know how to keep you busy, don't they?" She sat down in the chair that Jen had vacated and rolled Harvie's blanket to the side. "Let me have a look. Don't worry, I'll be careful."

Harvie knew she would. Sabira's hands always smelt of regenigel and mediskin solution, just like her mum's once had. In fact, if Harvie closed her eyes, she could make the walls of the medical unit shrink about three times in size, to a crammed compartment inside a battleship. White spotlights overhead would grow brighter and more persistent, constantly humming a pitchless tune, occasionally broken with a high-frequency whirl of the regenigel mixer. And then she'd see her mum's hands with a pair of headphones. *Here. Take this.* The headphones never played any music, just some white noise interspersed with crackles and short beeps, but it would clear the fog in her head and Mum's face would slowly come into focus. The only face she remembered from her first two years of life. Even Dad's was a blur in her earliest memories. Harvie knew his smell, but she didn't connect it to a face until much later.

"Try to move your right leg," Sabira said.

Harvie held her breath and pulled her knee up. It moved, but it didn't quite feel like her limb, as if Harvie were operating an android's body attached to her head. Sabira took a few scans and gave a short satisfied nod. "Looks like the fractures are fusing just fine. Let me check something."

The doctor took a plastic spatula from a cup. "Close your eyes."

Harvie knew what was coming. She shut her eyes and felt a feather-light touch at the tips of her fingers.

"Do you taste anything?" Sabira asked.

"Sweet. A little bit salty. And there's a hue."

"What kind of hue. Can you describe it?"

"Not sure, it's coming and going. The taste – " Harvie frowned, remembering. "Caramel?"

"Yep, we have our Harvie back, synaesthesia and all!" Sabira chuckled and put the spatula in the bin.

Synaesthesia. That mouthful of a word Harvie had heard from Sabira a lot. And the other long ones: hyposensitivity to pain; hypersensitivity to weak stimuli; endemic visual memory; residual prosopagnosia. The last one was Sabira's favourite. Apparently, Harvie never remembered people by their faces, yet she could instantly recall almost anyone she had met in her life. Dr Sabira had always been kind to her, but Harvie could never quite figure out what the doctor liked more: her or the thick soup of multi-syllable medical terms that Harvie carried inside her body. In any case, it felt better to be called a synaesthetic than a freak.

"Bel needs to have her girl's head checked," she'd once overheard one of *The Ranger* crew say. "A battleship is not a place for a toddler. She's clearly traumatised."

She had learned to stay clear of the other crew on *The Ranger* and taken to wandering alone around the decks, tracing metal mesh walls with the tip of her fingers, tasting the sensation. She never got lost. In fact, as Dad later found out, she could instantly find any place inside the ship's identical looking labyrinths. For Harvie, every deck and passageway had its own unique imprint.

"I think I can let you go now." Sabira gently wrapped her arm around Harvie's shoulders and helped her stand up. Her muscles buzzed and ached, but she could stand.

"What about my training? Are you sure about two weeks?"

"Yes." Sabira's face became cold. "The regened bones are still brittle. Try to stick to t'ai chi for the time being."

Jen greeted Harvie with a brisk nod and slid to the side a silkscreen partition printed with blooming irises over a golden field, guarded by a drowsy dragon. The screen hid a small room adjacent to her office. The cadets referred to this place between themselves as "The Backstage." It was, Jen used to say, where the magic happened.

"Sit." Jen pushed a black leather armchair over to a full-length mirror and turned on side spotlights. Harvie squinted, getting used to the blinding brightness. "We'll need to have your hair done."

Harvie clenched her teeth. "Is that absolutely necessary?"

"Yes, and the nails too."

Harvie sat down and glanced in despair at Jen's reflection in the mirror. The woman looked determined. "Paul Gulescu's alias is a stinky rich socialite, and he needs a girl who can pass for his daughter. You have to look the part."

Harvie bit her lip and put her hands inside a black box that immediately grabbed her fingers. Her mouth filled with the taste of dry ground coffee.

"It won't be long," Jen assured her and picked up a brush. "Sit still."

"Does Captain Gulescu know that you want me to try out?" Harvie said, jerking with every tug and pull from Jen's hairbrush.

"Yes." Jen took a couple of delicate crystal-encrusted hair-clips into her mouth and tilted Harvie's head to one side.

"What did he say?"

"That…" Jen squinted, and put the first hairclip on, "he can't possibly take to Delanue's black-tie dinner a girl who still thinks that a fork and a knife are hand-to-hand combat weapons." She put Harvie's head straight and checked the mirror, then moved the clip a notch, pulling a few hairs. "And that even Henry Higgins wouldn't be able to domesticate this Mowgli."

Now it all added up. One thing Jen Takura would never allow was when someone questioned *her* skills. She had risen to the challenge and was getting her own Eliza Doolittle ready for the embassy ball. No surprises here.

The manicure station beeped and released Harvie's hands.

"Let me see." Jen grabbed Harvie's palm and turned her fingers to the light. Once short and unevenly bitten, the nails now formed perfect ovals, glazed with a transparent coat. Milky, slightly bluish spirals coiled underneath and then burst with golden sparkles. Jen clicked her tongue. "Not quite what I expected, but that'll do. Should go well with the dress."

The *dress*. Of course.

Harvie hated slipping into an unfamiliar garment even more than having someone mess with her hair. Another one of the things she had learned to accept as an unavoidable part of her future job. If she could get one.

"What if he does take me?"

"Then you'll go with him to the dinner at Eugene Delanue's cruiser, impress the host with your manners, and go back to your homework. Gulescu will take care of the rest."

"Eugene Delanue?" The name had a soapy taste. She must have heard it before. Some story that made her want to wash her hands afterwards. "Eugene the Paedophile?"

Jen cleared her throat. "Let's say, he has some peculiar interests. But I'm surprised you've heard about that."

"There was one girl in my pack. She used to be in an orphanage – only, that's not what it really was." Harvie took a deep breath, trying not to let her Litter sister's face enter her mind. "Delanue was her regular customer."

"Interesting," Jen said in the way she always did when she heard something she already knew. "Which reminds me…" She put on the second hairclip, opposite the first one. "If you do get the assignment, try to keep your cutlery next to your plate. No matter how you may feel about Eugene Delanue, your mission is not to kill him. Your mission is to sit down, have small talk, eat canapés and get out. Do it without a glitch, and I may – no promises yet – put your name up for this year's graduation."

Harvie jumped in the chair. "Seriously?"

"I said no promises. Now come, let's see the dress."

Harvie followed Jen to the cubicle behind another silk-screen partition. The dress was still sitting in a lilac box with a moving pattern of dancing flowers.

"Open it."

Harvie touched the box, unsure whether she was doing it right. The flowers stopped twirling and the box glowed and expanded before bursting open with an explosion of paper strings that evaporated into a fragrant mist, revealing the folded white garment. Harvie touched the stretchy fabric and her tongue tinged with a crispy taste of fresh snow. She unfolded the dress. Unlike her thick, sweat-absorbing hoodies, it felt weightless. Harvie took off the crumpled olive T-shirt and baggy trousers the medical unit had issued her with, and dived into a silky wave.

***

"You must be my cousin. What's your name? Grandpa never told me, he always calls you 'Bel's Laika bastard.'" A tall, suave girl in a shiny white dress smiles at her, and stretches her hand. "I'm Francesca."

Harvie doesn't know what "Laika bastard" means, but she doesn't like how the girl says it. The phrase has an aftertaste of tinned broccoli.

"Denise. Denise Dubois," Dad says behind Harvie's back. "She doesn't speak."

The girl laughs as if she's heard a joke and suddenly leans forward, presses her nose towards Harvie's neck, sniffs, and pulls away. "So it's true. You do smell."

Harvie feels her cheeks burn.

"Your hair. It's that chemical – what do they call it? Octilen?"

"Octalon." Dad's fingers grip Harvie's hand. "We are going, sweetie."

"*Au revoir,*" says the girl in the white dress, but Harvie has a feeling she won't see her again.

"Stupid little Krot scum," Dad says.

Harvie knows about Krots. Krots are people who live on the Mainland, or Earth, as it's also called – a big blue ball with coloured shapes. Dad said the word means "a mole" in another language. That's a funny thing about Krots; they all speak different languages. Mum could do that. She said Harvie too must learn, but how can she if Mum is gone?

Maybe she still can. She understands more than people think she does. She hears more than they think. And she remembers.

That girl is creepy… Does she even know her mother is dead? She's three, should already be speaking. No, I don't think Dubois will take her. A Laika? Here?

Laika was a very brave dog, Mum said. She died in space. But when these voices say it, it sounds bad.

Without looking up she finds her dad in the forest of legs and torsos, takes his hand and whispers her first words ever.

"I want to go home."

***

"Flemming? Are you still with me?"

Harvie realised that Jen had already called her name twice.

"Are you ready? It's time to go." Jen lightly squeezed Harvie's fingers. Her touch tasted of cinnamon.

"Yes." Harvie straightened the hem of the dress and checked once again the reflection of the girl who looked like Francesca Dubois. Pampered. Spoilt. Rich. Never knowing how it feels to see her mother's coffin disappear inside a loading dock of a shuttle that would take it to the place where she never belonged.

Yes, she was ready. Today at the lunch with Paul she would become Francesca.

Harvie followed Jen to the officers' restaurant where the tables were already set, awaiting first arrivals. A fresh ocean breeze ruffled the tablecloths. Paul Gulescu chose a window seat, looking fully immersed in the illusion of a beach vacation. He even sported a tan.

Jen Takura greeted him like an old friend, exchanging hugs and pleasantries.

"You old rascal. Look at you! Another year as Marcel Jacopo and I might need to take you back to lose some fat in the sims."

"Hey, I remember you always telling me I needed to build up." Paul smiled. He did look rounder than Harvie remembered. "So, who have you got for me?"

"Just as I promised: The best of the best." Jen nudged Harvie forward. "Cadet Flemming."

"Bonjour, monsieur." Harvie looked Gulescu in the eye with an air of elegant superiority. "Did you have a nice trip?"

"But…" Paul frowned and looked at Harvie from head to toe, his face gradually changing from confusion to surprise, and then, to a barely disguised admiration.

"That's – this is Harvie?" Gulesku raised from his seat, grinning widely. "Girl… You did grow up, didn't you?" He turned to Jen Takura and punched her shoulder. "Damn it, Jen-sensei, you are truly something."

Jen's face beamed with a victorious smile.

"Now, Mr Jacopo, I would like you to meet your daughter Clara."

Gulesku bowed his head and took Harvie's hand in his as if it was made of delicate porcelain that could burst into shards and a tiniest squeeze. *"Très enchanté, mademoiselle. Très, très enchanté."*

Coming from the man, who used to slam her to the wall in the martial arts class and once broke her a pair of ribs, it was courteous to the point of barely credible, but Harvie smiled and played along.

Gulesku pulled a chair next to him and gestured her to take a seat at the table. Jen sat opposite him, no doubt to be able to scrutinise every shade of emotion on Captain's face. A suit-clad waiter appeared from nowhere without a sound, pulling along a vintage serving trolley with cast iron wheels, rearranged a few things on the table and filled everyone's glasses. Harvie's stomach churned. She was too hungry by now to sit through all those ceremonies. She fidgeted with the napkin on her lap, but then caught Jen's disapproving glance and leaved the thick cloth in peace.

They didn't have to wait for long, it turned out. As soon as the waiter set down three steaming plates, Jen made a brisk nod, and Harvie dug her cutlery in.

"There is something you need to know about this assignment, Jenni." Gulesku moved his plate closer and gave it a skeptical look. "Before you commit any of your girls, especially – " he pointed the tip of his fork at Harvie. "This one."

Harvie got long ago used to people talking about her in her presence as if she wasn't in the room. "That *orokana* is not even there," Himiko had said to the clique of her sidekicks sitting right in front of Harvie at the mess hall table. Being called a "retard" in Japanese didn't make it any less insulting. What Harvie said back in perfect Tokyo accent would make even Jen blush, and the clique vacated the table in a fraction of a second.

But this time it was different. Now she felt like she was made privy to the things that used to be discussed out of her earshot, by people not aware of how sharp her hearing was.

Jen gave Harvie a fleeting glance as if deciding whether to ask her to leave. "Go on, Captain."

"Confederal Nearspace Security are advising us to pull out. Gonzales said, a cover breach is likely, but she didn't delve into detail over the comms." Gulesku took a few bites from his plate and made an approving nod. "She wants to send a personal CNS envoy to General Takura."

"What a change of heart! That Krot witch didn't even want to talk to USF six months ago." Jen chuckled and cut her chicken breast in half. "Who's the envoy?"

"Stan Kozerski."

"Stanko?" A thin line crossed Jen's forehead. A bad omen, as Harvie knew from experience. "Kato won't talk to him." Jen shook her head. "Hasn't done it once in the past in sixteen years, won't do it now."

"Maybe he should, Jenni-sensei. Maybe he should." Paul took another bite from his plate.

"Kozerski is a Krot. He'd say anything to get us out of their way." Jen made a familiar sarcastic chuckle. "That guy would sell his firstborn son's kidneys if it helped him to score points with the Confeds. And even if he's right – " she arched her eyebrow. "What are you going to do about that?"

"Even if he's right, I can live with that risk. You know that, Jenni. But" – Paul moved the pieces of chopped asparagus around the plate with the tip of his knife and looked up. "Do you guys really want to send this girl? I mean, she's a *Flemming*."

Harvie's heart skipped. She'd never heard Gulesku say her name this way before. Like it was a spell too powerful for the uninitiated to say out loud, and those knowing its power treated every phoneme with extreme caution, lest it brought to life the forces beyond anyone's control.

"Yes, she's a Flemming." Jen gave Harvie another fleeting

glance. "And she wants to live up to this name, if I understand it right. So far she had kicked the fat asses of each and every other cadet in my boot camp. Compared to what she has to deal with day in day out, this mission is child's play."

"You're kidding me, Jen-sensei. She'll be breaking into and infecting with spyware an encrypted data server." Paul paused. "On a ship guarded by Legion-trained hired guns. If *this* is child's play, then I've been indeed having just an extended vacation."

"Weren't you?" Jen smiled. "You sure look that way."

Sounds about right. Harvie put a morsel of grilled chicken in her mouth and rolled it on the tongue. Low to medium complexity sim level. She wouldn't even bother to pick that one up for a sim run: added zilch to her score and bored her socks off. If this was all she needed to get her chance to graduate this year, then who cared about that guy Stanko and his warnings? She could live with that risk, just like Gulesku.

"It's your call, Jen." Paul cleared up his plate and pushed it to the side. "If you're sure you want to send her – "

"I'm sure." Now Jen looked straight at Harvie. "One hundred percent sure."

"Do me a favour, Jen." Paul took a napkin from the silver holder in the centre of the table and carefully wiped each finger. "Ask Kato to talk to Kozerski for once. Maybe he'll change his mind. If he doesn't, I'll take her."

"You know General Takura is not the one who makes mission staffing decisions, do you?"

"Then you have nothing to lose by asking. And – " Paul stood up and stretched his hand towards Harvie for a handshake. "Good hunting, *Mowgli*."

5

"Mr Kozerski?"

Stan Kozerski jumped to his feet at the sound of his name and rushed towards a glaring glass column where a digitised female border control officer inspected his file. The glass reflected a slightly balding man in his forties, dressed in a dark blue Confederal uniform, whose crumpled trousers, puffy eyes and weary face suggested that he had come off a very long spaceflight, most likely the sort of duty rather than pleasure. Stan felt his hands tremble and wondered whether it was from too much caffeine or from a nagging desire to get done with the formalities once and for all. He straightened his shoulders and tried to look presentable.

The digi moved her chair down to make her face level with Stan's – an uncomfortable reminder of his height – and gave him several pensive looks, first at his face and then at a 3D mugshot where Stan still had longer brown hair sticking out in unruly spikes. He had received a few persistent reminders before to have his UID updated, and even took a few new pictures, but didn't upload them. The short-haired aging man looking back at him from those pictures with the sad and dis-illusioned brown eyes of an abandoned cocker-spaniel wasn't Stan, no matter what the UID office might say.

"You have been granted a thirty-six-hour stay," said the voice inside the column. It was flat, pitchless, the way lifts or coffee machines talk. "You will need to check out with border control upon your departure. If you expect your visit to last longer, you must notify Unian Immigration Authorities at once. Failure to comply with your stay conditions will result in an immediate deportation and possible refusal of future visits. Please confirm that you understand these terms."

A small red dot appeared on the glass at his chest level. Stan nodded with a short sigh, tucked the small leather brief-case in his right hand under his left arm, and pressed his thumb to the dot, waiting for the biosig scan to process.

"Welcome to New Albion, Mr Kozerski. Enjoy your visit."

A frosted varistate glass barrier scrolled to the side. Stan took his briefcase into his hand and stepped through with a short, irritated grunt.

Thirty-six hours. He shook his head.

The matter that brought Captain Kozerski to New Albion would only take him a couple of hours at worst. In fact, he already had a flight booked for tonight, non-refundable, as had always been the case with his department's business trips for as long as he could remember. Cheapest tickets, economy class. So much for fifteen years of Confederal Government service. Yet, being given the shortest of all Unian visa options annoyed him. As if someone wanted to remind the forty-two-year-old captain of the Confederal Nearspace Security how unwelcome he was in New Albion.

As soon as Stan got down the escalator and through the doors of the arrival lounge, a smell overwhelmed him. Delicate, exquisite yet strong, somewhat flowery, but not quite the smell of perfume or air fresheners. One could even call it pleasant, the way some people find pleasant a smell of fresh paint, or an animal they care about. It made Stan uneasy, as if it brought out something he didn't want to be reminded of, yet he couldn't help but stand still for a moment, absorbing it with his nostrils, drawing it into his lungs, feeling the chill down his spine.

Octalon.

This unmistakable smell of purified fumes had always been a sign of an octalon production factory; it would creep into air systems, soak into the walls. They used to be harmful, those fumes, but decades of research and advancement in purification technologies had reduced the health hazards to negligible. What they couldn't do was get rid of the smell.

The port must have been on the same stem as the production units. That's how they were usually built nowadays; cheaper, more efficient, convenient. Kozerski tried to remember how many stems New Albion had. Thirteen or fourteen, something around that – he recalled it being named "the second largest human settlement in space" in the in-flight video he'd watched just before he dozed off. The first was Universum, Confederal space capital, with seventeen.

He would have to take a taxi to Mandalay – a business district spanning two of the larger stems. It must be Upper Mandalay he needed, but Stan was not sure. He opened his briefcase and looked inside for his percom.

"Captain Kozerski?"

Jolted, Stan looked up into the face of a young, dark-skinned woman in military uniform, who stepped back and gestured towards the gate that led to the parking docks.

"General Takura asked me to take you to the headquarters."

Kozerski made an approving grunt. It was a neat social gesture on Kato Takura's side, to arrange a pickup. Perhaps General Takura's memory wasn't as short as Stan feared.

He followed the officer to a large black executive-style two-cabin pebble. The woman climbed into the front cabin and opened the passenger door. Stan got in and sank into a giant soft chair that felt like heaven after sixteen hours of torture in an economy-class seat of a commercial space shuttle designed, no doubt, by a sadistic midget. He stretched his legs and peered at the screen in front where a WBN news report broadcast had just started.

Stan liked WBN. The network had an air of naughtiness about the way it fed the news, a bit of inquisitive, cheeky humour. It was the kind of channel a bored government officer would turn to for a bit of intellectual gossip on politics, society, and people in power. Another reason Stan watched it was that the independent network, controlled by neither Unia nor Confederation, more than often leaked dirt on their mighty space neighbour. On the other hand, of course, WBN unearthed with disturbing regularity an equal share of Confederal under-carpet dealings, which made an even more compelling reason for Stan's fondness. He turned the volume up.

"The World Economic Council today debated on the proposed expansion of Unian octalon production capacities at New Albion, Saudade and Olympia. The ratified plan will make Unia the world's largest producer of octalon, with more than a third's share of the world's fuel supply. A heated debate is expected. Many councillors indicated concern over Unia's proposal, saying it will pose a threat to the balance of the energy markets. Unian representatives on the Council state that the proposed expansion is a necessary protection against the increase in octalon output by independent fuel producers. 'We have undeniable proof,' said Councillor Ivan Graft, 'that not everyone is sticking to the quotas drawn by the council, and we have no choice but to respond accordingly.' The debate will continue later this afternoon."

Octalon. *It's all about octalon now,* Stan thought. A century ago, it used to be about oil. Before, it was about land. But as always, it was all about power.

"The deadline is set for the final submission of the bids for Ophelia space station." A familiar word caught Stan's attention. "The bid winner will be announced in two weeks, when the station's governing board reviews all proposals and makes its final recommendation. The experts see the Legion as the one most likely to emerge as the new governor of Ophelia, the largest in the chain of their five acquisitions earlier this year. The rapid expansion of this paramilitary alliance has caused some voices of concern. As a well-informed source from Confederal Nearspace Security recently said to our reporter, 'We may be witnessing a rise of new power, and we must stay alert.'"

"Well-informed source." Stan sneered. They might very well have said the name – the views of General Amina Gonzales were *"le secret de Polichinelle"* anyway.

Every day Stan's boss was getting more and more vocal about her "concerns" with the Legion. Stan suspected it was the main reason the general had pulled him off the dead-end job that he'd dragged through for the past ten years and put him on this case, reporting directly to her. Amina needed someone who had the motives to hate the Leggies as much as she did. She must know that Stan had one. She had to know. She must have read through all his files, every single record, perhaps even his school grade sheets.

Stan went to school in the first year of the Separation. It wasn't called "Separation" yet. In fact, it wasn't called anything. It didn't exist. It wasn't on the news. It wasn't anywhere at all. Instead, there were conspiring looks and hushed voices, and empty desks in class, and talks of people "repatriated." At home, the tension was palpable. Dad would frown, Mum would cry, and neither would say what upset them. It wasn't until Stan met "the new boy," Rod Flemming, that he ever heard the word itself, but even then it didn't mean much to him. Things carried on; the tension became a way of life and stopped bothering him. Until – on the night of the day Stan turned fourteen – the Separation War broke out.

And once again, it wasn't called a war. It was "the conflict."

He thought of his son. Was Stan really the same age as him back then? Yes, almost. Two years younger, in fact: Tim had turned sixteen this February.

No, that couldn't be. Tim was still a child, a dreamy, wide-eyed boy who drew floating castles and rainbow-coloured towers. The toughest choice the boy had faced so far was which palette to apply to a 3D model, so it wouldn't look like it came out of a five-year-old's fantasy. For someone living on Earth for most of his life, Tim had an alarming lack of ground under his feet.

Yet Stan wished he could take his son to New Albion with him. If there were anything Tim could like about Nearspace, it would be here. Gravity that matched the Earth's so closely that even he wouldn't be able to tell the difference; or at least would stop complaining about his "space-sickness." Real, not synthesised or 3D-projected trees, flowers, and grass. And, most importantly, those amazing, floating, suspended buildings connected by var-istate walkways, dancing in the air filled with warm breeze that smelt of salt water close by, masking the all-permeating octalon scent. If Stan could be impressed, Tim's head would be blown away.

***

The scooter stopped and Stan realised that the ride was over. He must have been browsing through his memories for a good three quarters of an hour.

The driver opened his door and stepped out as well. "Just follow the signs for the visitors' entrance and you'll get straight to the reception," she said with a quick parting nod. "Have a nice day, Captain."

Stan looked around. The woman set him down on a narrow, dim platform with a few tunnel-like exits leading to escalators that disappeared inside a massive well-illuminated glass dome. A few dozen commuters were going up and down – more down than up. It must be the end of the office day. He hadn't checked the local time when he arrived, but he was sure Unia didn't use the same locale as Universum, synchronised with Greenwich.

The building, as Stan discovered from the floor plan next to one of the exits, had a pompous name, "Liberty Tower," and according to the department list, hosted quite a few govern-ment establishments, including the headquarters of the Uni-an Special Forces. Stan made a mental note of the layout and walked towards the exit at the end of the platform.

The escalator took him to an open-plan lobby built with a clear intent to impress and intimidate a first-time visitor. Twirling fountains of water danced around columns of multicoloured flames that surrounded giant morphing shapes of some hot contemporary art; flocks of palm-sized tropical butterflies fluttered around elaborate flower baskets hung from the ceiling on invisible strings. A shameless display of luxury and excess that screamed: "Like it or not, green chips are floating high, and that's the way to be."

Stan had seen a few places like this in Universum – banks, business hubs – but definitely not a government building. He remembered the ascetic and somewhat run-down look of the CNS office and felt a light touch of envy. He didn't try to suppress it – after all, for a nation that didn't exist a couple of decades ago, it was not such a bad job and Stan didn't mind giving the Unians a bit of credit.

"So, here you are."

The voice behind Stan's shoulder sounded familiar to the point of a painful jolt. It hadn't changed a bit, Stan thought, not even the accent. He turned around. A small, robust Japanese man with a haircut a tad too long for a military officer stretched out his hands, grabbed Stan's shoulders, and shook him so hard that the captain nearly dropped his briefcase.

"I couldn't believe my ears when they told me that Captain Kozerski was coming. I thought, 'Damn, why would the bastard decide to bring his old ass to my place?'" General Takura laughed, flashing a row of snow-white teeth. He looked much younger than his late forties. "Gosh, it's bizarre to see you in the Confed's outfit! How's Krot life been treating you?"

"Er… *ça va, Takura-kun*. Glad you are finally talking to me. Who could have expected that it would take you what, fifteen years?" Stan stopped mid-sentence. Not a good way to start a conversation, considering the delicate nature of the business that had brought him here.

Kato Takura turned solemn. "That was your decision. I made mine."

"Kato, please. I didn't come here to stir the ashes."

"I guessed so. Anyway, how may I help you?"

"Shall we not go to your office first?" Stan frowned. The thought of discussing the matters of state under the accompaniment of flapping butterfly wings didn't excite him.

"Sure, sure." Takura nodded and pointed towards the lift. "This way."

Stan dodged a fist-sized insect and followed Takura.

"So, did you have a nice flight?" said the general as soon as they got inside a small, tinted-glass capsule. "What did you take? The Arrows of Albion?"

"I wish!" Stan grumbled. "Unfortunately, they put me on ICE."

Takura smirked. The reputation of the International Charter Escorts needed no advertisement.

"They used to be a cargo-only spaceline, did you know that?"

"And they should have stayed that way," sneered Stan, listening to a burble in his stomach.

"You must be hungry like a dog, then. I'll arrange for something." Takura pulled out his percom and jotted a few lines.

The capsule stopped and the men stepped out into a small, narrow corridor panelled with fake oak. The only door at the end slid open without a sound, letting them inside a small office, furnished with a definite touch of style.

"Coffee?" Takura pointed at a round meeting table next to his surgically clean desk.

"Sure." Stan sank into the chair. "What locale are we in, by the way?"

"Sixteenth." Takura took the coffee pot off the tea tray that had just floated into the room and hung over the table like a tiny UFO. "It's 17:30 here."

Six hours behind, Stan figured out.

"So, what brought you all the way to our modest corner of the world?" Takura passed Stan a steaming cup that spread the bitter and intense mouth-watering smell of premium coffee.

Stan took a sip, paused for a moment, feeling hot liquid envelop his tongue, and put the cup down.

"I want to talk about Ophelia."

"Ophelia? Oh, yes, I remember! Prince Hamlet's girlfriend. She died, poor thing. You finally started reading books, Stan?"

"This is not funny, Kato. You know perfectly what I'm talking about." The bid for Ophelia has been on the news for a good four months by now. A huge industrial structure fitted with the latest technology, and issued a class C space station licence, which means it can be easily converted into a military base. A fortress impossible to break into. All about to fall into the hands of the Legion.

"So?" Takura shrugged and took a sip from his cup. "Ophelia is a private enterprise; they can do whatever they fancy."

Scheming bastard, Stan thought. The Legion isn't made up of the guys you'd flirt with the way you do with the Confeds, and you know that.

"Are you telling me that Unia feels comfortable about such a neighbour? Don't take me for a fool, Kato. How many factories did they acquire last year? Fourteen? They tripled their quota in twelve months."

"I thought you knew better than to buy into all that WBN hype: 'A new power is rising,' huh?" Kato looked at the bottom of his espresso cup, swung it a few times and took a sip. "If you want my opinion, they are nothing more than a bunch of dodgy weapon dealers looking for the best way to launder their money."

"Yep, and Unia once was nothing more than a bunch of whizz-kids who snapped up a few bankrupt factories wholesale."

"Times have changed."

"Times never change."

"Yes, times never change, only people..." Takura put the cup down. "Correct me if I am wrong, but I don't remember the Confederation ever declaring a war against the Legion. Am I missing something?"

"I think you're missing the point, Takura-kun." Stan leaned forward. "The stations that Rod Flemming wanted to set free are falling into the hands of the people who gas street children and call it 'ensuring the operational efficiency.'"

"Indeed." Takura's face darkened. "How mean of them. Perhaps they should just suffocate them in their sleep by blowing up the whole town's oxygen supply."

A ball of fire exploded in Stan's chest and rolled up his throat. Gonzales shouldn't have sent him. If she wanted to accuse Takura in playing for the "dark side", she should have sent someone who doesn't flinch when he faces himself in the mirror.

"I know what I've done, Kato. I sleep in the bed I've made. Every night. Why do you want to share it?"

"Because it's too big for you. It was too big even for Rod." Takura leaned back in his chair, staring into the space over Stan's head and sighed. "There are things no man can control, Stanko. *Shikata ga nai.*"

It can't be helped. Stan made a bitter smile.

"That's what you always said, Takura-kun." This canned phrase used to enrage Stan. But over the time he learned to make peace with it, accepting that he'd never fully grasp it's meaning. "You haven't changed a bit."

"And neither have you. I hoped you would." Takura put the coffee pot back onto the floating tray and sent it away. "So, do you suggest USF should fight the Legion?"

"I am not suggesting that you fight them. I am just asking for a little cooperation against them."

"By which you mean…?"

Stan leaned closer. "We know that your people are working on the project Ophelia. Undercover."

"That's nonsense!" Takura slammed his palm on the table. A tiny silver spoon on the side of the saucer jumped up and dropped onto the floor.

"Listen." Stan picked it up and put it back. "We know that the Legion's Colonel Moretti suspects one of your people."

Takura shrugged. "Marko Moretti is a pawn – he doesn't have any real clout in the Legion."

"Yes, and that's why he'll make sure that nothing goes wrong with the Ophelia bid that he oversees. He's after your guys, Kato. You can't get them out – it's too late. They are out of your control zone now. If we interfere, we might save them. The Legion wouldn't want to make noise in Confed's presence, so it'll back out, and we'll let your people go. For a small favour."

"Sure, would you ever do anything out of higher motives?"

Stan grind his teeth. "I need my share of the information that your people managed to get. We can't let the Legion have Ophelia, and we'd do anything to stop them."

"Anything? So why not send your people to do the dirty work? Or are your agents too precious to risk?" Takura narrowed his eyes into perfectly straight lines. "Anyway, you are talking rubbish. It's just your sick imagination, nothing else."

"You know it's not." Stan looked straight into the general's face.

"Kozerski, I am not going to make any comment on your not only erroneous, but also absolutely absurd supposition!"

"If you betray your own people, if you let them die there, you'll never forgive yourself!"

"Speaking from experience, Stanko?" Takura leaned closer, no doubt to make sure it hurt just as much as he intended.

Stan swallowed the pain. "I've made my choice. Will you make yours?"

"Are you blackmailing me, Captain Kozerski?"

"Exactly, General Takura."

The general leaned back, gazing into a softly glowing semi-transparent sphere: a reversed imitation of the space skyline. Floating a couple of inches above the black polished desk surface, it was the only decoration in the emphatically formal Takura's office. Billions of coloured sparkles shone inside: a captured infinity, a universe turned inside out.

"You may quote me, Captain Kozerski. It is an official statement." Takura stood up. "As a senior commandment officer of the Unian Special Forces I declare that..." he split the dry, cool office air with his palm, "... no one, I repeat, not a single Unian agent is presently involved with the bid for Ophelia. Is that clear, Captain?"

"Très enchanté, Monsieur Jacopo, très, très enchanté." A short, stout man, whose white tuxedo made him look more like a restaurant chef than a host of a VIP party, shifted a glass of champagne into his left hand, releasing the other one for a handshake. "Long time no see! Where have you been hiding?"

"Busy, busy..." Paul gave a quick, apologetic smile. "You know the business nowadays – watch your back or else."

The man in the tuxedo chuckled and made a compassionate nod, pressing the side of his flabby chin to the top of his collar, which made his resemblance to a gourmet cook even more striking.

"Tell me about it! And this must be..." His eyes stopped on Harvie's impeccably styled head, then followed along the neat set of bronze toned legs all the way down to the pair of matching soft-leather demi-boots with open toes, each decorated with a row of stick-on tiny diamonds.

"Oh, yes! I beg your pardon. I have not introduced my daughter." Paul gave her a wide, reassuring smile and stepped to the side, so the party host could have a better look. "Clara. My eldest. I thought it would be a good idea to bring her along while she is on vacation. Otherwise, she might start believing anything my ex-wife says about her father. Clara, meet Mr Delanue."

"*Bonsoir, monsieur.*" Harvie flaunted a row of perfect pearl teeth and flawless French pronunciation. The dress strap slid off her shoulder. She casually put it back and smiled.

"Are you serious? She is your daughter? Incredible! Know what? Some have already started spreading rumours of Marcel Jacopo's new affair!"

Paul burst with laughter. "No way! She is not even sixteen yet!"

"Incredible! Just incredible! *Incroyable! Mon plaisir, mademoiselle!*" Delanue sailed off to the banquet room, circling the guests with his never-ending '*Incroyable!*' and '*Magnifique!*'

Harvie watched Delanue's ample back disappear amongst mingling dinner suits and ball gowns, and leaned closer to Paul, who seemed preoccupied with the assortment of cold starters floating by on a large silver tray.

"The old jerk seems to have a crush on you, eh?" he whispered, his lips almost motionless.

She answered with a contemptuous grin and pinched a salmon canapé. "Surprise, surprise; I must be an old hag by his standards." Min Li, the Litter girl from the 'orphanage', was about twelve when Eugene Delanue chose her as his favourite. "So, do you suggest I should reciprocate?" Even standing close to Delanue made Harvie regret the promise she had made to Jen Takura: under any circumstances not to try to kill the man. But she couldn't stop thinking about Min Li, the stick-thin, willowy girl with almost translucent skin; Delanue's favourite concubine. She had always reminded Harvie of her Japanese doll.

"Erm… within reason," Paul said. "Ask him to show you around and most of all try to make it to the control room. Control room, not a bedroom, please!"

Harvie nearly choked on her snack.

"I'm just worried about you, Flemming, that's all. Given Delanue's reputation…"

"I can do my own worrying just fine." Harvie picked another canapé, smiled a quick apology to a formidable diamond-encrusted lady to her left and squeezed her way through the partying crowd, looking for the proud owner of the brand-new suborbital cruiser on its maiden voyage.

The security at the ship's inauguration rivalled that of the Nearspace Council assembly. No bioware or wearables were allowed, and each invitee had been scanned for possible concealed spyware. If the ship's system was to be breached, it would have to be done from within. Harvie had to earn Delanue's trust enough to get near his personal comms console. *Child's play.*

She found Eugene Delanue standing next to a giant projection screen with the panoramic images from outside cameras, his white silhouette even wider against the pitch-dark abyss. She stood next to him and sighed, pretending to be overtaken by the view.

"You know, I still cannot believe we are in space. It's all so… normal!" Harvie's voice trembled with excitement. A tiny drop of sweat glittered over her upper lip – she swiped it off with a brisk lick. "It makes me dizzy even to think that all there is around us is just endless space."

"It's your first time on a space cruiser, *mademoiselle*, isn't it?" Delanue squared his shoulders as if trying to look taller.

"Absolutely!" Harvie said, and gave an almost inaudible

sigh. "You know, Mr Delanue… I can't stop thinking, what if something happens? An emergency? Like an asteroid?"

"Oh, c'mon!" Delanue laughed and put his hand over Harvie's elbow. An electric jolt went through her arm, and her mouth filled with the taste of aluminium shavings. Harvie clenched her teeth and forced out a friendly smile. "People have inhabited space for ages! They're born; they die here like anywhere else. And what is Earth after all if not a giant spaceship? It's hard to believe, I know, but I still feel safer here than on a trans-metropolitan speedway. It's a matter of habit."

"You haven't given her a name yet, Mr Delanue?"

"Simply call me Eugene, Clara. Well, not yet. I'm not sure… maybe *Champion*? Sounds good, right? Hold on, you know what? You will name her! Let's have the ceremony tonight! You will break the bottle. Yes, that would be absolutely fantastic!"

Harvie giggled and looked around.

"Me? It's so… so… such an honour! I just don't know what to say." Her cheeks blushed with sweet adolescent innocence, as she watched Delanue melt into the state of a butter chunk left over on a terrace table on a sunny July afternoon.

"I'm not rushing you, take your time and let me know. It's not easy to be a godmother of something so beautiful. Want to see it all?"

"Eugene!" Harvie shrieked and threw her arms around him. "Can I? No, really. Can I?"

"Of course you can!" Delanue extended his arm. "After you, *mademoiselle!*"

Harvie grabbed his elbow and followed the man to the massive glass stairway, rolling an imaginary cotton wool ball in her mouth.

***

"There are two main servers on board, one on the navigation deck and one – in my office," Delanue advanced through his tour, "but they are interchangeable. Mine is slightly more powerful, and it serves as a communication centre, too. The one on the navigation deck is responsible for the ship: engines, air supply, light, gravity. Am I boring you with all the detail?"

"No, not at all, Eugene! You are the best guide anyone could ask for!" Harvie leaned over the dashboard. "So, you can go online even from here?"

"In a fraction of a second! Something on your mind?"

"Yeah…" Harvie bit her lip, "if it's not too much of a hassle."

"C'mon, don't be shy!"

"I wish I could talk to the girls at school from here. They would envy their shit off! Oh, sorry, Eugene, I did not mean to say that!!!"

Delanue nearly collapsed with laughter. He shook from side to side like a penguin with a hiccup fit.

"Come on, let's do it! Let them… how did you say that? 'Envy their shit off'? You're such a treasure! Your dad must be a lucky man indeed. Go on. Do it!"

"Awesome!" Clara leaped with joy. "Do I need some kind of password or something?"

"All you need is my biosig and that's it! You are in. Do you have your friend's call ID?" Delanue leaned over her shoulder.

"Yes, but… can I try?" She wriggled away.

"As you wish, Clara. Are you sure?"

Harvie gave him a fierce look. "I am not totally stupid! They've taught us something!"

"*Très bien, très bien,*" Delanue pulled back. "I won't even be looking, you independent young woman!"

Harvie messed with the machine for a while then cleared the screen.

"No reply. They must all be out."

"Well, bad luck. Maybe next time. By the way, shouldn't we go back to the party?"

"Holy shit! Dad must be furious!"

Harvie rushed to the doors, and ran into an agile shape that blocked the doorway. The intruder grinned and pushed her back into the room. She sized up the tall, muscular man in the black uniform of a Legion officer, and stepped aside, looking curious rather than scared. Her lip twitched.

"Marko? What are you doing here?" Delanue's hands trembled.

"We need to talk."

"But – I'm not alone!"

"No problem. She might also be interested." Marko put his hand on Harvie's shoulder and pulled her along.

"Excuse me, sir? I don't think I know you…"

Marko moved close to Harvie, his eyes flashing with a joyful irony.

"Alas. I must have missed the day when Captain Paul Gulescu was blessed with such a remarkable daughter."

"Paul Gulescu? Who is that?" Harvie looked at Marko with the sincerest bewilderment she could muster.

"You don't remember?" Marko raised his eyebrows in mock surprise. "Let me remind you." Marko's blow was sharp, fast and professional. Clara Jacopo shouldn't have seen it coming, so Harvie chose not to duck. Her mouth filled with a salty taste; real blood, not one of her synaesthetic phantoms.

Eugene Delanue jumped into the air and grabbed his arm. "You stop it! What are you doing?"

"Shut up, Delanue. When we let you in on the deal, I don't remember putting any Unian spies in the contract." Delanue frowned, not understanding. "Your best pal Jacopo, just for your information, is no more or less than a senior field agent of our respected USF friend Takura-san, and this underage slut… Well, we have yet to find out." He gave Harvie a courteous smile.

Harvie sat on the floor, preoccupied with exploring her broken lip with the tip of her tongue.

"Is that true, Clara?" Delanue glanced at her with panic.

She shrugged her shoulders.

"'Eugene' knows better, I presume." Marko seemed too informed to try to keep up appearances.

"*Merde!*" Delanue turned pale.

"Happens," she replied, somewhat philosophical.

"Clara, are you here?" a voice came from behind the doors.

"Do any trick, and you'll die a virgin," warned Marko as he pulled Harvie up onto her feet. "Go on, talk to your 'daddy'."

"All is fine, Paul, I'm here. Mr Delanue walked me around his ship."

Gulescu froze in the doorway, eyeing all three of them.

"Okay, I won't be disturbing you. I'll wait for you downstairs, honey. Don't stay for too long." He turned around and walked away.

Marko screwed up his face,. "Little scum! Now all of a sudden you call your daddy 'Paul'?"

Cupboard-like figures of the Legion troopers, each coupled with a pair of octaguns per head, crammed into Delanue's office.

"You two, watch that bitch, the rest follow me, now!" Marko barked.

The rattle of armoured boots echoed through the gangways. Marko grabbed Delanue's shoulder and pushed him towards the door. "Your guests are waiting. I don't need any fuss here. Go; make sure everyone is drunk and merry." He then turned around and gave Harvie a long, attentive look.

"We'll resume the conversation, kid, as soon as we get that 'daddy' of yours. So you'd better start practising your memory skills. Saves loads of pain, you know."

Harvie stretched her legs, nesting on the thick, soft carpet. She tried to appear unconcerned by the presence of two armed butchers at her side. An uneasy silence filled the room.

"I am thirsty," she declared, as she pulled off her blood-stained glove.

"So what?" grinned one of the cupboards.

"Nothing. Just thirsty. Is there water or something?" She rose onto her feet, looking around until she spotted a glass on Delanue's desk, with a water bottle standing next to it. "Ah, there!"

"Sit back down!" The second guard raised his octagun.

"Will you kill me for taking a glass of water? Don't be insane! I'm not going anywhere." She picked up the glass.

"I said, sit down!" The man's voice became exasperated.

Harvie stopped halfway. "Don't be hysterical. I just want to drink some water."

The man shoved the octagun behind his belt, dashed forward and grabbed her forearm.

"Do as you're told, you…!"

Before the butcher's companion knew what had happened, the two-metre heap of flesh collapsed with a noise of a middle-sized elephant, his head at an unnatural angle. For a fraction of the second Harvie admired the grotesque beauty of his broken shape, wondering when the idea to reach for his octagun would cross the other guard's mind. When he finally did, she added his body to the first one without much hesitation. Anyone armed was a legit kill.

Having disarmed the deceased, Harvie sprinted out to find Gulescu.

The "cupboards" in the Legion uniforms blocked the ways in and out of the ship, but kept clear of the banquet hall, as far as she could see. Harvie dashed towards the hall's stairway. Another uniformed Legion trooper ran after her along the gallery. Harvie didn't even need to stop and aim to hit a target of his size. With a long, deep groan, the man flipped over a barrier and landed right onto the partying crowd.

The soirée was ruined beyond recovery.

7

"Paul, I'm on VIP dock, level 3. Paul, where are you? Say something!"

Harvie's percom answered with a numb, depressing silence. What was she thinking? Paul wouldn't use this thing. All of Delanue's guests were issued with these ancient devices on entry, in case they wanted to go online through the ship's secure channels. No other devices were allowed; they had to check them in. Paul must have already ditched his, so Delanue's security couldn't trace him. She really should do the same. She swung her hand and hurled the device against the wall.

"Damn, where is he?"

Harvie curled into a Chinese hieroglyph and tiptoed between the rows of scooter shuttles that belonged to Delanue's renowned visitors, her feet freezing to cramps. She had had to say goodbye to her boots: they weren't quite made for frantic running. She wished it weren't so damn cold. The VIP shuttle dock, located right in the middle of the cruiser's underbelly, was clearly never intended to be heated to a comfortable temperature. Harvie exhaled, watching a white cloud of steam curl in front of her face. Definitely below zero.

"I could just kill you, Gulescu!" she hissed, hoping that Leggies haven't yet done that. No way of finding out now.

The broken percom by the wall spat out a hushed sound. Harvie dashed and picked it up. "Paul? Gulescu?"

The percom grunted twice and coughed out a frazzled voice: "Get outta here, Harvie. Do you hear me? Get out!"

"Gulescu, where are you?"

"I'm stuck in dock B. Don't come here, you won't make it. Get out while you can!"

Harvie scowled. "What the hell? Gulescu! Pa-aa-aul!"

"The subscriber is switched off, please call again later. The subscri…"

Dock B. Where was it, bloody crap?! She scrolled hastily through the images of docking maps Gulescu had made her memorise before they departed for the mission.

"Bingo! Dock B, East wing, level 2." She could now see it in her head clearly. "Damn! That's hell knows how far." She'd have to get to the opposite side of the cruiser, through hoards of the Legion troopers running amok. "Gulescu, you are such a son of a bitch! Why did you even go there?" Harvie anxiously bit her still perfectly round nail. An idea started to form in her mind.

If she couldn't get there from the inside, she could do it from the outside, right? Harvie jumped to her feet and ran.

VIP dock was becoming crowded with panicked guests who'd fled the party without paying any attention to the bare-foot girl, apparently searching for her parents. They'd arrived just in time. Harvie dashed into the crowd looking for the scooter she and Paul had parked here a few hours ago.

The shuttles kept launching one after another. The dock attendants could hardly manage to unblock the docking locks, let alone check the identity of every single one of the scared passengers rushing inside.

Harvie jumped into the cockpit of Marcel Jacopo's Porsche and swiped the UID token attached to a silver bracelet on her wrist. The dashboard lit up. Harvie turned the voice comms on and screamed on the verge of her vocal cords: "Get me out of here, quick, you morons!"

The dock attendant must have already heard quite a few such heated requests. The locks clicked softly and a tired, low voice floated from the speaker: "K 2465 BZ, Gate 5. Follow dark green vehicle number N24 LD 479. Have a good day!"

"I'm already having one." Harvie smirked and turned on the engines.

She gnawed her nails, unable to peel her eyes off the screen that showed the reverse docking process at Gate 5. The outer docking gates sluggishly closed, preparing the chamber for the next batch of departing shuttles. This was definitely her slowest escape ever.

"Come on, pump it up! What are you using, balloon blowers? Let me in already!"

Finally, the panel read that the pressure in the chamber had reached the needed level. Yet, the inward gates did not move.

"I'm sorry, madam." The voice in Harvie's headset struggled through some sort of interference. "We have a problem here. For your safety we recommend you stay inside. Colonel Moretti, our head of security, will be here in a few minutes to assist you."

"Damn." Harvie looked around in despair.

The docking lot seemed huge. The security had turned the lights off, leaving only dim blue trails of emergency lightings, which gleamed off sleek contours of lifeless cargo vans that rested peacefully upon their landing pads.

It occurred to Harvie that she should probably come up with some sort of a plan before Marko stormed in.

"Ta-ta-ta-taaah." Harvie leaned her forehead against the cool sheer siding inside the cockpit.

Getting out of the shuttle made no sense whatsoever. Marko's crowd was probably already somewhere near, and at least she could use the cockpit as a shield in a gunfight.

As if reading her mind, a fast, supple body clad in a skin-tight black overall approached the shuttle with a hasty gait. Harvie gripped her octagun and slid under the dashboard. He put his hand on the glass, trying to peer inside.

"Go away," Harvie whispered.

Instead the trooper reached to his belt and unclipped a police-type electronic lock jammer. The device buzzed, and the cockpit opened. The man leaned inside. Harvie pressed the gun barrel to his forehead. He froze.

"Where's Gulescu?" Harvie moved the trigger up a millimetre.

The man seemed to understand but didn't rush to answer. His percom played a jolly tune.

"Would you mind?" She detached the handset and answered the call.

"Markides, he is in the food storage," a frantic voice said. "Come here, quick!"

Harvie hung up and pulled the trigger.

The food storage that lay three decks down could only be accessed through a narrow flypass, wide enough for roboforklifts, but not for a scooter shuttle. Harvie couldn't care less. She assumed she had already caused enough noise to stop being extra prudent. With the grace of a proverbial behemoth in a china shop, she secured the cockpit, took hold of the controls, and plummeted her shuttle past the food containers neatly stacked inside mobile storage racks. She dodged a couple of autopiloted roboforklifts, still busy with kitchen deliveries for the party, and plunged under a descending rack, barely avoiding a collision with the container shelves.

A screech of metal against metal made her peep to the left. A heavy rack, brought to a crash with the scooter's tail wing, slowly collapsed, launching an avalanche of coloured crates. Hundreds of champagne bottles crashed towards the bottom deck and squashed into a mash of glass and liquid.

"Hey, Eugene, look! I've just launched your ship! How about a nice name? Maybe *Loser*?"

The percom in Harvie's hand squealed.

"I know only one little girl that can make such a mess. Is that you, Satan's daughter?"

"Gulescu!" Harvie screamed. "Where the hell are you?"

"I'm coming. Stay where you are. I must go off comms now. Will be with you in a couple of minutes."

More Legion troopers had arrived and started firing at the shuttle, but soon they figured out the incongruity of their weapons against the meteor-proof shield. They regrouped and formed an orderly defence line. Harvie fired back from time to time, trying not to waste gun battery on the targets she had no chance of hitting.

"Damn, where is he? What's taking him so long?"

At last, she saw a bent silhouette skipping from one van to

another. He dragged something that looked like a log with handles. Harvie gunned down the nearest trooper who had made a mistake of coming too close. The others stepped up the fire. She shot several times into the approaching squad, and yelled: "Gulescu, move your ass!" As if he could hear her.

"Help me! Hold this!" exhaled Gulescu, as he finally appeared near the scooter. He began to attach the log to one of the balance wings.

"A missile? No bloody way!"

"How were you planning to open those gates, I wonder?"

"Gulescu, you're a genius! Where did you get this?"

"Stumbled upon it. Go!"

Gulescu fired twice into the troopers and slid into the cockpit. Harvie engaged the manoeuvre jets and turned the scooter's nose toward the loading dock gates.

Gulescu slammed her shoulder. "Let's have some fun, partner." He handed her a small box.

"Lots of it!" Harvie grinned and pushed the button on the missile's remote control.

Nothing happened.

"It won't charge!"

"What?"

"The missile. It won't charge."

"Can't be! I checked. It was fine."

"Yet it won't. And – look there!"

Another, much larger group of troopers broke into the dock, circling it round the perimeter. In addition to octaguns, they'd brought in some heavier stuff.

"Either we'll make it through the gates now, or… we won't make it," Harvie said.

"I love your little summaries. Open the cockpit." Gulescu removed his safety harness.

"Why? What are you up to?" Harvie frowned.

"Open the cockpit and cover me!"

Gulescu wrapped the strap around his fist and hung out of the cockpit, propping himself against the outer cabin shell. She saw him struggling to keep balance as the scooter swung up and down.

"No contact with a charger. That's nothing, I'll fix it in a sec. Check it now!"

"Got it. Get in!"

Paul pulled up but suddenly slid back.

"Paul?"

"Help me. I'm hit."

Harvie grabbed Gulescu under his arms, and pulled him up. He clutched her shoulder so tightly it hurt. Twice he almost fell down; she was not ready for his body weight, but eventually she got him in. Harvie dumped him into the passenger seat and sealed the cockpit.

"And now we will have fun!" Harvie smiled.

The docking gates flapped like cardboard. The liberated air erupted, clearing the storage deck of all its contents: vans, cargo, guns, missiles, people. Harvie maxed out the engines, striving to surpass the cloud of fire and debris, trying hard not to let her imagination picture the hauntingly beautiful red flowers popping up amidst the thick, burning mash. She felt a sickening hairball move up her throat. She knew if she looked back, she would see something else: the explosion of *The Ranger*, forever imprinted into her mind. Human bodies thrown in space were not the best sight to those prone to occasional sentiments.

Finally, she dared to glance at the rear-view monitors.

"Wow! What a mess. The Leggies must be really pissed off." *And Delanue too*, she thought, secretly hoping that the cruiser's owner had perished in the explosion. "We've made it, Gulescu, can you believe that?"

Gulescu did not answer.

"Paul?" Harvie felt a sudden chill down her spine. "Are you okay?"

She switched to autopilot and unfastened her straps.

Gulescu lay still in the passenger chair, his eyes shut. Harvie leaned over and unbuttoned his shirt. Carefully, she stroked down his chest. Her fingers came across a characteristic thick brown spot, right below the nipple.

"Paul, you stop that, it's not funny!" She tried to feel his pulse, check his pupils, listen for a faintest hope of breath.

Nothing.

"Don't do this to me now; I'm fed up with this crap!" She shook her head and stared at Gulescu with a deep reproach. "How could you?"

Harvie crawled back into her seat and buckled up again. She only had three, five minutes at best, before the Legion interception fighters would catch up with her. Barely enough time to override the autopilot, shut down all extra features, recalibrate the engines to maximise the speed and response, scan the maps and pick the closest safe haven. She glanced again at the rear-view monitors. Several silver dots appeared above the slowly spinning shape of the gutted behemoth that still had no name. Two minutes, perhaps. She didn't move.

"Listen, Paul," she said and swallowed as if her throat had gone numb. "There will be a guy out there… waiting for you.

His name is Rod Flemming. He'll take care of you. He will."

She breathed in and out, her teeth clenching her lower lip. It felt coarse and salty. The dry crust split and started bleeding again; she wiped her mouth with her palm and lowered the touchscreens of the manual navigation system. Her fingers left dark red smear marks on magnolia-coloured interior trimmings.

Silent and focused, she worked her way through the screens.

***

The interceptors caught up with Harvie sooner than she'd expected. First three sleek shapes, glistening in the sunlight like large pointed drops of mercury, appeared in rear view monitors. Then another three. They followed her in an honourable escort, not shooting, simply hanging in space like a huge sparkling ring. She moved the speed control up. The ring centered on her and began to tighten.

Harvie zoomed on one of the shuttles and studied it for half a minute, then launched a browser screen and typed without looking: "spacetech walrus aurora ttz possib ttx 2pil tech spec?" A list of words and numbers rolled out on the screen. "fuel capac? max spd? burn at max?"

She looked up onto the screen and chuckled. "You lazy fat behemoths…"

A rush of adrenaline swept through her body, a hot wave that flushed over the dull sucking emptiness she felt every time her elbow would accidentally brush over the corpse to her left.

She turned simugrav off and checked the power distribution. 87% to the engines, 9% to the ambience support and impact shield, 3% to the onboard systems. Harvie dimmed the lights and turned off the air conditioning. 89% to the engines.

She hesitated and turned off the impact shield. 94%. Good.

Gulescu's white hand floated in the air beside her. She tucked it under safety straps. He looked peaceful, asleep.

"Wish me luck," she whispered.

She increased the thrust slowly at first, not to overload the engines. The escort stayed on her tail, as expected. Harvie counted to five and moved the thrust level to the maximum. The acceleration pushed her back into the chair, returning the sensation of weight to her body, the only indication of speed apart from the slight vibration of the pilot's seat. She looked at the fuel gauge and smiled. Should be fine.

Harvie scanned the map. Three stations nearby, all Confederal, all class C. She cringed. Jumping off the frying pan into the fire: Krots would be waiting for her there with their arms spread wide. She had to get to a place where a Unian shuttle could land safely to pick her up. She requested the nearest independent settlement and zoomed in on the first one in the row of pictures: a group of ugly black-and-silver shapes that looked like bundles of giant bagels. Xastor Module. A safe haven.

She tagged the picture and forwarded it to a mail bot account. If she made it there alive, the link would go to the USF team who then would arrange the pickup. If she didn't, it wouldn't go anywhere at all. No need to put the guys at risk for no reason.

Harvie locked the course and checked the situation behind her. The interceptors regrouped into a line, but still didn't shoot. They wanted to take her alive, she reckoned. They wouldn't shoot unless they absolutely have to.

"Ouch!"

Harvie crashed into the cockpit's siding. "Bastards."

A warning shot. Close enough to throw the scooter off course, but not to damage.

Smartasses.

She checked her speed. By now she should be outdoing them by 7-8% or so, and they'd have to slow down when their fuel tanks switched to reserve. Or so she hoped. She checked the fuel gauge and gave the Leggies another ten minutes before they would start shooting to hit.

The line began to break up. Two of the shuttles stayed behind; the rest of them no longer flew in a tight formation. Two more warning shots shook the scooter, then another three. The last one came so close she thought they'd hit her, but the systems reported no damage. Someone must be getting quite keen on playing cat and mouse. Another two shots. She swerved to avoid the impact and noticed five more blue traces coming her way. The scooter jumped up and down like a rubber duck hit by a splash of water. Her body, strapped to the seat, dangled like a rag doll. She checked the distance to Xastor. Forty-five minutes at max speed. She tightened the straps and took a deep breath.

The Leggies kept ramming the scooter every thirty seconds. Harvie grinned at each one of the impacts, even though she felt like an ice cube in a shaker. Every shot of an octalon-powered anti-spacecraft gun left the interceptors with less fuel for flying.

"Nice going, guys."

Twenty-five minutes to Xastor. She checked the monitors. Three left. The others switched to reserve and headed to the nearest base. Then another shuttle sent a trace of shots her way and made a gracious U-turn. She noticed that one of the remaining interceptors didn't shoot, trailing behind the other.

They must know by now where she was heading; it was just a question of whether she'd be able to dock before them. As soon as she got into the chamber, the gate approach would be locked by a security barrier field, and by the time the Leggies got in, she'd already be a face in the crowd: try, find her! She checked the relative speed: 10% above.

Another hit. This time she knew it was serious even before she checked the systems. Speed down 20%; she must have lost an engine. She rebalanced the power to the remaining ones and cursed. Leggies never had the reputation of good gunmen, but there was always one black sheep.

She looked at the monitor. It must have been a parting shot: only one chaser interceptor was left, the one that didn't fire. Relative speed: -3%. The Leggies were catching up.

"You are approaching the border space of Xastor Independent Settlement. Please identify youself"

Harvie jumped up at the voice in the speakers. Only now she realized that she had entered Xastor's safety zone. She breathed with relief and typed in Marcel Jacopo's UID code. Should still be okay.

"Welcome to Xastor Module, Mr. Jacopo. You are cleared for docking through gate Seven Alpha Charlie. Please confirm that you are familiar with the International Docking Safety Regulations paragraph 17 through 46 concerning individual private vehicles with load capacity under…"

Harvie cringed and accepted before the voice read out the rest of the sentence. Bunch of byte-pushers… Worse than the Confeds.

She slowed down and followed the docking beacon through the maze of grey bagel-like structures connected by spikes covered in glistering scales of solar panels, keeping an eye on her back. The Leggies were catching up fast. She switched all controls to manual. Unbalanced by its damages, the scooter lost most of its handling; it moved in tacks, like a sail yacht against the wind. The docking chamber gate slid open, oozing a string of bright light, like a huge grin. Harvie didn't bother to wait until the gate opened all the way. As soon as the illuminated grin widened enough to squeeze the scooter between its flat teeth, she cut the main engine and plunged in on the remaining set of docking jets.

A bright flash of light tore her head apart and went off, leaving her with an intense, pulsing buzz in her ears. For a few seconds Harvie felt wrapped in a thick blanket, unable to see or hear. When she regained her vision, she discovered she was lying on her side, with Gulescu's body floating on the seat straps above her, like a life-size puppet.

She tried to get vertical but a sudden sharp pain in the legs made her reconsider. She looked around. The head monitors were all gone, and the rear one didn't produce much more than a blurred image of a metal wall painted with yellow diagonal stripes. Twisting herself into a sort of advanced asana, she stretched her arm to the dashboard, pulled up the monitors, unshaded the front visor and swore.

The scooter lay stuck in the gutter between two lower rows of the chamber gate's "teeth," the upper rows overhanging just meters above her head. The chamber gate automatics had been racking its brain trying to figure out the paradox: a ship entered the docking zone, got in the gates, but never got into the chamber. The "jaws" froze, hesitant whether to close or to open.

Harvie swept her hand across the dashboard, looking for the main switch. Nothing responded. She wondered if the scooter triggered the sensors to lock the gate's safety barrier.

A quick shadow cast over her head, then a flush of light made her shut her eyes. The Legionnaires' shuttle burst into the chamber. Now the "jaws" interpreted that correctly. With a dumb clang they jerked and commenced a sluggish downward movement.

Harvie went numb.

Tons of extra-resistant plastic and metal plus the pressure lock to cut the chamber from the outside vacuum. If ever in her life she wished to be slimmer, she never intended to turn two-dimensional.

She pulled herself out of the straps and almost fell onto the dashboards, trying to kick the engines alive. "You damn stupid thing, you freaking piece of garbage! Come on!" she pleaded. She did not look up. If it was coming, it would come. She'd fight till it came. She suppressed the urge to unseal the cockpit and jump out – not smart, as it was still perfect vacuum outside.

The monitors lit up. Harvie hardly managed to hold a scream. The system slowly started to reboot. She finally looked up and her heart jolted: the "jaws" kept descending.

"Systems testing" the monitor blinked and then: "Core engine failure."

That's it.

Harvie grabbed Gulescu's hand and squeezed her eyes shut. Then a sudden force thrust her forward and she crashed head-on into the dashboard panel.

8

Rod Flemming came to their school class when Stan was eleven. He was older and taller than the rest of the boys – or perhaps that was just the way Stan remembered him. Rod always seemed to stick out: bold, loud, daring, he'd never miss a school fight or a heated dispute with a teacher. If not for his grades – consistently in the top ten, to his teachers' amazement, since Rod never seemed to bother with studying – he'd long ago have landed in deep trouble. He sought it out. On his very first day he declared, not without certain pride, that he was a bona fide "Laika", a slur nickname for one born in space. In fact, he said to his mostly recently immigrated classmates, unlike them he had never in his life set foot on Earth.

Celesta was a brand-new facility with the majority of the staff recruited from a recent wave of settlers. Stan's classmates still swapped stories of weekends in the forest, seaside breaks and snowstorms; things Stan saw only on the net. He could never quite partake in those conversations. He hardly remembered Earth, and at times he felt he'd missed out on something important. Stan always tried to glaze over the fact that his parents never took him "down", not even for a vacation.

For the first three years after Rod Flemming had joined his class, they simply co-existed as if in parallel universes. Until one day Stan took Rod's side in a heated debate with their history teacher when he felt that Rod's sarcastic comments were making a bit of sense. Stan's true intention at the time was more to restore peace in the classroom; the sight of a red-faced teacher barking at Rod made him uncomfortable. They both ended up in detention. With four hours to kill and not much homework to do, they started to swap stories and found that they shared, among a few radical political views, a common dislike towards "the Krots" who thought they were better than anyone else only because "they've seen what a real sunset looks like". Then Rod told him about the Separation movement, and the people who wanted to make space colonies independent.

Stan didn't pay much attention to his story at first, but then it all started to come together: the hushed talks, "repatriations", odd inconsistencies in the news, the gossip, the glances.

Two weeks after Stan's sixteenth birthday, Rod disappeared.

Stan was told that Rod simply took off one day, leaving everyone, including his parents, in the dark. Meanwhile, things became even tenser at Celesta. People in military uniforms patrolled every nook and cranny of the station. A new net policy was announced: only approved sites would from then on be accessible from school computers. There was no need for that; students had stopped talking to each other online long ago. In fact, they stopped talking to each other at all. Stan felt as if they were locked in a basement, with a tornado lashing outside, waiting for it to blow off. He missed Rod, but his attempts to track his pal led to nothing except a three-week ban on his net access. Cut off from the rest of the world, Stan joined the gloomy crowds hanging aimlessly around the school corridors.

Little by little he started to forget his friend. Things were moving along, the end of the school year approached, and high-school selection tests loomed large on the horizon. Stan aced his, and together with a few of his pals was rewarded with a school trip to one of the amusement parks in Universum, the largest and poshest settlement at the time.

They never made it. Halfway through the trip came the news of an accident at Celesta's main production unit, where Stan's and most of his classmates' parents worked. By the time their cruiser reached Celesta, it was dubbed by the news channels "The Orphans' Ship".

The investigation that followed left Stan with an inconclusive report, a modest insurance payout and the option of either going back to Earth to live with his grandparents, or to move, with a few of his classmates who didn't have any close relatives left, to a boarding school in another settlement. Stan chose the latter (a lesser evil, perhaps), and was in the middle of packing a few essential things and throwing the rest of his possessions into the rubbish compactor. That's when Rod Flemming appeared in the doorway, almost unrecognisable.

"There is a war," he said. "A big war. There are things happening we can't miss."

At that very moment Stan knew he wouldn't be going to the boarding school. He would leave with Rod in the middle of the night; they would sneak into a service tunnel, past Confederal guards that looked more like soldiers than policemen. They would cash Stan's parents' insurance, pay some cyberthugs to forge their UID tokens so they would be eighteen and free to go about their business, and use the rest to buy and refit a small second-hand cargo ship that they would call *The Ranger*. Then they would join the Separation, recruit a bunch of similar breaknecks and capture their first Confederal cruiser.

But before that knowing settled in, he glanced at Rod and said: "You look like shit. I'll get you something to eat from the kitchen."

***

Another sixteen-and-a-half-hour-long spaceflight later, Stan stormed into the CNS office with the graciousness of a middle-sized grizzly, still outraged with General Takura's humongous idiocy. To boot Stan out of the door like that, just because Kato still held a grudge for Stan leaving Rod Flemming's side! Unia never had done much themselves to support the Rangers during their final days. The best they could do was harbouring the remaining few who survived after the Legion, encouraged by their successful attempt to take Commander Flemming to his grave, began wiping them off one by one. Yet it was Stan who had been forever branded a traitor, for he hadn't just left Rod.

He had joined the Krots.

Stan nodded briskly to his partner, and thrust himself into a screeching plastic armchair that complained with a choked squeak.

"What's up?" Nik turned his dark face away from the glimmering screens.

Stan made a wry smile. "Not much, apart from the fact that my old friend, acting, no doubt, out of his best intentions, has all but slaughtered two of his people." He shook his head. The lengths Kato Takura would go to make his point! "I guess there go all our hopes to interfere with the outcome of the bid for Ophelia. I'll make a report to Amina now."

"Well, hold that thought." Mgamba stretched his lips into a conspiratorial smile. "Have a look. Might be interesting."

"What's that?" Stan leaned towards muted figures on the monitors that gulped soundless words while wearing the expressions of extreme concern on their faces.

"Long story. In brief, a few hours ago we got a call from Xastor's security…"

"Xastor?"

"Independent modular settlement, industrial class F. Greenhouses and stuff. We patrol it under Amendment 377."

"Peacekeeping Agreement?"

"Yep."

"Go on."

"They found a scooter with what turned out to be the body of USF Captain Paul Gulescu."

"How do they know?"

"They don't. CNS patrol took over the body and established the identity. I got the files right before you came. Our source in the Legion confirmed that it's the guy they were after on suspicion that he works for Takura. He called himself Marcel Jacopo. Was closely involved with the Ophelia bid. Too involved, apparently."

"Where did you get his real name from? List 17?" Stan nervously rubbed his chin, feeling alarming symptoms of nicotine withdrawal. His fingers habitually rolled an imaginary cigarette.

"Exactly. Got a complete file on him, yet – too late." Mgamba frowned. "Not one of our own, but still. It sucks."

"It's not our fault, Nik," Stan tried to convince himself. He felt a slight pinch of guilt – perhaps Kato would've been less stubborn if Stan had not demanded a full disclosure on Ophelia in return – but then he brushed the thought away. CNS wasn't a charity; they couldn't flutter around like fairies, rescuing everyone from their blunders for nothing. Kato should have understood, but he wouldn't even listen. Maybe he'd listen now.

"Contact the Unian Embassy. We need to return the body to them."

Mgamba shrugged his shoulders. "I doubt they'll admit it's theirs."

"Shit." Stan rubbed his chin. "OK, I'll talk to Takura. They must give the guy a proper funeral."

"Getting sentimental, Captain?"

"Shut up."

"I haven't finished yet. There was a second pilot in the scooter." Nik launched another projection screen.

Stan moved closer. "Yes?"

"We found some bloodstains inside the cockpit. Sent them to DNA check straight away. The cockpit was not depressurised; most likely it was opened by hand when the scooter got inside. She might still be alive."

"*She?*" Stan scrolled through the report.

"That's what the lab guys say."

"What else do they say?" The forensics report was too thick with bio-med mumbo-jumbo for his liking. Stan leaned over the table covered with all sorts of debris and generously decorated with coffee mug stains and started to read aloud. "The sample was compared to the matching records from the databank of common civil cases... blah-blah-blah ..."

"Not much. She's not in our records, not even List 17. They found a relative's record though."

"Did they?"

"Yep; some minor legal offence. Should have been spent and destroyed long ago, but nobody bothered. Here." Nik pointed.

"…a first-line direct descendant relation traced to the record 13480GH08-349 of Ms Isabelle Marie Dubois (see the corresponding reference)…" Stan's scrolling finger froze. "Born on— Shit!"

Stan's pupils ran amok along the lines of the text.

"No way…" He rubbed his forehead.

"What's the problem, Stan?" Mgamba moved his coffee cup to the side. "Did you find something I missed?"

Stan did not respond. He looked at Nik as if his partner's words were stuck in mid-air, not reaching his ears.

"I need to talk to Takura. Now." Stan jumped to his feet. "Would you mind leaving me alone for a second?"

"Are you sure? You don't seem safe to be left alone."

Stan gave Mgamba a very special look, usually reserved for the moments he asked Nik to clean up the rubbish-compactor chamber they called their office.

"Okay, okay," Nik said. "I'll be at forensics if you need me."

When Nikolai left, Stan stomped heavily from the desk to the door and back, waiting for his heart to stop pounding. He then rubbed his palms, took a deep breath and leaned over the desk.

"General Takura, coded USF line." The screen remained blank then a fringed face appeared.

"Sorry, Captain, your call is declined."

"Tell the general we found a body."

A dust-coloured Takura's face popped up on the screen in less than twenty seconds.

"I'm listening, Stan."

Stan's throat suddenly went dry. What if he was wrong? Too late. He needed to know.

Kozerski looked straight into Takura's eyes, as if he wanted to read every single thought that passed Kato's mind.

"You never told me that Bel had a daughter."

For a second Stan thought that he had lost the connection and was staring at a still frame of the last transmitted image. But then he noticed a drop of sweat creeping down the general's temple.

"So you know now," Takura said finally. "Good for you."

Stan shook his head. Up to this moment he'd still hoped that it could be some weird mistake, that Kato would give him some logical explanation: undeniably a lie, but a lie Kozerski could live with. But instead he read in Takura's eyes a cold determination to make Stan share the full extent of his own pain and grief.

"You bastard..." Stan was lost for words. "Why, Kato? Why didn't you tell me?"

"Tell you what, Stan?" Kato's face turned as impenetrable as ever. After a moment of softness, he now resumed his official duty of blatant denial.

Stan felt a hot wave rising from inside. "Would you just stop that crap, for hell's sake? As if you haven't done enough damage yet. Your Gulescu guy is dead and now—"

"Did you say Gulescu?" A stony expression on Takura's face broke.

Stan instantly realised. "Yes, Kato, I did. *She* might still be alive. If you pray hard enough."

Takura closed his eyes for a swift second. "Where is she?"

"You did not answer my question." Stan shook his head.

"Why, what will it change?"

"Why?" Stan's felt sudden pain down his throat. All anger disappeared, leaving nothing but a bitter aftertaste. "Don't you think I have a right to know?"

"Know what? And what for? What difference would it make? Would it bring Bel back? Would it make you forgive Rod? Would it, at least, help to save their child?"

"I never blamed Rod."

"Yes, you did. You still do."

"How do you know? Why should you care?" Stan almost screamed. "You don't even care if Rod's girl dies! Takura, how could you make her do that? Shit, it's not even legal, she must be what? Fifteen? Sixteen? Rod must have trusted you if he let you take care of his daughter and you— You bastard!" Stan slammed his fist against the desk. "Don't you have enough adults in your fucking Special Forces? Or does the Legion kill them so fast you have a hard time finding a replacement?"

"Shut up, Stan."

"Oh, I sure will." Stan paused and took a breath. "I'll let you know if we find the girl. If the Leggies don't get her first." He stretched his hand to cut the connection.

"Wait."

Stan's hand froze midway.

"Yes, Bel Dubois had a child. I don't know why Rod never told you, but I think he had good reasons. You really had some guts to become a Krot. *Baka, yo.*" You idiot.

Stan skipped the insult. "But how come *you* never told me?"

"Stan, she's Rod's daughter, not yours!"

Stan screeched his teeth and changed the subject. "How could you send the kid to do this job? Are you out of your mind?"

"Stan, I never made her do anything. You don't understand,

you don't know the whole story…"

"Oh, sure, I've just found out there's a hell of a lot I don't know! Like, her name, to start with."

"Stan." The general's voice steeled. "Where is she?"

Kozerski pressed his finger down. The screen went blank, *Connection Ended* blinking across in red letters. He rubbed his temples, as if applying extra pressure could squeeze out the headache that was crushing his skull like a chainsaw.

Rod Flemming had a daughter.

No matter how many times he repeated that, it did not sound less absurd. How did Takura put it? 'Rod's daughter, not yours.' Stan clenched his fists.

Bel's daughter, he thought. *Don't you get that, Kato? Bel's.*

***

Stan and Bel stood in the shuttle dock of the Rangers' flagship cruiser. His hands were still shaking even though more than an hour had passed since his once best friend had told him to get off the ship once and for good.

"Come with me," he said. "He's gone crazy, don't you see? He'll kill you both."

"I hope you know what you're doing, Stan." Bel shook her head and backed off.

Her last words. Then four years of silence followed, and his frenetic attempts to break it. His messages returned unanswered until one day a short, typed mail came from Rod: *Bel's dead. The funeral is on the 14th. You can come. RF.*

He didn't.

'If you go, I'll leave you,' Irina threatened. Stan looked at her pale, drawn face and then at three-year-old Tim asleep on her lap with his favourite stuffed dolphin tucked under his arm, and didn't go. Irina left him in less than a year anyway and took their son with her.

He didn't go to Bel's funeral, he never saw Rod again, and he never met their daughter. She ended up with Takura and he turned her into one of his killing machines.

***

The door to Stan's office jumped aside as if trying to avoid a collision with the healthy ninety-five kilos of Mgamba's body. Nik slid into a chair and triumphantly installed another weather-beaten mug atop the pile of classified debris, spilling a few steamy drops of opaque liquid.

Stan frowned, yet said nothing but: "Any news from Xastor?"

"Nah…" Mgamba waved his hand. "Nothing special, except—" Nik moved his chair closer. "They registered the landing of a Legion shuttle at the same time as Gulescu's."

Stan gulped and wiped his forehead covered with drops of cold sweat despite the blasting chill of air conditioning.

"I have to go there, now. Can you get me the clearance?"

"I'll try, but it will take pulling some long strings." Nik frowned. "I'm not sure I have that kind of leverage."

"I'm sure you do. And not a word to anyone until I speak to her, understand? Especially Amina."

"Are you getting us in trouble?"

"Me? No. If *she* finds out, she will."

"Appreciate your honesty, partner." Mgamba picked up his mug, took a slow sip and put it back. "You want me to cover your ass and you won't even tell me which side to watch. Ain't that fair!"

Stan bit his lip, thinking how much he should divulge to Mgamba. "Remember the forensics report, DNA match? I know this girl's father. "

"Oh." Nik looked perplexed. He rubbed the tip of his dark, slender nose. "She can't be yours, Stan. The lab has your full DNA profile. Who's the father, then? And how you can be sure?"

"Will you get me the clearance?"

"Will you answer?"

"Rod Flemming, her husband, was her first and only man." Stan glanced at Mgamba's stunned face. Nik's eyes looked like two ping-pong balls shoved into eye sockets.

"You mean, Takura's other guy – sorry, girl – is Commander Flemming's child? Rod Flemming, *the* Commander?"

Stan blinked a "yes".

"Jees." Nik shook his head. "I didn't know he was married."

"Not many people knew. I thought you were of game-console age when Rod was *the* Commander."

"C'mon! If we don't mention Rod and Stanko around here it's only because a certain well-respected captain is known to get very edgy when the subject is touched."

"Uh-huh. Who's Stanko?"

"My point exactly." Nik nearly knocked his drink over his trousers, but caught it midway. "Do you realise how much hell is going to rise around here when you spill the news?"

"Nikolai." Stan put both his hands on his partner's shoulders. "Just think. Would Stanko-whoever-this-guy-is *not* realise how much hell one little girl with a drop of Flemming blood could raise?"

Mgamba looked up and shook his head. "I don't think so."

"Then get me the fucking clearance."

Two hours later, when Kozerski was boarding the shuttle, his secure line percom buzzed. Stan reached into his pocket and took it out, wondering who it could be. The sender's UID was blocked. He opened the inbox.

There was a message from Kato, two brief sentences:

Her name is Harvie. Harvie Flemming.

For what seemed like hours Harvie had been trying to locate her body parts. One at a time. They did not quite belong to her body, no matter how hard she tried to reconnect them. A dull pain of indefinite origin felt, however, like hers; the only sign that she was still alive.

The place didn't smell of the shuttle's cockpit, the last thing in her conscious memory. A blend of fruity air fresheners, laundry detergents, and stale cigarette smoke blended with the stench of damp upholstery. The room felt small, with not enough air to dilute the smells. Her back rested against a soft surface, while her head propped against something harder. Probably a cot. A monotone rattle came from an adjacent room – a bathroom, judging by the reek of floor sanitisers and cheap generic hand soap common for public facilities.

Someone else was here with her. She tried not to move, in case that someone was watching, waiting for her to come round.

A whiff of cigar smoke, thin, exquisite, came from her left, and a leather chair squeaked. She didn't need to look to know who sat there.

"It was rather rude of you to cut short our little conversation, don't you think?" The chair squeaked again and the cigar smell intensified, now coming almost directly into Harvie's nostrils. "Teenagers and good manners... Never go well together, do they?"

Another whiff of smoke flew directly into Harvie's face, bringing a painful spasm to her throat. She coughed and opened her eyes.

Marko's face hovered above her. His dark hair, sleek and in a tight ponytail when she last saw him at Delanue's, now hung loose at the sides of his long clean-shaved cheeks. He leaned forwards looking at her the way a bug collector looks at a rare tropical butterfly he has just pulled out of his ring-net. "By the way, my condolences about Captain Gulescu. Such a violent, untimely end... terrible."

Harvie said nothing, just clenched her fists. A tape pulled the skin around her wrists.

"I just thought you might feel a bit sad. But I guess you weren't really that close." Marko chuckled.

"If I could kill you I would sure feel better," Harvie said.

"There, there." Marko patted her on the shoulder. "Don't strain your voice. You'll need it."

"You'll be wasting your time, you know that," she said and stared at the ceiling, away from Marko's probing eyes. It was covered with creeks and dirty brown circles from seeping condensate. Some efforts seemed to have been made to fix it but the rust still showed through the fresh coating of paint. A half-peeled sticker on the side of an air conditioner with a broken front panel read: 'Property of Nebula Inn, Xastor.'

"I'm not in a hurry." Marko moved closer so she couldn't

escape seeing his face. "Take your time."

He turned around, walked up to the door and let in three men in civilian clothes. Without much ado, the tallest one, a tanned silent man with long blonde hair hiding half of his face, clutched Harvie's shoulders and pulled her off the bed. She shrieked as her broken legs hit the floor, but nevertheless tried to punch him with her head. The blonde grabbed her hair and crushed her face into a minibar stand, scattering the bottles all over the floor.

"Go to the bathroom," ordered Marko. "Don't leave any mess here. We don't need trouble."

"I thought you said we wouldn't have any," grunted the blonde over his shoulder, while struggling with Harvie as she tried to wriggle out of his grip.

"I said if you are careful." Marko picked up another cigar from the box. "I don't want to go broke covering up your shit."

"Why not take her to the base then?"

"Since when are my decisions any of your business?" barked Marko.

"Stay still, you bitch!" The blonde man wrenched Harvie's arms back and up, almost dislocating her shoulders. She screamed with pain and stopped twisting.

"Since you don't want Band A to find out about your screw-up with Delanue," the henchman said, resuming his conversation with Marko, "and I don't know why they shouldn't."

Marko's face darkened. For a few moments he stood silent then bit off the tip of his cigar.

"Get her talking first. If she doesn't, your ass is in as much trouble as mine. If she does, we can discuss how to handle our little arrangement."

"Sounds good to me." The blonde nodded. "I just don't want the guys doing overtime for no good reason."

"Keep working," Marko dropped grimly. "I want to know the kind of virus she uploaded into the servers and how to disable it."

"Shouldn't take long." The blonde grinned. "Go have a beer, boss. You look tense. We'll be done in an hour."

Some boss you have here, Harvie thought watching the blonde handcuff her to the radiator that ran from the top to the bottom of the bathroom like a ladder, *if he lets you talk to him like that. Scary guy, isn't he?*

She knew it would hurt, and the pain wouldn't be good, but there wasn't much she could do about it right now, other than try to step out of her immobilised body and watch, not without a certain spectator interest, the blonde deliver his first cannon-ball punch to her face.

***

Two hours later the trio hadn't made much progress. Not that they didn't try hard enough; they left no punch undelivered. But Harvie stubbornly refused to cooperate, letting out nothing more than short shrieks of pain and swears.

"She's not talking yet," the henchmen squad leader complained when Marko walked in. Moretti pushed the man aside and stepped into the bathroom. Harvie sat on the marble tiled floor, her elbows fixed to the radiator, head leaning back against glass tubes filled with magenta-coloured bubbling water. She was still conscious enough to acknowledge Marko's appearance with a weak grimace. He had changed his clothes, now sporting a black leather biking jacket over a stretchy turtleneck of the same colour. *He too knows how to blend in,* Harvie thought.

"She won't last overnight, boss." The henchman shook his head. "She already passed out twice."

Marko picked up a towel, bent down and carefully sopped up the blood dripping from the side of Harvie's mouth. His hands smelt of barley brew.

"You silly thing… Why are you doing this to yourself?" The beers he'd had while his crew was roughing up Harvie softened his voice. He pressed the towel to her cheekbone. Harvie saw red stains oozing through the cloth. "You are too young to play these games. Let's finish it and I'll let you go."

Harvie turned her head and articulated with her lips only: "Fuck. Off."

"You don't believe me, do you?" Marko put the towel down. "You should. You are a brave soldier, I respect that. But I must know what you know. There's no way round it."

Harvie jerked and coughed out a thick string of clotted blood. It landed on the embroidered top of what was left of a once elegant white dress. Marko grabbed Harvie's head with both palms. She had no choice but to stare right into his long, tired face, at his thin, pale lips that made his mouth look like a hole slit in his head with a carving knife.

"Just think: do you really want to die? Now? Here? Like this? Look at you! You know you deserve better."

Harvie shut her eyes. She didn't want this face to become one of her last memories.

"C'mon, let's get it sorted." Marko let go of her head. "I'll call the ambulance and leave you alone. They'll get you fixed in no time."

"You won't let me live. Because if you do, I'll make sure that you are dead." Harvie looked up.

Marko chuckled. "I'm ready to take the risk. Although…" he leaned on his right knee, eyeing Harvie with the same kind of entomological curiosity she had already seen. "Maybe I over-estimated you. Maybe you just don't have what it takes. Maybe you are just looking for an easy way out, huh?"

He stretched his hand and tried to touch the side of her neck with the tips of his fingers. Harvie jerked instinctively and recoiled. Marko moved his hand back in surprise.

"You…" He shook his head in disbelief and let out a burst of hearty laughter. "You are ticklish?"

Marko clicked his tongue and rubbed the side of his mouth like a boy who had just dumped on his desk a disassembled toy spaceship kit. "Who would have thought? Perhaps I should take you to the base after all." He stood up. "They'd love to have you there. Just think: a girl who feels no pain, but can be literally tickled to death." Marko folded his arms on his chest. "I wonder what else you're afraid of."

Harvie clenched her teeth, hating herself for betraying one of her sensory weak spots. She should have learned to control it long ago, was it really that difficult? She remembered the sensa-tion of Marko's fingertips on her neck and jolted as if hit with an electric discharge. Apparently it was difficult. And when stressed out, tired and worn out with two hours of bushwhack-ing, it became downright impossible.

"Listen." Marko frowned as if working out a plan in his head. "How about I change my mind? I'll take you to some people who would love to pull your head apart and see what's inside. They'll find everything about you. Everything that you hate. The sounds that drive you mad. The touches that make your skin burn. The smells that make you curl in the corner and wish you had never been born. They can do that, can't they?"

Harvie gulped. Yes, they could.

"You have an Achilles heel the size of an elephant's bottom, girl." Marko laughed. "And you delude yourself thinking you can make it because you can hold a few punches."

Harvie narrowed her eyes. She could take much more than a few punches. There were days when living in her skin, just going through the usual things of the day, felt worse than anything she had endured in the hands of Marko's 'pressure crew'. But she went on, taking each day in her stride, living. Not letting her own body scare her into a helpless wreck of a human.

"I'd be delighted to meet your employers." She grinned. "We have lots of things to talk about. Like the way you let your own goons blackmail you. Good career move."

"You…" Marko clenched his fist.

"The virus I put in Delanue's server can't be disabled," Harvie continued. "It has already transmitted everything that was there to transmit, and destroyed itself. Nothing I can say will save your ass. You've botched this one."

Marko's lips trembled. Harvie could see he was barely holding himself back from hitting her.

"Go ahead. Do it." Harvie lifted her chin. "As you've said, I can hold a few punches."

"Really? How about this?" Marko pulled the shower head off the stand, pointed it into her face and slammed the cold tap on. Millions of icy needles pierced Harvie's skin. Each one bore deep in, and she could feel them all. She pulled, kicked and wriggled, trying to get away from the sprout. Her heel hit against the glass shower screen. It shattered, cutting through her frantically jerking legs. "Turn it off!" She couldn't hear her own voice, but she knew she was screaming. "Off!"

"Wow, boss," one of the goons said in the distance. "We should have tried *that*."

Marko turned the tap off. "I've changed my mind," he said, "about taking you to the base. I think there's still some work to be done here."

Harvie pulled her bleeding legs to her chest, as if trying to shield herself. Drenching her with cold water wouldn't work on her a second time. The effect was the strongest when unexpected. But a few more surprises like that and her panic would become uncontrollable.

"I want to make you a deal," Marko said.

He squatted down, playing with the shower head in his hands. "Forget the virus. Whatever it lifted from Delanue's files was not that important. Not really worth the effort you guys have put in."

He was probably lying, but Harvie didn't care whether he spoke the truth. She'd been given a job and she had to finish it. For Gulescu, at least, if not for her.

"But you're right, it doesn't reflect well on my career, to let some cute teen take us for a ride like that."

Marko bent down and pulled a large shred of glass out of Harvie's leg. She had no idea it had been stuck there. He looked it over and tossed it in the bin. "I want you to do a few things for me. Help me play a little game with your boss."

Harvie didn't say anything. *Play along,* she thought. She needed time to get her body back in order.

"You contact your boss, and you tell him that you've escaped and you need to be picked up. Give your location. They'll come to collect you, but you won't go with them. You'll move. You'll keep moving until they figure it out. Knowing Unians' intellectual capacity, it may take them a while."

Yes, Harvie thought, they would keep trying to retrieve her. And it would expose a good deal of their undercover network.

"What happens when they do figure it out?"

"I don't know. Perhaps that's the question we'll ask your boss?" Marko grinned. "I'm sure you're smart enough to play it so well that they won't."

"Give me a minute," Harvie said. "I need to think."

She leaned back and stared at the transparent glass pipes with boiling water encircling the bathroom. Hosts of bubbles, large and small, drifted clockwise, popping, merging, breaking up in a mesmerising ballet. *How high is the water pressure inside that pipe?* Harvie wondered. *What if it breaks?*

They'd done a run on a small hotel once, she and Growler; looking, as usual, for edibles and medicine. Growler ransacked the whole minibar. He had just lost the girl he'd grown very attached to, and had taken to the habit of dumbing with grownup liquids the pain that often drove him to violent outbursts. Only it didn't help much, and he let his wild side go loose on every object that happened to be in his way when the anger hit. That was how they had learned about anti-vandal alarms in hotel rooms. *Learn and live.*

"I'll do it," Harvie said. "When do you want me to start?"

"How about now?" Marko released one of her arms. "Right here."

It will work, Harvie thought.

She focused on a large water bubble that swelled up, about to pop, and wondered for a second how much it would hurt. Then she drove her free fist through the pipes.

The scalding water burst out into her face, and she gasped, taken way over her sensory threshold. Her nerve system went into a full shutdown, as Harvie watched, quite fascinated, her skin turning red under the steaming stream.

"Holy fuck." Marko backed off, not even trying to move her away. "You are mad."

His voice drowned in an ear-piercing shriek of an anti-vandal alarm siren.

"Boss." The blonde henchman pulled his sleeve. "We need to get out. The police will be here any minute."

Marko nodded. "Yes," he said, panting. "Yes."

The blonde pulled out a gun and pointed it at Harvie's head.

"Don't." Marko pushed his hand away.

"Whatever you say." The man shrugged and waved to his men to follow him.

"I'll come back for you, girl," Marko said, throwing one last parting look at Harvie. "I will come and I will get you. This is my word."

When Marko's wet back disappeared from her sight, Harvie crawled onto the bathroom floor away from the scorching water that now leaked out in pulsating bursts, and closed her eyes, letting the exhaustion take over at last. She didn't feel fingers checking her pulse, or six muscled arms picking her up and putting her onto a stretcher, or an oxygen mask on her face, or ice blankets all over her body. She had slid into the world beyond pain and beyond fear, the one run by the forces outside her control.

10

They were young, they were foolish and zealous; the world lay in their hands like a little bouncy ball. Things fell apart, and Stan and Rod sat on the ruins with their cheap smuggled beers and celebrated. Every day made the day before seem like a walk in the park, and every tomorrow came upon them like a cannonball. They cheered each one they dodged, wondering why they were still alive. Rod became silent and serious, often disappearing for days, and then bringing along a few guys with classified station plans, or docking codes to Confederal warehouses, or crateloads of octaguns and other top-notch weapons for closed-space combat. He didn't order anyone around, he didn't argue; he simply said a few quiet words and things appeared and disappeared, as if by magic. People too; but it was even harder to keep track of people those days than to keep track of things.

The Confeds came from behind when Stan least expected it. He fought with all the might of his nineteen-year-old body, but they knew their job and they were ready. The drill hadn't changed much over the years: a shot of immobiliser drug into the base of the neck, a pair of remotely-controlled restraints in case the drug wore off sooner than expected, and a gag mask over the face that would provide the prisoner with oxygen, but keep him mute, deaf and blind. He could feel the heat and the smell of other bodies packed into the cargo compartment of a patrol ship and wondered if Rod had been captured too. They never discussed what they should do if the Confeds got them – the possibility simply didn't exist in their agenda.

Stan ended up in a dingy, stuffy cell that stank of a broken waste collector. The immobiliser wore off in a few hours, leaving him jerky and sluggish at the same time, and along with the freedom to move his limbs came a bout of desperate rage. Stan slammed his fists against the door and yelped obscenities in every language known to him, in a frantic bid to get some attention. He got what he asked for, and a little extra. Lucky for him, the senior guard noticed that he was coughing blood onto the floor and stopped short of rupturing his lung with a splinter of his broken rib.

They knew that drill too. A quick clean-up while the prisoner was being patched in the med block, a short log entry from a couple of eyewitnesses to make sure that HumanAid lawyers stayed cool, and everything would once again run like clockwork until Stan's next dumb act. A grim Slavic doctor explained all that to him in three short but eloquent expletives in his native language, and left him to the mercy of HumanAid volunteer nursing staff.

"Don't speak, don't move, don't breathe." The nurse didn't need to say the last one. Stan stopped breathing the moment she walked over the partition screen. He simply stared, not daring to believe that this ethereal dream-world being was going to touch his mortal body. The dream creature pulled over a mobile diagnostic station and smiled; to reassure herself, Stan assumed, because no way this dainty blonde pixie could know how to operate it.

"Need help?" Stan pointed at the station. "I've seen these things before."

"Bog off!" The pixie's velvety green eyes shot angry needles that made him twitch. "I'm a sophomore at Sorbonne Med School. So now lie down and let *me* help you."

She bent over to his ear, pretending to examine a deep cut on his scalp, and whispered: "Rod said they'll be taking over the prison tonight. Get ready."

The takeover of Base DG-6-D was the first large-scale coordinated Rangers' attack on a Confederal facility. That night the Rangers stopped being a bunch of breaknecks and became an armed force. Six lightweight ships force-docked at the main gates of the base, blocking access for any Confederal troops; the remote locks, overridden from the inside, threw the cell doors open, and Stan, who'd already worked out the plan in his head while cooling off in the med block, led the bewildered prisoners to the nearest assembly point. Rod waited there with crates of firearms, water, food and first aid kits. They hugged each other briskly, without exchanging too many words, and then again Stan saw the stunning blonde who'd fixed him up. He stumbled towards her, afraid she would disappear in the commotion, but Rod got there first. He smiled, grabbed her hand and turned to Stan, beaming like never before.

"Have you met Bel? She is – she is my wife."

"We will be waking her up now. You may come in."

Stan nodded and followed a small, dark-haired woman in loose blue overalls who met him at the entrance to the intensive care ward. Hospitals always made him uneasy. Too clean, too quiet. Hostile. They reeked of medicine, pain and death – things he preferred to avoid.

Stan landed at Xastor at noon local. A grim police officer checked his UID and informed him they'd acquired another item of interest to CNS, beyond the body of a man identified as Marcel Jacopo that now rested in the station's morgue. Xastor's security had delivered a badly injured teenage girl to the ER, and her profile didn't match any of the station's residents. The only way she could have got inside was aboard the dead man's shuttle, and a quick DNA check proved the theory right.

The officer escorted Stan to his vehicle, and then to a run-down hospital building that looked seriously understaffed. Stan had to wait for a good forty minutes before the woman came down to collect him.

"Dr Zhang?" Stan read the name tag on her chest. "Would it be possible to talk to the girl?"

"We'll see. Depends on how she feels, can't really tell. I suppose you want to find out who did this to her?"

"You mean the accident?" The police officer hadn't mentioned anything about the nature of the girl's injuries, so Stan guessed she was hurt in the shuttle crash.

"Accident?" Dr Zhang raised an eyebrow.

Apparently not, Stan realised, and felt a knot in his stomach. Had the Leggies got to her, just as he'd feared?

"Someone boiled her alive. I wouldn't call it an accident."

Dr Zhang looked at Stan with suspicion. "Have you not spoken to the police squad?"

"Haven't had a chance yet," Stan lied. Indep security would never answer a single question beyond what they had chosen to report without first asking for a CNS special investigator's warrant, which he didn't have. "I came straight here. Where did they find her?"

"Nebula Inn."

"Do they know who checked her in?"

"No. The room had no reservation – someone simply had a key. They are doing an investigation in the hotel right now. Looks like someone made good friends with one of the staff." Dr Zhang looked up, and again Kozerski could see the doubt in her eyes. "You said there was a crash, Captain?"

"Yes, I thought they found her in the docking park. That's where the crashed shuttle was."

"And you think it is linked?"

"Can't really tell you that. It's classified information. Sorry." Stan made the kind of solemn face that in conjunction with a CNS officer's badge often helped to stop unneeded questions.

Dr Zhang nodded. "I understand."

"Did you or the police find any items of identification on her?" He pressed on.

"They said she was with some men in the room, but…" The doctor looked away while she wiped her hands with a surgical towel. "She's not a hooker, that's one thing I can tell you. Too clean, honed. And the dress – do you know Borschanov's?"

"Not quite sure. Is that a shop?"

"A damned expensive one."

"Well, some escort girls make quite good money, if you

think about it." Stan shrugged his shoulders. Maybe he still could make the Indeps believe that it was just a teen hooker's job gone wrong. The less they knew the better.

Dr Zhang shook her head. "With that kind of money, you wouldn't need to be an escort girl. You could buy the whole franchise."

Stan took a close look at the surgeon. "You are a very observant woman, Dr Zhang," he said, stressing each word.

"I've spent nine hours putting this kid together. If I can do anything to get to those who did this, I will sleep much better. And I need it, trust me."

"Sorry, Doctor. I'm afraid I won't be able to keep you in the loop. No offence."

"I understand. Please, put this on." She handed Kozerski a disposable gown and led him upstairs to the intensive care wards. She opened one of the doors with her UID token and let Stan inside a dimly lit room filled with blinking monitors and buzzing machinery that made Stan squirm.

Dr Zhang lifted a matte screen that separated them from the life-support bed. Stan looked over her shoulder.

"Not a pretty sight, Captain, I must warn you."

A thick layer of dark yellow gel covered the girl's naked body up to her neck, leaving visible only her swollen, deformed face. Several coloured tubes protruded from under the surface and disappeared inside humming and buzzing machinery above the bed. Stan thought of a museum display of the insects trapped in drops of amber and shuddered.

"What's that stuff?" He pointed at the gooey mass.

"It keeps the skin sterile and is also a mild painkiller. Too many surface injuries: cuts, burns. This way we make sure they don't get infected. We'll remove it in a day or so, when most of the skin regenerates."

"I see." Stan had heard of regen treatment before, but never seen it in action. He just hoped it worked; or rather, prayed it would. Hoping didn't feel enough right now. "Can she hear us?"

"She is coming round. Might take some time; she was asleep for nearly twenty hours. Very long surgery. We were afraid she wouldn't make it."

"Can't believe what they did to the kid." Stan leaned closer to the bed, trying to detach from the burning ember in his stomach. "Bastards."

"I'd think you were used to seeing lots of things, Captain."

"So would I." He'd seen worse, in fact. But never before had it felt like his own body floating in a viscid tawny marinade. He gulped.

"Shame." Dr Zhang flipped through the screens and changed a few settings. "She must be a really good-looking girl, but you can't even tell now, can you?"

Her mother was, that's for sure, Kozerski thought. If Harvie had a quarter of her looks, she should be stunning. Stan bent over, hoping to see the familiar features once belonging to a brave and beautiful young woman who had by now become no more than an obscure memory.

He met with the sharp, stubborn grey eyes of his long-gone friend and rival.

"Can you hear me?" Dr Zhang flashed a pen light into the girl's face. Her pupils constricted. "Blink if yes."

Harvie's lips moved but only produced a coarse, breath-like "wkhe…"

"Sh-shh… Don't talk." Dr Zhang pressed a palm to the girl's mouth. "You are safe now. I'm Caroline Zhang, your doctor, and this is Captain Kozerski from Confederal Nearspace Security. He just wants to find out who hurt you."

"Hi there." Stan moved closer, so she could see him. "I'm Stan Kozerski." He glanced at Dr Zhang and hesitated. The surgeon looked like she knew how to keep her patient's privacy, but – "I used to know your mum and dad."

"Did you?" Harvie's voice came from deep inside her throat, articulated with vocal cords only. The girl's face didn't express any emotion. Stan wondered if that was the effect of the anaesthetics or if she had remarkable self-control.

"Yes, I did." Stan rubbed his temples, fighting off a headache.

"Then you already know too much." She closed her eyes. "So get lost, Captain."

"You are Rod's kid, goddamit. You sure are." Stan turned to Dr Zhang. "Can you leave us for a few minutes?"

"I'm not sure, Captain." The surgeon looked at Harvie, then at the flickering projection monitors at her side and shook her head. "She's extremely weak. You really shouldn't be bothering her right now if she doesn't want to talk."

"That's okay." Harvie's lips barely moved. Every word she said came out in a voiceless whisper. "I can handle it."

"You have five minutes, Captain." Dr Zhang pressed a few controls on the screens and disappeared behind the glass door.

Stan dragged a chair next to the bed and sat down, not sure what to say. Only five minutes to tell everything he had been carrying along for years. He didn't know where to start.

"Me and your father… We used to be best friends once." He finally broke the silence.

"Him and you." Harvie stared at Stan again, as if scanning him through. "A Krot."

"I used to be a Ranger. In fact, it was the two of us who started the Rangers." Stan wriggled, thinking of how absurd it must sound.

"How come he never mentioned you, then?"

"I don't know. You must have been too little to talk about these things."

"He talked about the Rangers a lot. Never mentioned you. Strange."

Stan felt the familiar hot wave rising inside him. "We went separate ways before you were born. He must have held a grudge, I guess."

"For switching to the Krots, I guess?"

Stan jerked and held his breath. *Easy, Stanko,* he thought, *she's just a kid, don't bring her into this old squabble.* "That's one way of putting it."

"Nice story."

"I know it's very hard to believe, but..."

"It's perfectly fine to believe, Captain. But it doesn't change anything." She pulled her right hand free of the gel, looked down at her fingers and twitched them one at a time. "What happened here is none of your business. Feel free to go back to your job."

"I will," said Kozerski. "And I'm taking you with me."

"Are you?" Harvie still didn't look at him.

Stan stared at the girl for another few long silent seconds, and then crossed his arms on his chest.

"You don't quite understand, young lady." His tone became official. "You and Paul Gulescu were identified as Unian agents performing a clandestine operation in Confederal space. We have sufficient evidence to put you under arrest."

Harvie kept twitching the fingers on her hand. "You won't be able to prove it."

"Maybe not, but we certainly can make sure that your operative career is over. And we sure will."

"Unless what? Carry on! There's an 'unless', isn't there?"

"I want you to quit, Harvie. On your own, voluntarily. Quit this job, go to school, get a normal life. This is not a job for a teenage girl. You shouldn't be putting yourself in harm's way, not like this. Just look at you!"

"So it's not really a choice, huh?"

"If you mean going back to Takura, no, you don't have that choice."

"Thanks for making this clear, Captain." Harvie pointed with her eyes towards Dr Zhang as she entered the ward. "I guess you have to leave now."

"We'll talk again, Harvie."

She didn't reply, pretending to be absorbed with Zhang's manipulations around the machines.

"Take care, kid." Stan got up and left the ward without taking another look.

He didn't get too far. A trio of his colleagues greeted him at the reception. He recognised the uniform of the CNS peacekeeping unit stationed at Xastor.

"Captain Kozerski?"

Stan acknowledged them with a quick nod.

"I have an order from CNS Headquarters to place you under arrest. Follow me, please." The sergeant stepped aside and pointed to the doors. Two others framed Stan from left and right.

Stan shook his head and obeyed.

"Amina, Amina…" He muttered under his breath. "You sure work fast."

On some days Stan couldn't but admire the professional demeanour of his boss. Well into her fifties, General Amina Gonzales could easily write a decade or so off her age without anyone taking notice. She moved in brisk dashes, sprinting from office to office, from desk to desk and then freezing next to one of her subjects in a pose of almost perfect stillness, like a drop of water in mid-air when the gravity field glitched momentarily before re-taking its grip. Amina Gonzales was, no doubt, the Boss – of the kind whose slight tilt of head or a twitch of the corner of her mouth, or simply a sudden pause or a change in tone could make one's armpits sweat profusely and heart rate drum a fire drill. Hardly reaching the shoulder height of many of her subordinates, she was nevertheless a force to be reckoned with. Yet she preferred to keep her style rather informal, as would anyone who had reached a position beyond any worries of authority and respect.

Yet at this very moment, Amina Gonzales fumed and spat flame and fire the way her people hardly ever saw; or would ever see, since the flame-throwing took place behind the explosives-proof doors of the Secure Detention Unit. The prison-style section didn't even appear on the floor plans of CNS Headquarters facility, and it made General Gonzales more at ease with her raging fury. Unfortunately for Stan Kozerski, he was on the receiving end.

"Are you out of you mind, Kozerski?" Amina barked as soon as she stepped into the cell where Stan sat contemplating whether someone was going to take him to a shower and bring him a change of clothes. "What kind of games are you and Mgamba playing here?"

There'd been plenty of time for Stan to rehearse his answer to this one. First, on his way back from Xastor, handcuffed and held at gunpoint; then locked up for ten hours in this dim, hot shoebox with a foam bed, a toilet and a water tap. "Lieutenant Mgamba has nothing to do with this. I accept full responsibility..."

"Cut the crap, Kozerski. You two are a pair of gloves in one pocket. But I expected at least a grain of common sense from you, Captain. How did you intend to hide that you have stumbled upon Rod Flemming's child?"

"She's a child, General. Flemming or not Flemming, she's only fifteen. I'm not sure anyone in CNS remembers that." Stan didn't bother to stand up. He knew he'd stepped way out of line, but so had General Gonzales, by coming down to SDU to chew him up in person.

"So what did you plan to do with her? Kidnap and hide her in some private orphanage? Or keep her in the drawer under your desk?"

Stan clenched his teeth and looked over Amina's shoulder.

"Answer me, Kozerski. You are still a CNS officer and I'm still your boss."

"I assume not for long."

"You wish."

"Oh." Stan raised his eyebrows and scrapped the plan to start a snorkelling franchise on Varadero beach after his conditional release was granted in about twenty-five years. "Shall we talk business, then? If you're done sawing my neck, of course."

"When I'm done with you, Kozerski, you'll be a cadaver." The general leaned against the wall and crossed her arms. "I want to make a deal with Takura."

"She can't go back to Takura. It's madness!" Harvie's mangled face on the hospital bed flashed in Stan's head. He wouldn't forget it soon.

"So make sure she doesn't, and I'll make sure this little incident never happened. Clear?" Amina tilted her head.

Stan frowned, estimating his chances to win Kato over. Not even zero. How about negative? "What happens if I don't make the deal?"

"What do you think will happen? The best we can do for the kid is to lock her up out of harm's way."

"That's the best you can do?" Stan looked around. "Keep her here?"

"What's your suggestion, Kozerski? Do you have a better option?"

Stan jumped at the chance. "She is a legal minor. We could place her into a foster home."

Amina shook her head. "The girl is a loaded weapon, emotionally unstable and trained to kill. CNS won't put a civilian family in that kind of danger; at least not if she's still a Unian agent."

She was right, of course. The 'Enemy of State' clause. They couldn't even send her to regular juvie, not to mention releasing her. And the child protection laws wouldn't apply either.

CNS could hold Harvie indefinitely, regardless of her age.

"And what will happen if Takura lets her go?"

"One step at a time, Kozerski." Amina stood up. "I'll leave you to think about it." She signalled to the guard to open the cell door. "When you make up your mind, let me know."

The heavy reinforced door closed behind General Gonzales with a tad more noise than would become a woman of her stature.

The comms pod came shortly through the food chute, together with a packed lunch, a disposable white T-shirt and a hygiene kit. Stan gave a satisfied grunt and took care of the life necessities before sitting down to play with the pod.

He pulled out the contacts list, hesitated over whether to call Mgamba, then decided not to. His every contact would be monitored, and Nik had already earned his share of trouble. Stan went through a few names on the Legal Dep list, thinking of a possible loophole he could pull Harvie through to safety, then sighed and set the pod down. He rolled his jacket into a ball, placed it at the head of his bed, lay down and closed his eyes.

Quiet, it's so quiet in here, he thought. Sometimes you wish you could spend more time in a place like this. Have time to think.

He stretched, releasing the tension in his back. What a luxury.

Stan picked up the pod again, found the apps screen and projected it to about a metre and a half over his head, so he could still lie on his back while browsing. Instead of launching the comms link, he went to see if he could log onto a music channel. It came up, with a slight delay. Stan selected classics and turned up the volume; the piano chords reverberated in the empty space. The acoustics of the prison cell astonished him. Who would have thought?

Stan closed his eyes and smiled, letting the music flush over his tired body.

Take that, Gonzales. You think you can get me by locking me here alone with my memories. The truth of the matter is, General, they are not the worst company in the world.

***

Stan called Amina eventually, and agreed to the talks with Takura. He didn't put much hope in the conversation, though. It would be a surprise if Kato answered the call, Stan thought, pacing across his atypically roomy and spacious office. Nik Mgamba must've had it cleaned up as a welcome-back gesture; another fringe benefit of Stan spending a few hours in solitary.

It was unlikely Stan would get a second chance, so he had to stack his deck right. As soon as a slice of Kato Takura's office appeared in the reception space of his 3Dcom, Stan jumped onto his feet as if ready for a fight. Thank goodness they were separated by a few thousand miles, he thought, feeling an itch in his fists. He rubbed his hands to calm down and cleared his throat.

"How is she?" General Takura did not bother with a greeting.

"How is she...?" Stan shook his head. "*Now* you ask."

He reached into his pocket, took out a pod, and pointed at the data receiver on Takura's desk.

"Look here." Stan pulled up a full-screen picture of a battered body spread on a blood-smeared marble floor. "That's from when Xastor police found her. And this..." He pulled another one – a close-up of a face, bruised and swollen beyond recognition. "This is from her medical record. Look." Stan flipped through the pictures, each more gruesome than the one before. He went faster and faster, until the images blurred into a kaleidoscope of torn flesh and blackened blood.

"Stan!" Takura stood up. "Get a grip, you!"

Stan turned the screen off. "Had enough, General? So fast?" He put the pod down. "She had to take it for hours. Her legs were broken in the crash. She could neither run, nor fight! Leggies just tenderised her like a piece of steak."

Takura exhaled through his teeth and sank back into his chair. "So how *is* she? Are you going to tell me or not?"

Stan took a cup from a water cooler, poured himself a drink and took a large sip.

"She is at the CNS high-security detention unit: solitary cell, restraints, and twenty-four-hour surveillance. All medical treatment she's now getting is vitamin supplements once a day."

Takura rubbed his chin. "You know that we'll bargain for her, Captain. Just name your price."

"CNS won't let you have her. And neither will I."

"You'd rather let her rot in Krots' jail?"

"I'd rather not see her wrecked by the Legion's henchmen again."

Takura stood up and paced towards the antique book cabinet. "So what do you want from me, then?"

"You need to talk to the Unian Board, Kato. You are the only person they will listen to." Stan stepped through the ghost of a half-rendered chair as if wanting to grab the general's shoulder. "They'll listen to you," he repeated.

"Talk about what?" Takura frowned. "I'm not following."

"They have to let Harvie go. CNS can't detain a minor, unless she's considered a state security threat. If the board fires her, Amina won't have any legal ground to keep her here."

Takura shook his head. "Fire Harvie Flemming? You are out of your mind, Stanko. The board just made her the youngest USF officer in their history. The girl has delivered billions worth of data to them, in a single mission!"

A chill slid through Stan's stomach. He knew what USF was after: Legion's acquisition plans for octalon-producing stations. Delanue must have had it all: the timelines, the blueprints, the suggested prices, the key contacts in the Nearspace Council's lobby. No secret service in the world would sack an agent who could deliver things like that.

"If I fire her now, Stanko, I'll have to resign too."

"I understand." Stan looked up. "But if you don't, Gonzales will keep her locked up until she's eighteen. Then, if she behaves, she may get a probationary release. She'll have to wear a chip though, like a tagged dog. For the rest of her life." Stan took a few rapid gulps from his cup. "They'll try to break her. Gently, but persistently. Confeds might be pro human rights and stuff, but the System is the System. It has been that way for centuries, and it won't change. You've been inside, Kato. You know."

"Krots will trade her, I'm sure. Everyone has a price. We got Ludo Hakada, we'll get Harvie."

"Yes, you got Ludo. That's right. It only took you what? About seven years?" Stan smirked. "It will destroy her. *You* will destroy her."

"So, you are asking me to betray her instead."

"I'm asking you to give the girl a chance!"

Takura took a random book from the shelf, flipped the pages and put it back. For a few moments he stood there, tapping his index finger on the book's spine then turned to Kozerski.

"I need to see her. Face to face. In private."

"Kato, I can't," Stan protested. "I don't have that sort of authority."

"Then find someone who does. Prove you can make things happen for Harvie. I want to know I can trust you with her."

"She's Bel's child – don't you think I'd do everything I could…" Stan swallowed.

"Prove it. You make it happen – I'll talk to the board. Tell Amina Gonzales that's my condition."

Stan nodded. "Thanks, Kato. I will."

***

Stan spent the next morning packing. He wasn't sure where he was going or whether leaving was a good idea. Right now he wanted one thing: to get out of the office, get some space, calm down, weigh his options, think. His request for General Gonzales to let Takura see Harvie had been declined, and he had no other business to do here, except to pack up and leave. He should have done it years ago. Even better, he should never have set foot into this place.

"I've heard you're resigning?" Amina's head popped out of his 3Dcom without forewarning.

"You should have received my letter four hours ago, General, and I assume you've read it." Stan didn't look at her. "I made it explicitly clear that I no longer see it possible to represent CNS interests; at least not the way you interpret them, General Gonzales."

"By which you mean Flemming's case, of course."

"By which I mean denying a child her basic human rights." Stan looked up and met Amina's piercing glance.

"Come to see me, Kozerski, for a second."

Stan trudged to the general's office, stopping on his way to grab a coffee and compose himself. As the door behind them closed, Amina pulled a squeaky leather chair next to her immaculate desk.

"Tell me something, Kozerski," she narrowed her eyes as if

focusing on his face as she sat down. "It's the girl's mother, am I right? She's the daughter of a woman you loved."

"General, I'm not going to—"

"Don't. I'm not asking for a yes or no. All I'm asking is to consider whether a man can count on his reason when it comes to the passion of his life."

Stan's face went red. "You've got the girl, what else do you want, General?"

"Calm down, Kozerski." Amina pointed at the chair next to her. "Sit."

Stan did.

"Look." She opened her tablet. "That's a psychologist's report on little Flemming. See here? 'Determined', 'manipulative', 'evasive', 'crafty', 'cunning'. And here: 'It can be concluded with certainty that Harvie has a significant number of neurological traits consistent with a pervasive autism spectrum disorder.'" Amina let Stan read a few paragraphs, then blackened the screen. "Do you know what this means, Captain? This girl doesn't know what love or loyalty is; it's not how her brain works. She is essentially selfish. If you let the memory of her mother run your mind, she'll twist you around her little finger before you know it."

"Can I repeat my question, General?" Stan lifted his chin and looked Amina in the eye. "What do you want from *me*?"

General Gonzales sighed. "I once did a background check on the man called Stanko." She glanced at Stan's face to see his reaction. None followed, so Amina went on. "Some sources said he was the first of the Rangers to object to the impetuous decision-making of Commander Flemming. Some even went as far as to suggest that it would be Stanko, not Rod you would need to go to if you'd want to reason with the Rangers."

Stan shrugged with resentment. "Rod Flemming was a great man, that's all I can say."

"He was also a very driven man: Focused, obsessed, hot-tempered at times. I'm not judging – many great leaders are like that." Amina paused. "Stanko, on the contrary, was referred to as 'diplomatic, rational, calculating,' but also 'extremely loyal'. It was Stanko we approached to offer the Rangers an honourable exit that saved hundreds of lives in the end."

Stan gulped and looked away, avoiding Amina's piercing eyes.

"It's Stanko", she continued, "I would want to take care of Rod Flemming's daughter. He's the only man up to this job. But I don't know if he's around anymore."

"I see." Stan sighed and stood up. "Let Harvie talk to Kato Takura, and you'll get your Stanko. If that's what you want."

"That's what I thought." Amina grinned and turned the screen back on. "Tell Takura to be here at 1700 standard. He'll have an hour. That should be more than enough."

"Yes, General."

"Anything else?"

"No, madam."

"You can go now, Captain. And—" Amina's eyes steeled. "Next time I really would like to see Stanko."

A tall medic in a Confederal uniform pressed the injection gun to Harvie's shoulder and pulled the trigger. Harvie ground her teeth.

Dr Zhang picked up the discarded capsule. "This is quite a strong drug for a kid, don't you think?"

"She is a strong kid, Doctor. Now if you'll excuse me…" The man moved Dr Zhang aside and stretched his arm to power down the mobile bed's flotation device. The man's arm detached and hung in the air, only to be replaced by another one, which also detached and hung up below the first one, still connected to the main body with a snot-like string.

"It's an adult man's dose; she's hardly over 50 kilos." Zhang's protesting voice gurgled over Harvie's head. Speech bubbles came out of her fish mouth in rainbow-coloured spheres and popped with a firecracker sound.

"We can't take chances with this young lady." The Confederal medic tilted his bird head and blinked with yellow bulging eyes. The feathers on his head ruffled. His ten arms danced around his scaled body in a sophisticated jig. "It will keep her quiet. Now, would you sign off the transfer? Here. Then you can go."

Dr Zhang gurgled again and splashed off a wave of turbid foamy water, leaving behind an intense stench of rotting seaweed. The water filled up all corners of the ward and then disappeared, sucked in by a black viscous hump in the doorway. With each gulp the hump grew; it spat dark red balls that floated around chirping, tiny, snickering giggles, and splat to the floor, the walls and the ceiling. The splatters steamed and smelled of burnt flesh.

The black protuberance rippled and turned into a human figure. It then stepped aside, letting the hundred-handed birdman walk Dr Zhang through the ward doors, and laughed with Marko's wry chuckle:

"How's my little girl doing? Have you missed me? I sure missed you."

Harvie turned her head away and faced another man, staring at her through a white mesh wall.

"You're dead," she said. "What the hell are you doing here?"

Paul Gulescu looked younger, more like the man she'd met during her first term at the USF cadet programme than road-weary Marcel Jacopo. He walked through the wall of aluminium mesh and squatted down, so his face came level with Harvie's.

Gulescu grinned. "Being dead has its advantages. So, how are you, anyway?"

"Tired," she confessed. The continuing waves of lucid hallucinations had begun to wear her out. Even the lunch box on her bedstand blinked with multiple curious orbs' on little curly stems. Closing her eyes made no difference; the visions remained. So now she could see dead people. Great.

"I want to see Dad. If I can see you, why not him?"

"He's not here, and neither am I. I'm just your sick imagination, Flemming. You're sick. And you won't get better if you don't eat."

A dark shadow bulged in the corner.

"What about that one?" She pointed at the bulge that once again started to look like Marko. "I don't remember him dying."

"Don't pay any attention, he's not real either. Will you eat?"

"I'm cold."

"Stop whimpering and eat your lunch before they clear it and put you on a forced feed. You won't like it, trust me."

Harvie sat up. The cell walls pulsated like the body of a giant white jellyfish, changing shape and hew. She could smell dead fish too. She suppressed the urge to throw up and grabbed the lunch tray.

She held a bite in her mouth, unsure whether to swallow, then gulped and felt it slide down her throat. It stayed there. She took another bite and looked around to check if Paul was watching her. He wasn't there. She sat on the floor of a small, narrow cell with metal walls painted greyish white, holding a black plastic lunch tray, all alone, and hungry as a wild dog. She finished the rest of the tray in less than three minutes, washed it down with tepid water from a plastic bottle, and climbed under the sheet, still shivering and dizzy.

Harvie closed her eyes but sleep wasn't coming. She sighed and curled into a ball, nursing her broken arm. The bulge in the corner moved and chuckled.

"Get lost," Harvie whispered. "I'm tired. Just wait till I get to you for real."

She tried to focus on the spots of residual pain that began

their creeping return to her body, bundling them up in imaginary cocoons of cool blue bands. One by one she stretched the bands and wrapped them around her, sinking into a pool of milky glow, then dimming, dimming it until she was half asleep, then three-quarters asleep, then nine-tenths…

A blast of bright light over her head hurt like a blow with a wooden board. She jumped up, gasping for air, unsure whether the figure towering over her was real or imaginary. A sullen man in the uniform of a CNS lieutenant waited for Harvie to gather her bearings and handed her a pair of handcuffs.

"Put these on and follow me. You have a visitor."

Harvie put her shivering legs down to the floor and complied.

The cell had two exits: one a mesh door with a reinforced metal shutter and another, varistate one, with a small red light on the side. As Harvie stared at the light, it turned green and the door dilated like a giant grey iris, revealing a small, dim lift cabin with a mirror that reflected the two people who had walked inside. The first one was a sullen girl in a crumpled bright-orange shirt and slacks, arms behind her back. Next to her stood a Confederal sergeant, a tall, tanned man in his twenties with a dark face framed with a small, trimmed beard.

Harvie took in her face, a puffy, jaundiced mask with sunken cheeks and stitched-up cuts that made her look like a scrawny street cat. She pictured the animal getting into a bin of freshly dumped rubbish and suppressed a cough. Her mouth filled with the taste of sour clotted milk. The door dilated again, its uneven edges pulsating with an iridescent indigo hue that made Harvie feel queasy. She had enough hallucinations up to now to put up with the solid objects that behaved like illusions. Her temples throbbed as she tried to keep inside the contents of her stomach.

The Confeds brought her into a scarcely lit room, grey and morbid, with matte wall panels that Harvie knew masked one-way glass. Someone out there must be watching them. In the middle stood a plain desk with an office chair, and beyond it there was another chair bolted to the floor, with solid metal clamps welded to the arms. The sight of the man at the desk made Harvie flinch. She hoped that he too would turn out to be just another phantom of her drug-spiked brain.

Stan Kozerski sat at the desk, tapping his fingers on the scratched plastic surface.

"Captain Kozerski?" inquired the Confeds sergeant.

"That's right." Stan stood up.

"Stay there, Captain." The sergeant led Harvie to the bolted-down chair. "Sit down." He slightly but firmly pushed her into the chair. Harvie didn't resist.

"Lean forward." The man took off her handcuffs. "Hands."

She put her hands on top of the arms of the chair. The clamps clicked shut around her wrists. She jerked and looked at her right arm, the arm she'd used to crush the glass water pipe at Nebula Inn. It was still raw and swollen.

"You have fifteen minutes, Captain. When you're done, the buzzer is under the desk." The sergeant stepped back and disappeared behind the sliding doors.

Harvie looked up.

"Let's spare the preaching. What do you want?" She squirmed. "It hurts like shit when I sit here, so if we can keep it brief, you'd do me a big favour."

Stan came up to Harvie, bent down and released the right clamp, then returned to the desk.

"Better?"

"Thanks." Harvie put the arm down on her lap. "What about the other one?"

"Not so fast. I don't want to end up with a sock around my neck."

Harvie smirked. "I don't have socks, as you can see." She wiggled her bare toes in their oversized orange slippers. Her feet were freezing despite the burning sensation all over her body, an onset of a high fever.

"Well, *I* do, not mentioning the shoelaces."

Harvie looked at Stan's feet. He in fact wore old-fashioned formal shoes. Harvie mentally thanked him for the tip. Might one day come in handy. "So you are saying you're scared of me?"

"Aren't you scared?"

"Of what?"

"Yourself." Stan stood up and paced across the room. Harvie wished he wouldn't. The floor tilted and wobbled with his every step as if he were rocking a giant swing.

She felt chunks of semi-digested food travel up her gullet and focused on a transparent plastic cup on the desk. The water stayed level with the rim despite all the ducking and swaying. Harvie gulped and shook her head. "I get along with myself just fine. Do you?"

Kozerski looked uncomfortable. He glanced to the side and tried to change the subject. "Are they treating you all right?" He ran his fingers through his hair. "It can be rough here, but they are nothing like the Legion."

Harvie sneered. "I've noticed. Apart from 3 a.m. interrogations, it's pretty humane. I even got cheesecake for dinner."

"That's rather sarcastic for someone who not so long ago enjoyed the hospitality of Colonel Moretti."

"I haven't been with him for that long. He was in a hurry."

"I've heard that he's efficient." Stan sat down. "However, for better or worse, that's not our way."

"So what is your way, Captain?" The floor finally stopped swinging and tilted to one side.

"I—" Stan paused, as if hesitating. "We want you to go free."

"So, what's stopping you? Can I go now?"

"You know it's not that easy."

"If you want me to work for you, the answer is 'no.'" Harvie leaned to the side to feel level with the floor and suppressed another bout of nausea.

"No, Harvie. We don't want you to work for us. In fact, we don't want you to work for anyone, at least not in your current capacity. As I said before at Xastor, we want you to quit."

"Go to school, get a life, blah-blah-blah..." Harvie grimaced, feeling an oily taste on her tongue.

"Exactly."

"So what is the catch, Captain? What is there to keep me from flanking school one day and jumping onto the next shuttle to New Albion?"

"You'll be released under my custody. I will assume a full responsibility over you until you are twenty-one. In essence, I will adopt you."

"You will... what?" Harvie grimaced again. The room began to stink of fried eggs, one of the smells she could hardly bear.

"Technically speaking, I will be your new father."

Harvie laughed. The strands of hair dropped over her face.

"There are certain conditions attached. If you try to run away, you'll go to jail. For a very long time. And don't rely on us not finding you."

Harvie slowly bent her free arm and pressed it to her chest. The smell of fried eggs intensified, and she could see the side of the whites getting brown and crusty, as if they were searing in oil. The yolks looked at her from the pan with two wide, inquiring eyes.

"Hurts?" asked Stan.

"A little. Nothing to fuss about." She put it back onto her lap. "You are not telling me something, Captain. I know there must be something else."

"Yes, Harvie." Stan rubbed his knees. "I know it will be a bit hard for you to hear this." He tilted his head. "I'm really sorry." He took a deep breath. "We have got an agreement with the Unia's board, that if you ever come to their territory without our consent, they will detain you and ship you back to us."

Harvie opened her mouth as if about to swallow a whole apple. She could even taste it now, wilted and mushy, stuck in her teeth.

"Oh yeah… right!" She moved her jaw to get rid of the phantom taste. "Do you really expect me to buy that?"

Stan looked straight at her, quiet and composed. "No, I don't. All I want from you is to have a talk with someone who will make you believe it." He rubbed his temples. "And above all, to understand. This is all for your own future. For your best."

He pressed the buzzer. "There is someone here to meet you. I will leave you guys alone." He stood up and waited for the door behind him to open, then stepped aside, letting another person enter the room. "I was promised that this conversation wouldn't be listened to or recorded."

Harvie felt a rush of joy as she recognised the man, but the next moment she pulled back and clenched the armrests.

"You— This is not true, is it?"

She could no longer hold it. The food chunks burst out of her mouth, drenched in foamy liquid. It splashed onto her lap, burning through her skin. Harvie instinctively jerked her knees apart and the sick landed on the floor between her legs.

Kozerski rushed to her, but Kato Takura stopped him. "I'll get this, Stan."

He pulled a couple of disposable towels out of the wall dispenser and bent over Harvie, who sat rocking back and forth, staring at the puddle. "It's okay, girl. I'll get it."

Kato tried to wipe her face. The wet towel felt like sandpaper.

"Get away from me!" Harvie screamed and pushed him with her free arm. If the broken wrist hurt, she didn't feel it. "Get out!" She shouted at the top of her lungs. "Get out, both of you!"

You have an Achilles heel the size of an elephant's bottom, girl… Marko's face grinned at her from the puddle of vomit.

Kozerski stepped back. "I will leave you alone now. Sorry, Harvie."

"Everything will be all right, Stan." Kato Takura pressed on the captain's shoulder. "She will be okay."

The general sat down and took off his cap. "You can leave now, Stan."

Kozerski made one last glance at Harvie who sat there breathless, with her arm pressed to her stomach. He jerked his lips as if about to say something, but instead just nodded and left the room.

***

General Gonzales looked down at her notes as if taking stock in a grocery shop. It was close to eleven o'clock in the evening, and the woman looked a bit off colour, with dark shades beginning to set under her eyes. Looking at her, Harvie couldn't help but feel fatigued as well. She'd had a much longer day than Gonzales, after all.

"Denise Harvie Flemming." Amina raised her eyebrows, which made a deep vertical line appear in the middle of her forehead. "Quite a file you have, Deni."

"My name is Harvie, to start with."

Harvie had taken a shower and changed into a fresh set of clothes, but she still smelled the sour stench, even though she'd drunk up all the syrupy medicine they gave her to offset the effect of the drug.

"Look, Denise. If we are going to have arguments about every little thing, this is going to be a very long conversation."

"My name is not a little thing. And I'm not in a hurry."

"Well, you want a new life, you need a new name. And I think Denise is a very nice one. That's the one your parents gave you, didn't they?"

"My parents are dead."

"And you buried your name with them?"

Harvie didn't reply. She felt dead too. The medicine dumbed down her senses, but it was not that. The inside of her chest felt hollow; a gust of wind could easily blow through it.

"I shall call you Denise. You need to get used to it again." Amina looked down at her notes. "I assume you are fully aware of all details of the arrangement between you and Captain Kozerski?"

"Yes, I am."

"Nevertheless, I shall highlight a few very important points." Amina bent forward and put her elbows on the table. "I want you to listen very carefully, Denise, and take note. It's not just your future on the line, but also that of Stan Kozerski, who, I must say, went a very long way to make sure we would be having this conversation."

"You bet."

General Gonzales picked up her tablet and scrolled down the document with her short, polished fingernail.

"Under no circumstances shall you attempt to contact your former employers either in person or by any other means of communication." She looked up as if checking that her words were getting through; then continued. "You are not allowed to possess or use firearms or weapons of any kind. In plain English, if you so much as lay your finger on anything sharper than a table knife, this arrangement is over. You get into a fight, it's over. You hack into any computer system, even if it's downloading a movie, it's over. You fail to keep up your school attendance, it's over. From now on, you will need to be an exemplary girl, Denise. One step out of line…"

"And it's over. I get it." Harvie chewed her lip. "There's one thing I don't understand, madam. How does all this differ from what I've got going on now?"

Amina smiled. "You won't wear handcuffs. And you can choose your desserts."

Harvie snorted and turned her head. Then she looked back at Amina and shrugged her shoulders. "Thanks at least for not telling me it's all for my own good."

"It is, Denise, but you will need some time to appreciate it."

"What if I don't?"

"Then it's over. For you and for Captain Kozerski. I hope you understand."

Harvie nodded. "Where shall I sign?" She looked over Amina's shoulder, avoiding her eyes.

"Right here." Amina turned the tablet over and put it down in front of the girl.

Harvie pulled the stylus out and shuffled, looking for a way to place her tied hands over the tablet.

"Wait," Amina said. She waved to the sergeant. "Take off the handcuffs."

The man touched the control on his belt; cuff rings clicked and pulled open. Harvie took them off and put them to the side of the table, then rubbed her wrists and picked up the stylus. She hesitated for a moment then wrote in large, flying letters: 'Harvie Flemming'.

Amina produced a wide, satisfied smile.

"You did the right thing, Deni. Your father would be proud of you."

Harvie swallowed as if she wanted to say something, but instead she just bit her lip and nodded.

"Captain Kozerski is coming to pick you up at 2300. We'll bring you some civilian clothes."

Harvie stood up and moved towards the exit. Amina grabbed the tablet and empty paper cups.

"There is no shame in defeat, Denise."

Harvie stopped but didn't look back. "Is that what you tell your people, General?"

"Sometimes. I suppose your father didn't teach you that."

"He didn't." Harvie stepped through the doors. "Have a good day, madam."

Stan paced the tiny windowless room, waiting for Harvie to come out. He was desperate for a smoke; he had not had one for days. He cursed under his breath for leaving his 'emergency' supply at home after yet another ill-conceived resolution to quit. It came back on him with a vengeance.

They brought Harvie out at eleven, as agreed. At first, he didn't recognise her. Out of prison clothes she looked taller and bigger, although she still could use a proper meal or two. She wore a pair of classic blue jeans and a black T-shirt with a manga heroine kicking some serious ass. Stan thought it was ironic on the border of being cruel.

The sergeant gave the girl a tap on the shoulder: "Move." Harvie stepped forwards into the light and Stan could see her face. Most of the swelling and bruises were gone, leaving just a few stitched scars that made her look odd, but not deformed or ugly. Her blonde, shoulder-long hair was tied into a ponytail, with a few loose strands dangling at the sides. Now he finally saw what he was looking for when they first met at the hospital.

A few vague lines, an obscure semblance to Bel Dubois: fine, rounded chin, high cheekbones, and that special way she moved her upper lip when angry. Yet her eyes were cold grey steel, nothing like Bel's green velvet with light golden sparkles. It was as if he were looking at both of his friends at the same time, merged into one body; yet it was a body with a life of its own. It wasn't them anymore.

They took an unpiloted pebble cab to the living compounds. On the way down, neither of them said much. Harvie stared at the labyrinth of steel structures outside the pebble window; Stan stared at her out of the corner of his eye. The guilt he'd felt yesterday, when Takura left CNS office without shaking his hand, gradually started to dissolve, leaving him more and more convinced he'd done the right thing.

"Kato said you've finished most of the high school programme." Stan finally broke the silence. "I've seen your grades. Quite impressive."

"What did you expect?" she retorted. "That I'd be an illiterate?"

"I'm just trying to say, 'well done.'"

Harvie huffed. "Pass the water, please, would you?"

Stan looked around and saw a bottle in the holder next to the pebble navigation dashboard, a freebie from the cab company. He picked it up and handed it to Harvie. "Still cross, are you?"

Harvie took a few gulps. "Now I know how he felt," she said.

"Erm?"

"My father. When people like you left him. You and Kato." She took another gulp.

"Kato didn't leave Rod. Unia stayed on his side to the end. They took in most of the remaining Rangers."

"You mean those who didn't switch over to the Krots already."

"If you mean me, I don't regret what I did. If Rod had done the same, he would still be alive. Your mother would still be alive."

"So you're saying staying alive is more important than staying loyal?"

"Staying loyal…" Stan pressed his thumbs together. "Yes, that's what Rod would say." He looked at Harvie. "And now what? What use is he dead to anyone? To the Rangers? To his daughter? Shouldn't he be here, with you?"

Harvie squeezed the bottle so hard that the liquid nearly spilled on her brand new jeans. Then she carefully relaxed her grip and put the drink down.

"I have a few high school tests left. Need to get them sorted," she said as if the rest of their conversation never took place. "Did they say which school I will go to?"

"You'll have a private tutor for the first term, and also a child psychologist." Stan felt relieved to change the subject.

"Do they think I might bite other kids?"

"They think you'll need time to adjust."

Harvie snickered. "Locked up alone in your place? Some adjustment!"

"My son and his little brother will be coming over for the holidays. They'll keep you company for a while."

"'My son and his brother?' Strange way to put it."

"Jem's got another father. But he's a nice kid. You'll like him. He's a little tornado." Stan realised he hadn't yet told Irina about Harvie. That would be some conversation. He flinched.

"What about the other one?"

"Tim?" Stan frowned. "What can I say…? He's a quiet one. Very much like his mum. We split when he was three."

"You have a habit of abandoning people, don't you, Captain?"

Kozerski's face reddened. "Some things are just none of your business, young lady."

"I see." Harvie twitched the corner of her mouth.

Stan sighed. "One day I might tell you the whole story. But not today." He looked out of the window. "We are almost there."

***

Stan's was a modest flat, even though by now he could probably afford a much bigger one. It never seemed to bother him; he hardly spent any time there. He liked the feel of the place, its cramminess, much like the family compartment he grew up in, when living space was still a luxury, and the cubic metres of breathing air per head were the way to measure a family's status. Back then his parents had a tiny one-bedroom section, but at least they 'lived at sea level', never having to reduce the pressure in the house to conserve oxygen.

Stan had moved into this flat about ten years ago, when it became clear that his CNS job was there to stay. He did invite a designer over to give the place a more 'Earthy' look and feel after he had arranged custody time with his son. He was hoping that Tim would feel less frightened in a more familiar environment, so he went out of his way to make sure that the flat got all the features of a terrestrial suburban house, including shamelessly expensive VR window panels that now broadcast an all-too-real view of moonlit snowy mountains. He set it on a twenty-four-hour daylight cycle at his doctor's advice, to help with his sleep, but it didn't seem to work the promised wonder. Stan thought he might just as well switch it to permanent daylight; at least he would see some of it when he came home.

He'd left one room unchanged though: his 'den', as he called it, with bare walls of titanium mesh through which you could see all the wiring and piping. That's where he dumped his Rangers' memorabilia, out of other people's sight. He didn't want too many questions asked by occasional visitors. Not that he had many around anyway.

"Nice place." Harvie kicked her shoes off, shoved her hands into back pockets of her jeans and looked around. "You don't live here much, do you?"

"Why?" Stan felt a pinch of guilt. Had he somehow made it obvious that this spotless home was badly neglected by its owner?

"Don't know, just a feeling. It's surgical."

"I've just got it tidied up, that's all. I like it clean." He remembered his office had won the 'Fire Hazard of the Month' award four times in a row and felt another pinch. "Feel free to mess it up anyway, if that's the way you like it. Sorry you can't have your 'toys' here though. Anything else – just ask."

Harvie nodded. "So what happens to my 'toys'?"

"Kato will take care of them until you are legally allowed to possess firearms."

"Won't be of any use then. They are custom-made. My body will be different. Can they at least be modified for target practice?"

"There won't be any target practice, Harvie. Not here, not back in New Alb. Did Amina not make that clear?"

"Not even for sports?"

"One of the local schools has an award-winning wall-climbing team. I'm sure they'd be delighted for you to join them." Stan caught the sour look on Harvie's face and rushed to make amends. "I'm just trying to make a joke! You don't have to if you don't want to."

"I'll think about it. Martial arts?"

"Hmmm… It's sort of a grey area. I doubt they would let a pro fighter compete for an amateur team."

"But can I still train?"

"The coach will have to be vetted by Amina. We need to make sure it's non-combat training. She may prefer not to take risks, though."

"I see." Harvie turned away and stared at the framed pictures on top of an artificial fireplace, tracing the edge of the shelf with her fingertips. "I think I'll stick with wall-climbing. Beats banging my head against one."

Stan laughed. "You sound like you're being locked up in a convent!"

"Do I?" It didn't seem a question.

"Just for your information, young lady," Stan once again tried to sound jocular, "Universum, as guidebooks say, is 'widely acclaimed as a place with the most opportunities for people under eighteen'. Even Tim had to admit that, and he's not easily convinced."

Stan pointed at a 3D picture of a teenage boy with long dark hair and a slightly annoyed, detached, scholastic look. He picked it up and handed it to Harvie. "That's him. Tim."

Harvie gave the picture a quick, indifferent glance, still tracing the shelf. "How old is he?"

"Sixteen." Stan put the frame back. "You can probably put two and two together now. I found out my girlfriend was pregnant and… Well, I couldn't let my son grow up without a father."

Harvie's fingers stopped. "It didn't work out?"

"Not too well. But at least I gave it a shot." Stan paused.

"C'mon, say it!" snapped Harvie.

"Say what?" Kozerski said, taken aback by her sudden anger.

"Unlike *your* father. Isn't that what you wanted to say?"

"Harvie…"

"He *was* with me! He wouldn't let anyone take me away. I was there, on his ship the day he…" she swallowed. "Whatever. Doesn't matter." She slammed herself onto the armchair and curled into a ball.

Stan grabbed another chair and sat down next to Harvie. She didn't look his way, staring instead blankly into the distance.

"C'mon. Let's eat something." Stan stood up. "I'm starving."

Harvie nodded and followed him to the kitchen, down a level from the living room. As they walked down the stairs, Stan noticed her tracing the wall with the tips of her fingers, as if stroking. Bel used to do that too. One time Stan joked that she was putting some secret spell on *The Ranger*, to make the ship invincible. And then Bel was gone, and the spell stopped working.

"How did Rod die? Nobody told me." Stan opened the fridge and looked inside. They'd have to settle with half a chocolate bar and a dried slice of brie for tea. A feast.

"He blew the ship," Harvie said in a dry, coarse voice. "Put me on a rescue pod, fired into space, and blew his ship, with all the Leggies inside."

"God…" Stan exhaled.

"Nope, *He* wasn't involved much. Just observed."

"So, General Takura…?" Stan put the kettle on and took two cups off the shelf, checking the insides for dust.

"He found me by accident, three years later. I was eleven." She paused, as if unsure whether to say more, then continued. "The Legion took over a defunct octalon factory and cleansed it. Cleared all the hobos out then got to us."

"Us?" The kettle clicked and stopped boiling.

"The kids. You know. The Litter."

"The Litter." Back in his school years, that's what they used to call runaway Laika children who lived in the engineering tunnel network, feeding on whatever they managed to steal from warehouses. There were more of them later, when the war raged on. "I didn't know the Litter was still out there. Were there many?" Stan rinsed the cups, dropped a teabag into each, and searched the cupboards for sugar.

"Some," Harvie said with a hesitation. "Back then there were a hundred of us perhaps, maybe fewer."

"What happened to them?"

"Do you *really* want to know?" Harvie sat down in a black carbonplastic kitchen chair and again pulled her knees to her chest.

Stan looked down and said nothing, only shook his head, pouring hot water into the cups.

"We gave the Leggies a bit of a hard time," she continued. "I knew how to use firearms. And I was a good teacher." There was an unmistakable pride in her voice.

"Harvie!"

She shrugged her shoulders: "If the Litter has to kill, it kills."

Stan noted the use of the singular and felt a creeping chill. He took the cups to the breakfast table, grabbed the chocolate and sat down. "So what happened then?"

"Takura pulled me out, before…" She stopped and coughed.

"How did he recognise you?" Stan rushed to change the subject.

"He didn't. I did. I saw him once with Dad. I've got a good visual memory." Harvie's pupils jumped, as if scrolling through the pictures, visible only to her.

"And you told him about yourself?"

Harvie shrugged. "I thought it would give me a better bargaining position."

"A better bargaining position? You were eleven!"

"I was old enough to kill, sure, but not old enough to bargain for my life?"

Stan rubbed his face. "I just – I can't even imagine."

"Then don't." Harvie put her bare feet down. "Why would you even try?"

"I don't know how you live with all this." Stan shoved the chocolate bar her way.

"Yet, I do. Or did, until now." She broke a bit off and put it into her mouth.

"You're talking as if your life is over." Stan took one as well, even though he didn't feel like eating at all.

"Is it not?" She shrugged and looked around. "You call this life?"

"Call it whatever you want, I still think it's better for you." Stan took a sip out of his cup and grimaced. The brew tasted like soaked woodchips. Where did he buy this shit?

Harvie pulled away. "I *am* going to be twenty-one one day, you know. Or do you hope to break me before it happens?"

"I'm not trying to break you. I just want to show you another option to live your life; to be!"

"Having been is not being, even if it is 'the surest kind.'"

"You read Frankl?" Stan recognised the quote. "You keep surprising me."

Harvie took a few sips from her cup. "I read shedloads of stuff, what's your point?"

"You are a strong, brave, smart young woman, Harvie. You've got a lot in you and there will be more. And just to think," Stan squeezed his thumb and index finger, "that all of it came this close to being destroyed by a bunch of thugs. Why? What for?"

"My mother was a fine woman, too. Don't you think?"

Stan's face grew red. "So, it's all about revenge. Is it?"

Harvie shrugged. "Kato said you loved her. I thought if someone you love is murdered…" She stopped.

"You'd want to get every last one of those bastards? That's what you want to say?"

"Have you never felt that way?"

"I have. But you? I don't think so."

Harvie looked up and narrowed her eyes. "Right. And you think that because…?"

"It's not revenge that drives you. It's the guilt; the shame and helplessness of a little girl who watched her parents die and couldn't stop it. You think you failed them and you want to make it right. You want to make your parents proud. You play with death because you think your life isn't worth living, not without them around. And you want to end it the way you think they'd approve of. That's how I see it."

Harvie's eyes didn't reflect even a slightest shade of emotion.

"Sometimes I think all you're doing here is waiting for a suitable moment to run off. Always on the lookout, always ready. Can't you just *relax*? Harvie, you are a child, not a Ranger!"

Harvie's cheeks flushed. "I don't have to wait for a suitable moment. There are plenty of suitable moments." She stood up, breathing like a she-wolf ready for a fight. "I don't even need – look! In here, in this kitchen… "

Before Stan could blink, she pulled out a heavy deba knife from the block and thrust it into the wall. A fountain of electric sparkles burst out. The kitchen lights blinked and went off.

"There is a five-minute delay between the short circuit and the emergency power backup launch. Enough time for me to cut your throat and everyone else's in this house, if I wanted to. I'd be long gone before the compound security even noticed something had happened." Another burst of sparkles lit up Harvie's face. Her eyes glistened with moisture. "This is *me*. This is who I am. Do you understand?"

Stan stepped back, pulled out a kitchen drawer, and found a torch by feel. "If you know how to break it, then I guess you know how to fix it, so do me a favour."

Harvie took the torch and pulled the knife out of the wall. The lights blinked again and went back on; the power backup kicked in.

"I'll have to take the panel off; that's about an hour's work." She rubbed her forehead.

"You can do it tomorrow afternoon then. Dr Sharon Riesley from Children's Mental Health is expecting you at 9 a.m. Don't be late." Stan collected the cups from the table and emptied them into the sink.

"You're not going with me?" Harvie put the knife back into the block and then handed the torch to Stan.

"I have to be at the office. I'll give you the address and some pocket money to get there. Just come back here when you're done." Stan placed it back in the drawer and put the cups into the dishwasher. "Goodnight, Harvie."

"Goodnight, Captain." Harvie didn't move. "Or shall I now call you 'Dad'? What's the protocol?"

"Goodnight." Stan walked to his bedroom and closed the door behind him.

Inside, he hesitated for a moment, looking at his bed, straight and square as a brick, and then walked to a small corner desk of thick black glass where a slick shell of a matching

3Dcom glowed in aquamarine hue. Stan powered it up and sat down into an office-style rolling mesh chair, stretching his legs. Long day… The fatigue started to get to him, but not the sleepy, drowsy kind; more like heaviness, that pressed him down with a leaden blanket. He opened a wide, shallow drawer underneath the desktop, took out a pack of cigarettes and checked the contents. Six. There were ten two days ago. Stan sighed. He held the pack in his hand, rubbing smooth edges of the plastic box, then put it back and called.

"Irina."

The 3Dcom hesitated for a second then spat out a glowing yellow balloon with a rotating orange 'G' inside. A line of text circled the balloon's perimeter: *G-Link gives you the cheapest calls to Earth from anywhere in Nearspace*, then another one appeared under: *Irina Rostokina, Utrecht, Europe: 23478-47899-5599.*

"Call."

Stan listened to the first few 'ta-da-dams' of the *Moonlight Sonata* and had already stretched his hand to abort the call when a mop-like head appeared, followed by the top of the shoulders of a sleepy boy dressed in blue pyjamas. Green goggle-eyed monsters danced and jumped all over the desktop behind the boy's back.

"Oh. Oh! Uncle Stan!"

"Hi, Jem. Is your mother home?"

"She's sleeping." Jem looked away, at a flickering parallel screen in his room.

"Can I talk to her? Please? It's sort of urgent."

14

At half past two, Tim Rostokin sneaked into his house and tip-toed through the kitchen, careful not to wake his parents. The house lay asleep, dark and silent. A choir of domestic gadgets hummed peacefully as they worked through the dishes and the laundry. The fridge beeped and offloaded a portion of frozen vegetables into the slow defroster. Without turning on the lights, Tim pulled from the top shelf an empty glass and filled it with icy water. He took a few quick sips, put it down and turned around to the stairs that led to his bedroom. He met face to face with his mother, Irina.

Tim saw no point in hiding anymore. He turned on the lights and pulled a face of utter and genuine remorse, expecting a rhetorical 'And what time do you suppose it is?' Instead, he heard:

"Good, you're back. We need to talk."

"Something's happened?" His mother looked serious, but not in a usual sort of way; perhaps, even confused. "Where's Dad?"

"Sleeping." Irina sat down onto a round kitchen settee. "I haven't told him yet."

"Told him what?"

"Sit." Irina pointed at the settee next to her.

"Are you going to tell me that we are expecting a little bro or sis?" Tim paused. "You look kind of…" He looked for a suitable word. "Different."

"What?" Irina looked stunned. "God, no! No."

He sat down and put a hand on her knee, trying to keep a straight face and wondering if she could smell out that his late-night study group had freshened up their brain cells with something a bit more exciting than fruit squash. "Tell me then."

"It's about your father."

"Stan?" He didn't have to ask. Ian Nielssen was always 'Dad'; Stan Kozerski – always 'your father'.

"Yes." Irina nodded. "I don't think you and Jem should go there this summer."

"What? Why? I mean, I don't mind much, but Jem will. You know Squirrel." Any major change of plans would send Tim's brother off the handle. Their summer trip to Universum had always been one of the cornerstones, no matter how much Tim wished he could avoid it. "What happened? Did you have another fight?"

"Yes, we did. But that's not the point. Your father…" Irina clasped her shoulders as if shivering. "He decided to adopt his old friend's daughter."

"Did he?" The alcohol made Tim giggly. He tried to keep a sober face as much as he could. "What happened to his friend?"

"He died. Long ago."

"That's fine then, I suppose." Tim shrugged. "I mean, not his friend's dying, of course. The girl. I don't have a problem with it." He pictured Stan with a bubbly toddler in his arms, and suppressed a chuckle.

"I do."

Tim gave his mother a puzzled look.

"Did your father ever talk about his past? The time before we met?"

"Very little. He was in some war, or something. He doesn't dwell on it much."

"It's – complicated."

"Okay." Tim knew it was a bit more than 'complicated'. His father Stan used to be one of the leaders of the Separation, the largest armed conflict in post-industrial history. The war that took nearly a million lives in Nearspace settlements. They had a three-month unit on that subject last year at the academy, and Tim sat through all the lectures wishing he could drop out and join an Amish village every time the visiting professor mentioned 'the Rangers'.

"The girl he wants to take is the daughter of another Ranger, Rod Flemming." Irina joined her fingers together and pressed them against her chin. "And even if she is one-hundredth of her father, I don't want my children to be around her."

Tim shrugged his shoulders. Whatever business Stan had with his former war buddies was none of his concern. Stan had joint custody over him, but it soon would be over. Perhaps it was about time he found some other kid to care for, and left Tim in peace. The last thing Tim wanted right now was a protracted court battle between his biological parents. "That's nonsense, Mum. Do you think she's going to spit in Jem's soup and scratch his face? Okay, I'll make sure they don't get to sit next to each other."

"She's a bit past the spitting age. She's about as old as you."

"Tough. She might spit in my soup then."

Irina laughed and hugged him. Her face lightened up. "You're my little optimist. Anyway, you are not going, full stop."

"Fine. Tell Jem, not me, and see what he says."

"Will you be on my side?"

"And have an octalon-powered piranha as my sworn enemy?" Jem's temper tantrums were epic. "Thanks Mum!"

"At least promise you'll try to talk him out of it. He listens to you."

"I can try." Tim's brother did seem to accept him as the only authority in the house. Mum and Dad mentioned it often in their friendly bickering over who was the laxest parent of the two. Tim would give Ian the first prize, hands down.

"Thanks." Irina hugged him and pressed his head to her chest. Tim grunted and wriggled out.

"This doesn't mean you can walk around in your street shoes." Irina's voice had a familiar tingle.

Tim hastily took off the soiled trainers.

"And if you think you're off the hook with your 'study group' bash…" Irina lowered her voice another notch.

"Oh. Sorry Mum! It won't happen again," he lied without flinching and sprinted upstairs.

Tim dashed up the first flight of stairs and gave out a sigh of relief. His mother was still herself, after all. It couldn't then be *that* bad. To be on the safe side, Tim took off his socks and loose, checkered shirt, then looked sceptically over his faded sea-green jeans and decided to give them another day. He rolled the laundry into a ball and dropped it down the washing-machine chute. House rule: no disposable clothes, not even underwear.

The glass steps of the steep, round stairway felt cool and velvety against his bare feet. Once, the stairs were transparent, but now they were matte in the middle, all scratched and worn out. The house looked older than its age, almost twentieth century, even though Tim knew for sure it was built in the 2020s. He ran his fingers along the rough cork wall, his mind going through the useless facts and figures that only he, of all members of this household, knew. 2024: Miiki Tiinnenenn's eco-housing project was commissioned for De Uithof residential area, part of Utrecht University campus. Miiki won his first design award for this project, at age twenty-three. 'I'm not building a home – I'm building a dream, a vision. A future.'

No point in dwelling on it too much. Mum and Dad had never heard of Miiki; Mum simply wanted a house that could run without octalon (House rule: no Nearspace shit under this roof!), Dad wanted to be close to work, and both wanted something cheap. Tim kept the story of Het Hoge Bospad's architect to himself; one of his private things, between him and this house.

The door to his brother's room was closed, but a bright strip of light glared from underneath. He pushed the door open, a real door of chipboard and plastic, not a varistate solid. No transformable walls, no reshaping the interior at will, no floating beds and chairs, no fancies, nothing that would require an octalon power unit installed. House rule.

"Squirrel?"

Jem lay in his bed, fast asleep, breathing through a half-opened mouth. A dozen or so 2- and 3D projections flickered over his head.

Tim moved his hand to wrap the screens, but they didn't respond.

"Andy!" Tim whistled. "Andy, come here!"

A small sluggish tortoise crawled out from under Jem's pillow and blinked quizzically.

"Comms server: hibernate."

The screens went off. The tortoise closed its eyes and pulled in all six legs and a bald, scaly yellow-greyish head. Tim picked up the toy and pushed it back under the pillow.

He looked down and noticed a frown on Jem's face.

"Okay, I touched it. Sorry." Tim jerked his hand out.

Jem shook his head and looked away, then lifted his pillow, checked on Andy and put it on standby. The tortoise blinked and pulled its head back into the shell. Jem sniffed.

"Squirrel?" Tim knew that look too well. "I won't touch Andy again, I promise!"

Jem pushed Andy deeper under the pillow and blurted out. "You're not dropping your art & design class, are you?"

"What – why?" Tim had got used to Jem's conversation starters often coming out of left field, but this one caught him off-guard.

"Mum said – I heard her talking to your mentor."

"Alberta?" Tim's shoulders tightened. "Jem, I've told you many times! It's not polite to listen in on others' conversations."

Jem pouted. "But that woman is *loud*."

Tim smiled. Ninety-two-year-old Alberta von Haussmann could be heard through the noise of a shuttle taking off. "You bet. What did she say?"

"She said your work is very strong, but it's not *competitive* enough." Jem kept looking away.

I know, Tim thought. *I'm not blind. I just hoped she wouldn't say that to Mum.*

"She thinks you should focus on legal studies. Your grades will get you a good internship." Jem briskly looked up and took Andy out again.

That was it. It was all being planned for Tim, behind his

back. All decided.

Jem blinked and swallowed. "I don't think you should drop it." He looked serious, more serious than Tim ever remembered.

"I don't know, Squirrel. I need to talk to Mum in the morning."

"It's just not right." Jem turned the tortoise over and started to take off the bottom panels. He bit his upper lip, and pulled the lower one over it, just like Mum always did when upset. "Not right."

"Jem, it's almost three in the morning, you really shouldn't play with Andy right now."

Jem ignored him and pulled out a few circuit boards. "I just want to check the variables."

"Jem, tomorrow." That conversation, once started, could go on forever. "Mum is upset. I don't want her to come in here."

"Upset," echoed Jem. "I know."

He pushed the boards back inside the tortoise. "Tim?"

"What else?"

"What is an 'autistic killer'?"

Tim clenched his fists. "Did someone call you that? At school?" How much longer would this go on? Even at the academy, the school that swarmed with weirdoes of all shapes and sizes, Tim had already rubbed a few middle-schoolers' noses to the ground for picking on Jem. It was only getting worse. And his brother was only eight.

"No, not me. The girl. Mum called her that when she talked to Uncle Stan."

"Mum?" Of all people on Earth, Tim's mother would never use these two words in conjunction.

"She said the girl should go to back to her space gang." Jem lifted his head. "I want to go to the space gang too!"

He really should stop eavesdropping, Tim thought in despair. But then, when did Jem ever do what he *should*?

"You need to sleep now. You'll go to the space gang tomorrow." A tried and tested way to make Jem stop arguing. Jem sighed and climbed under the blanket.

It always amazed Tim how fast Jem would fall asleep once in his bed. Getting him there was a whole other story. Tim stayed for a minute over his brother, listening to Jem's breath and occasional sniffs then pulled the blanket over his shoulders, turned around and left the room, silently closing the door behind.

Tim didn't turn on the lights in his room, didn't have to. He knew the place inside out, every crack and spot on the low glass ceiling, every pattern of the cork walls covered with old, faded hand drawings of buildings and bridges. Dust magnets, Mum called them. He'd bought the whole bunch at Oudegracht Vrijmarkt flea market a couple of years ago, and would fight for them tooth and nail. 'It's for school,' he explained, knowing she wouldn't believe him.

He found the hatch that released the window frame and pushed it. It stuck, once again; he leaned the weight of his body against cold glass and pushed harder.

"C'mon. Be good."

The frame gave in. Brisk summer-night wind hit him in the face; it smelt of rain and grass, with a faint undertone of wet concrete. A dog barked in the distance. A couple of hovercars whooshed northside, above the glaring renovated towers of De Bisschopen. In summers De Uithof always felt like a ghost town, until the new wave of students arrived in September. The best time of year; he could have the whole place to himself.

Tim stepped away from the window and went to his desk,

planning to go through a few old paper books his stepfather picked up for him. Dad had a knack for finding non-digitised rarities in Oudegracht antique shops – one of the passions they shared. The Circle crowd knew: need a kinky old paper brick, ask Tim.

He pulled up the sheet of drawing paper that divided his room in half and yelped. A spider sat on top of his desk, purple and hairy, the size of a large coconut; a purple coconut with lobster legs coming out of a black-and-orange-striped cephalothorax. The legs twitched and a gooey string of yellow saliva dripped from finger-long fangs that moved up and down in slow motion.

Tim could swear he didn't take anything heavier than a few alcopops, but the thing looked real to the point of nausea. He shook his head, picked up a tennis ball, and threw it at the beast. It flew through and landed on top of his unmade bed.

"I beg the noble Sir to hear out his humble friend," the spider screeched and spat another blob of saliva.

"Dork," Tim hissed and gave the spider a stern look. "Accept."

The round Buryat face of Marat Kazyev popped out of the 3Dcom, blurred and shadowy at first, then more solid, as soon as bootleg link boosters kicked in after the initial delay.

"Do you look like crap or do I need to take my receiver to the dustbin where it belongs?" Marat squinted and bent over. "Nah, that's definitely your side."

"Did you just set up another holomonster in my gear?" Tim complained. "Scared me shitless. I thought I was seeing pink elephants."

Marat snorted.

"Funny, huh!" Tim grumbled and zoomed Marat's image to full body size. "Ran my reserve batteries to the ground again.

It's my neck Mum's gonna chew up if she finds out that I hooked up to the octalon grid."

Marat laughed. "Did you get back okay? You looked a bit shaky when you left. Any grief from your mum?"

"Not much. She's got other stuff on her mind. Some troubles with my father."

"Which one?"

"Very funny." Tim changed the subject. "Are you coming to the Circle tomorrow? I've got your *Gray's Anatomy*, thirty-ninth British edition. The best one you can get without selling one's own liver. Dad said these are becoming rarer than dodo birds."

"No can do." Marat sighed. "I'll stop by your place later. Got some work to finish."

"Oh yeah!" Tim smirked. "The mighty, magnificent Nacamura BiomedTech Student Grant! Do you reckon you have a chance?"

"Kidding? I've got it in the pocket. Two or three more lab trials and we'll be good to go. Gonna be big." Marat rocked back and forth in his floating chair. His head disappeared for a second from the transmission zone then came back into view. "See, the regen scripts they have got now on the market are only good for smooth muscle and occasionally some simple skeletal shit like palmar interosseous. There was a guy in Shanghai who regened some intervertebral discs, but never a whole thoracic…"

"Mara? Spare the jingle, would you? My brain hurts. Amygdala or whatever."

"C'mon! Even your brother can understand me. And stop calling me Mara. Or I'll come to you in your sleep!"

"My brother is a geek. Do you know he's already been tagged by MechTech?"

"No shit! Congratulations!"

"Yeah, at least someone in this family is good for something."

"Don't know about you, but I'm going to Nearspace as soon as I get my licence. Do you know how much a qualified biomed programmer makes up there?"

"Your parents will kill you."

"I don't care. What can I get here? Twenty years of pushing some shit around before I can even start thinking about my own lab."

Tim kicked his friend's virtual leg. His bare toe smashed against a massive antique photographic tripod that supported the hanging paper. He grabbed his foot and hissed.

"Hallux? That would hurt." Marat sneered. "I said, don't call me Mara. Karma, see? What goes around…"

"Says a biotech flesh-ripper." Tim got up and dragged the tripod out of the reception zone, just in case.

"Boo-ha-ha! Speaking of flesh…" Marat peeled the percom band off his upper arm and spread it on his lap. "Just watch this." A small holo of a group of four senior schoolgirls popped out of the band. They walked, chatting and giggling, along what Tim recognised as the floating pavement between the Circle and the concrete monstrosity of Educatorium, one of the few historic buildings of De Uithof. Marat froze the picture and zoomed on the tallest one, a blonde with long, swaying hair, in a dark blue T-shirt.

"Helena de Rijke… 'Helen of Troy'. Let's see what you've got." He twitched his fingers. The shirt began to dissolve, leaving the blonde stark naked from waist up. "Wicked!" Marat rotated the image a few degrees so his pal could get a better view of Helena's endowment.

"You're a perv!" Tim chuckled. "Did you write it?"

"Hah, that's from Li-Chang. Cool, huh? Now, let's see…" Marat squinted, picking his next target. "How about this one?" He zoomed on a tanned, stern-looking girl with short dark hair framing her oval face and high cheek bones. "Maria. Masha, full of passion. 'Virgin Mary.'"

"Stop it!" Tim jumped up and realised that he had tried to grab his friend's hand. Marat laughed.

"Oops! Did I pick the wrong one?"

"Go to hell. Or play with your dissected frogs."

"They don't dissect frogs anymore. It's illegal." Marat made a disappointed face.

"What a loss it must be for one of your kind!"

"Nah. There's still no shortage of fresh human cadavers."

"Get your grant first then you can be a proper biomed cynic."

"I told you, it's a done deal. In fact, I've even got an indulgence from Dad for another house party; this Friday. Are you coming?"

"Depends." Tim rubbed his forehead. In fact, he had other plans that he had not the slightest intention of sharing with his friend. He had in his backpack a neatly folded invitation to see a new production of a promising young playwright Chris Thomsen. With Masha. Tim could easily give the play a miss, but not the companion. "Who else will be there?"

"Alas, not Mary the Enchantress. She'll be gone to Heaven. Going to Rietveld Centre with the man of her dreams. Some mortals are that lucky."

Tim swallowed. "Shit. Does *everyone* already know?"

Marat laughed. "What do you think? Anyway, have to go. Frogs are waiting!"

"Go play with your wankadrome; just leave Masha out of it."

"Deal."

Marat's body shrunk into a bright ball of light that morphed into a blue and purple logo of the link provider, hovered in the air for a few seconds then went off, leaving a yellow-green after-image. Tim blinked and rubbed his eyes. A hangover started to kick in with a sandy feeling under the eyelids. He walked over to his narrow built-in wardrobe and slid the door that hid a small marble sink over a glass recycling tank flaking with residue. An insistent: 'Clean me!' scribbled across in blue fluorescent marker already began to fade, yet still stomped hard on Tim's guilty conscience. He checked the descaler drawer. Empty.

He closed the wardrobe door and walked to the bathroom. The main tank, Dad's responsibility, ran like clockwork. Tim filled his cupped hands with ice cold, slightly iron-tasting water and made a few slow gulps, savouring the sensation of clean fresh liquid in his throat. He took two more handfuls and wiped his face with his palm. His fingers felt soft stubble, not yet visible on his chin. Digits on the bathroom mirror blinked and changed to 03:14.

Back in his room, Tim crawled under the blanket and closed his eyes. Too late to sleep, too early to get up. He twitched and looked up. The glass roof over his head still was of a dark indigo colour. He had perhaps another hour before it would start to lighten. He tried to imagine what a night sky would look like, if the mesh of a solar cell grid didn't block the view: A few constellations, perhaps, and the bright, thick dots of Nearspace orbipolises. Not Universum – you needed to be in the southern hemisphere for that – but perhaps New Alb and a few smaller ones, like Saudade and Nadejda. Tim wondered: if Universum was visible, would he want to see it from here, every night?

He sighed and pulled the blanket over his head.

15

The building of Abu Ali Ibn Sina Medical Centre looked like a giant splotch of a microbial culture blown up to about ten million times its original size. The commuter train stopped in the middle of white membrane connecting the underside of the porous charcoal black dome to the surface of a shallow lake. Harvie made a mental note to check on the way back whether the lake water was real, just out of curiosity.

The train's perforated side spat out a dose of rush-hour travellers, who scuffled along suspended walkways and disappeared into the pores. Harvie looked around and limped towards the one most resembling the main entrance, slowing for a quick second to check her reflection in a mirrored memorial plaque. She shuffled her hair about, made a few faces and decided she looked respectable enough for the first meeting with her shrink.

The reception was staffed by a DigiGuide, a ubiquitous varistate core type she had already noticed in a couple of places. Harvie waited for the digi to acknowledge her presence, and leaned over the reception barrier.

"Good morning." Harvie smiled the Clara Jacopo's private-schooled smile she had rehearsed many times with Jen. "I have a 9 o'clock appointment with Dr Riesley."

"Your name, please." The digi launched a screen with the day's schedule.

"Harvie Flemming."

The receptionist scrolled through the list suspended in front of her eyes. "I don't seem to – I have a Denise Flemming though."

Harvie shook her head and smirked. "Yeah, that would be me, I guess."

"Harvie?"

She turned around. A lean, upper-middle-aged woman with unkempt greying red hair extended her hand. "Harvie, that's your name? I'm Dr Sharon Riesley." Her handshake was nutty with a hint of Styrofoam.

Harvie once again produced a smile-like grimace social enough to seem polite.

"I'm glad you've made it. Captain Kozerski said you were coming on your own."

"Did he worry I may *not* make it?" Yesterday's anger, which had almost subsided by now, returned. Harvie fidgeted with Stan's spare UID bracelet he'd given her so she could have some cash, and grumbled, not without certain acid: "Captain Kozerski worries too much, that's not healthy. Don't you think, Dr Riesley?"

"You may call me Sharon. Shall we go to the office?"

They walked in silence along a pastel-coloured corridor dimly lit with an amberish hue seeping through the walls. Harvie felt anxiety building up inside, a panicky voice whispering: 'Run, run, run!' and another one, cold and mechanical: 'There's a VR window system in the lobby, easiest panel to break, must have unsecured access to service ducts, can't be more than three levels away from pipeline tunnels, possibly manned at this time, means a vehicle, a lunchbox and a medikit at least. No gun. That's a pity but no big deal...'

She breathed in and out. Nobody was running anywhere, not yet.

The hue brightened as they approached what she at first took for a staff cafeteria: a shallow bowl in the floor, about fifty metres wide. Four opaque cylinders protruded from the white marble bottom, surrounded by small islands of soft-looking semicircular benches of the same milky shade.

"Not too busy today, I think we can find some place here." Sharon stepped into the bowl and looked around. "Anywhere in particular?"

Harvie shook her head. To her all the benches looked identical.

"Then let's go to the other side – a bit more private."

Is there an 'other side' of a circle? Harvie wondered as she limped behind Dr Riesley. Her left ankle was starting to throb. She sank onto one of the bench blocks, spongy and velvety under her palms, and stretched her legs with a loud sigh of relief.

Sharon sat down across from her and pulled out of her shoulder bag an old-fashioned foldable tablet for handwritten notes.

"Still can't get used to those virtual keyboards," she confessed. "Drives me crazy, which is not a good thing to say for someone in my job."

Harvie smiled politely.

"Where is it? – Did they refit it again?" Dr Riesley shuffled and looked around. "A-ha!" She touched a small bulge at the side of her bench, and a matte varistate column rose around them. "That's better. We've got about an hour today; it's really just a chit-chat."

Harvie shrugged her shoulders and noted the location of the varistate switch, just in case.

"So why are you here today, Harvie?" Sharon clasped her hands. She had long, thin fingers, no nail polish or jewellery, apart from a well-worn wedding band.

"Does it not say that?" Harvie nodded at the tablet on Sharon's lap.

"It does," Dr Riesely said. "What I'm asking is why *you* are here today."

Harvie raised her eyebrows in mock surprise. "Because I have to be?"

"Do you?" Sharon smiled.

"I was told I'd get a cookie if I came. So far I don't see any."

"I think I can sort something out." Sharon jotted a few notes, ignoring her sarcasm. "Do you like cookies?"

"Ice cream is better. Or chocolate." Harvie grinned with another Clara's smile, wide enough to make it clear she didn't mean it.

"Fair enough." Sharon put the tablet aside and hunched forward. "So, tell me about yourself."

"You have the file, Dr Riesley." Harvie leaned back, grabbed her knee and pulled it to her chest. "I'm sure you've read it."

"Yes, but I don't think it's complete." Dr Riesley clasped her hands and put them under her chin.

"In what sense?" Harvie frowned.

I'll take you to some people who would love to pull your head apart and see what's inside...

"Well, it says, for example, that you took up the government offer of a conditional fostering placement with Mr Kozerski, but it doesn't say *why* you did it."

Harvie propped her chin with her palm and bit the tip of the nail on her index finger. "I prefer talking about ice cream," she said, looking straight at Sharon.

"Can you answer my question, Harvie?" Dr Riesley's voice was soft, but insistent.

"You know that I don't answer questions that I don't like."

"Even for ice cream?" Sharon smiled.

"Especially for ice cream."

Harvie noticed the muscles around Sharon's lips tighten.

"That's why I asked you why you're here. A girl like you doesn't do things unless she wants to, the Confederal Government orders notwithstanding. Am I right?"

Harvie sighed and put her knee down. The anger pulsated in her chest like a hurried jellyfish. "Does your file mention that the Confeds can be no less persuasive than the Legion? In their own 'highly humane' ways, of course." She looked away and squeezed through her teeth: "You want an honest talk? So let's be honest about everything."

Sharon didn't flinch. "I was under the impression that you are not afraid of pain, Harvie."

"It doesn't mean that I don't feel it." In fact, her pain thresholds varied from near average on some days to that of a bionic android on others, but the last thing Harvie wanted was for Sharon to put her through a battery of tests to find out whether it was safe to leave her alone with a hot stove.

"So you are biding your time. That's wise. You need time to recover and you know that."

"Does that answer your question, Dr Riesley?" The smell of coconut pastry drifted in from somewhere, and Harvie wrinkled her nose.

"Not entirely, but we're getting closer." Sharon opened a gap in the varistate column, took a plate off the hovering tray that had appeared beside their table, and put it on the bench next to Harvie. "Cookies?"

"Closer to what?" Harvie ignored the question.

"To knowing you." Sharon took one off the plate and put it into her mouth. "We are going to spend quite a lot of time together and I want to get to know you."

"What for?" Harvie stared at the cookies, considering whether she should try them. They looked unfamiliar. And she didn't like the smell.

"To help you."

Harvie jerked. "Who said I need help?"

Sharon tilted her head. "Can I ask you something, Harvie?" She took the plate and moved it away from Harvie's sight. "How does it feel to lose your friends? To turn into a helpless punching bag, praying that you'll stay lucid enough to control yourself, to not betray people who matter to you?"

Harvie clenched her teeth. She knew what Dr Riesley was driving towards; Harvie'd had conversations like this with Sabira. Only the USF medic had never done it to see Harvie's reaction, to challenge her. Harvie wanted to respond with another sarcastic remark but couldn't. There was real sadness and softness in Sharon's eyes. For some reason Harvie thought of Paul. *Being dead has its advantages...*

"You have dreams at night, do you?" Sharon said, tilting her head. "Nightmares. You scream in your sleep."

"You're starting to sound like Colonel Moretti, Dr Riesley. He loves this kind of talk."

"I'd imagine he does. That's the Legion officer who

tortured you, right?"

Sharon leaned forward, but Harvie felt the invisible pool of cold, dark water between them widen. She shuffled in her seat and tried to joke:

"Did you guys go to the same college or something?"

Sharon grinned. "Maybe so; one never knows." She sobered and put her hand on Harvie's. "You have a lot of pain inside you. You can't carry all this baggage with you; it's too heavy for a young girl."

"I could do without a memory or two, that's true," Harvie quipped. She felt a pressing urge to turn around and look over her shoulder. "Like this conversation, for example."

Dr Riesley stood up. "I'll tell you what. Let's go and get some ice cream. I won't ask you any more questions today. Deal?"

"Does that mean you'll be neglecting your job, Dr Riesley?" Harvie frowned. Still trying to make her sell out for a snack. Pathetic.

Sharon shrugged. "I prefer butterscotch vanilla. You?"

"Mocha." Harvie stood up. "With apple sauce on top."

Dr Riesley kept her promise. They discussed ice cream flavours, moaned about calories, sampled acid-looking shakes, and even tried on a pair of Nirvana Visors and jointly discarded them as they were nothing more than cheap VR glasses preloaded with moor landscapes and soothing music.

After checking the time and wondering how quickly the hour had gone, they parted with a handshake. Sharon's fingers felt dry and cold. Just like Gulescu's, when Harvie had dragged him into the scooter. She twitched. *I'm just your sick imagination, Flemming.*

Before walking off to the train station, Harvie finally looked at Sharon, then again down at the top of her shoes and said, as if addressing no one in particular:

"It sucks, losing people you've known. You never get used to it." She looked up. "I'll see you on Monday, Dr Riesley."

***

Harvie decided to skip the next train and hang around a bit longer in the market square. She didn't want to go straight back to Stan's apartment, with its pristine surgical feel; more like a hotel than a house, as if he'd taken great care to remove everything that might betray a single weakness.

Harvie walked past glaring shop displays, not really knowing what she wanted to do. She watched for a while the faces of the midmorning shoppers that hurried past her: worried, happy, busy, relaxed, concerned, confused; listened to the jingle mix of Universum's accents, trying to spot Krot tourists. The ratio seemed to be around two to one in favour of locals, but she knew it anyway. She knew more about Universum than most if its citizens would ever care to find out. She could bring the whole place down if she had to, she thought, but then felt glad she never had to consider it for real. The Confederal Nearspacers were an annoying bunch, but certainly didn't deserve to die, in her opinion. Just very, very annoying.

She sighed and set out towards the train station, thinking that perhaps she should go for a run, regardless of the gnawing itchy pain in her half-healed legs. If things had gone better, she would've been back in New Alb right now doing her second sim track round of the day, shooting her way through a place like this one. Okay, probably not this one, since it would be too easy for her level. *Child's play...*

At the bottom of the market square she noticed something that wasn't there half an hour before: a steel rail cube about twenty metres in each dimension, filled with large floating shapes. A slow rhythmical beat came from underneath the podium that supported it. The cube spat out a dozen coloured spheres that unwrapped into twelve giant anthropomorphic holostatues. As she passed the installation, a tall, muscular black woman climbed atop the podium and jumped onto a floating cylinder, then somersaulted and landed, with cat-like grace, onto the next shape. Harvie stopped, turned around and walked up to the stage, gaze fixed on the dancer's feet that bounced off glossy cubes, cylinders and spheres in sync with hollow drum beats: Thump! Thump! Kerrum-pum-thump! Her eyes narrowed at every 'thump!' that resonated through the vibrating podium, making the holographic statues bend and morph.

Airdance. Set your body free! Clothes for the Freedom Generation. Words flashed across the dancer's tunic, but Harvie paid no attention. She watched the shoes.

A sales assistant appeared by her side, a small Asian girl with a surreal, wide smile, dressed in a promo tunic and red shoes matching the dancer's. Before the shop girl's mouth formed a question, Harvie interrupted: "May I try these? 5C." She pointed at the girl's feet. "Possibly D," she added. Her left foot still felt a bit swollen.

The assistant smiled even wider and disappeared behind the morphing shapes. Harvie sat down, took off the plain beige trainers the Confed's warden had issued her, rubbed her ankles and then massaged the thick rubbery scars masked by mediskin. Pins and needles travelled up her legs; she held her breath, waiting for the pain to pass.

The sales girl returned and put down a glowing white egg twice the size of a rugby ball. *Set your body free!* flashed over its pointy top. The egg whooshed and burst open, turning into a cushion with a pair of red shoes on top. Harvie picked up the left one and fingered the release pellet. The shoe softened; she stretched it on, rolled it up carefully over her ankle and pressed the pellet, feeling the fabric harden. She did the same with the other one, stood up and rocked heel to toe. Then she jumped.

Then she jumped once again, smiling.

16

"It's not too bad, but you should have seen him last year."

"What?" Tim stepped away from the almost invisible glass of a private spectator capsule, short of breath and smitten, and sat down. The image still stayed in his mind: a man in white, floating in darkness and then disappearing, as if consumed. Sucked into emptiness, the same one that had resided somewhere in his chest the whole afternoon, and now once again became almost painful.

"Chris Thomsen. I think he's losing it. 'The message is there but no one's listening anymore', as my dad says." Masha looked through her water glass, where a lonely and soggy strawberry floated at the bottom. "Shall we get some more drinks?"

She stretched her legs and sank back into a varistate version of a Rietveld's red-blue chair. The whole capsule was Rietveld-themed: matchstick shapes in primary colours, black ceiling and concrete-grey floor, yellow beams creating a cosy and private feel. Her open-sleeved dress matched the theme: silver-grey, with two coloured stripes, the vertical one red and horizontal one blue. Tim hadn't known that Masha liked the architect – well, did she? Or had she known *he* did?

"I'll get some." Tim jumped at the chance to play a gentleman. So far Masha had called all the shots. She rang him, she set the time and place to meet, she picked the show and she graciously mentioned at the booking booth that her father let her use one of his private capsules so they could have a better view, at which point Tim's heart skipped. Sure Rodion Furtzev knew his daughter wouldn't be there on her own; somehow, at some point he had already passed a stringent screening test, but he wasn't sure where and when, and, most important, what he needed to do to stay in favour. For he'd do anything to keep things that way a little bit longer. He couldn't deny it: Masha wasn't just good-looking, she was – Tim shook his head and pictured Mara throwing a bucket of ice-cold water all over him: *Don't get too carried away, man...* Mara said that when he first saw the sketches of her in his drafts folder. Tim smiled and wondered what Mara would say *now*.

He sat down, pulled up the hospitality screen, scrolled through the drinks menu and cursed in his head. He prayed that Dad hadn't forgotten to top up his cash account. This outing would swallow his monthly allowance sooner than Squirrel gulped a jumbo ice cream with double toppings.

"What are you having?" he asked.

"Let me see..." Masha bent over. Her dark hair brushed against his shoulder. Tim stopped breathing. She was now closer than he'd ever hoped to get. He could extend his fingers and touch her hands, long, even, bronzed with a smooth natural tan. The same hands that he'd watched for hours, from the safe cover of his workstation during arts and design class, hiding in the corner at Mara's wild parties, pretending to be engrossed into boys' talk at the Circle. He pulled away. She was too close for comfort; it almost hurt.

"Ugh." Masha wrinkled her nose, the way only she could; sophisticated rather than bratty. "Same old *kopie luwak*: fancy name, costs like a pint of octalon, tastes probably the same. Let's get out of here."

Tim felt relieved. He didn't belong in this place; it all seemed a fraud, a game of sorts that someone expected him to play, yet no one bothered explaining the rules. He followed Masha's lead with all the diligence he could muster, reading her face for any slight changes in mood. Not the hardest job by far, given how well he'd got to know her face. Yet he couldn't quite get rid of the stiff feeling in his shoulders, a tension similar to one he always had in Stan's presence. Something's not right. Something's gonna blow.

He looked over his shoulder to the empty stage, now the shape of a glowing blue bauble, pulsating to a low rhythmical beat. Most of the private capsules had already descended to the bottom of the theatre, strung together like eggs of a giant amphibian. A few that remained suspended now oozed a soft ultramarine glow that slightly changed its hue in response to the bauble's pulse. It seemed familiar. He frowned, remembering.

"*Lewendgebowconcept*", Alberta's cracked voice said in his head, "is a reminder that every construct of a human mind has its own living energy that connects it to the universe." Yes, last year, spring term, 'Living Building Design'. How could he forget?

"You seem quiet." Masha leaned against the wall and tilted her head. Her hair fell to the side, revealing a smooth, high brow that Tim rarely got to see, hidden as it was behind her dark fringe. Another reminder of the pleasure of being alone with her, the privilege to see things so private that even Marat's make-nude prankware couldn't reveal. What had he done right to deserve it, he wondered. And, most importantly, how could he keep from blowing it?

"Sorry." Tim shook his head. "I was thinking about Alberta for some reason."

Masha rolled her eyes. "Listen, Rostokin. Forget the hag. I'm serious. You'll get in."

Tim's face burned. How could she know about what Alberta had told his mum? Could she be telling other parents too? No, not possible.

"You'll get in." Masha's face looked all business. "Trust me. We'll both be there. You and me, same school, same programme. Understand?"

That 'understand' made Tim's shoulders tense up again. The way she said it: not as a word of hope or encouragement. A fact. A done deal.

"So what do you reckon octalon tastes like?" He rushed to change the subject.

Masha chuckled. "Guess what? I know the place that sells the shots they call 'octalon-on-the-rocks'; ever tried? It's a Laika's bar, but not too cheesy. Let's go. As Alberta says, we must expand our cross-cultural experience."

"Have I ever used a fake UID? Nope. Do I even have one?" Tim shook his head.

She pulled his sleeve. "C'mon. Trust me. I know the bar keeper. She's a charmer. Dad's former flame."

"Did he tell you that? I mean, you discuss such things?"

"Rostokin, you're something!" Masha laughed. "Mum's gonna love you. Quick, I have to be home by nine. Speaking of mums…"

✳✳✳

'Octalon-on-the-rocks' turned out to be an ultra-sweet, viscous minty green liquor. It burned Tim's throat, and he made a heroic effort not to cough. Masha took hers with a straight face.

"Crap. Is this the stuff they put in fuel tanks?" he said with a smirk.

"Don't know, don't care." Masha pushed her glass away. "Do you?"

Tim shrugged his shoulders. He may not have shared his mum's contempt with all things to do with the despised O-word, but some of her feelings still rubbed off on him. In the house where the way you washed your trousers was a political statement…

"It's quite a big thing up there." He tried to sound neutral.

"Everything is a big bloody thing up there!" Masha's eyes glistened. She seemed wilder, untamed. "Every Laika thinks they must be somehow closer to God or something. Have you ever heard how they talk about their place? 'Look, we have ballet in zero-g; look, we have cow farms in space; look, our babies drive spaceships!' Pathetic."

"My mother was born in space," Tim said mechanically. He wanted to add 'she didn't like it there', but realised that he'd already blurted out too much. A quick shadow went across Masha's face, like a flick of disappointment – or did he just imagine it?

"That's okay, I suppose…" She licked her upper lip. Tim remembered her doing that before, when she was nervous or concentrating. "Many great people managed to rise above their roots. It's not where you come from, but what you become."

"Yes, I think she did great – have you seen that documentary on Amazing Earth channel? About restoring the Neolithic village in Africa? That's my parents' work."

"Really? No, I haven't. Too much is going on." Masha's voice softened. She seemed to be trying to make amends without having to apologise.

"I'll send you the link; it's cool." Tim rocked his glass. The stinging in his throat was gone; now he felt adrift, floating on the waves of ambient noise. "I think there was a review in one of WBN's newscasts."

"I'll ask Dad to get me a studio copy. Better quality." She smiled, and leaned closer. "I have to hit the road soon. Let's get one more."

Masha disappeared to the bar, where her dad's alleged 'former flame', a purple-haired African woman with glow-in-the-dark tattoos covering every bit of flesh that her clothes failed to, greeted her like a long-lost little sister. While making the drinks, the woman threw a few approving glances Tim's way and winked.

Tim squirmed and pretended to be watching the projection on the opposite wall, a selection of documentary clips; a subdued spin on 'The Wonders of Universum'. A bit of history: the construction of the first wheel, now integrated into one of the stems, and the launch of the closed ecosystem. Nothing on the Separation War, as expected. It was still a raw subject, a bitter loss for the Confederation. Just a brief glimpse of a couple of stems being rebuilt and a brief mention of 'the testing times that pulled Universum's citizens together.' He caught himself thinking that he preferred the history this way. Where all bygones were bygones, and he no longer had to be reminded, whenever the charred skeleton of the destroyed Stem Four flashed on screen, whose side his birth father had played on. He wished he didn't know. Or didn't care. Like Masha.

The clip sequence concluded, to his surprise, with a quote from Wenzel Hablik projected over his 'Starry Sky' painting rendered in 3D. It jarred Tim. How dare they? To take the things that belonged to mainland Earth as their own, spruce them up and then flash back to him, enhanced, remastered and alienated. To take the things he cared about and keep them as their own. Just the way Universum had taken Stan away, forever, and made him into someone else. Not quite his father, not quite a stranger.

All of you represent humanity, a single great family of the same origin, and all are equally transient.

Yet some are more transient than others, Tim thought, washing off the bitter taste on his tongue with another dose of the sugary concoction Masha had brought. Her fine, slender fingers looked elegant and grown-up against the rim of her cocktail glass. He smiled at her with reassurance, finally letting it sink in: it had all been sorted; his future, his career, and he no longer had to worry. He could let go of his past, and let Universum have what it wanted. Let that space gang girl take his place in Stan's home. He didn't care anymore.

He saw Masha off to the taxi station. She slid, somewhat shaky, into the cab and tilted her head the same way she had in the theatre, but now it looked more deliberate.

"I'll see you at school then?" she said. Not a question, a statement. Tim made a gallant nod and stretched his hand. She laughed and pushed it away. "Save that show for my mum."

She wrapped her hand around his neck and pulled his face towards hers. He lost his breath for a second and then he felt the sweet taste of air that only a moment ago was in her mouth. It felt surreal: the taste of her lips, her soft cheek touching his. As if he'd stepped out of his body and now observed it, not without a flash of pride: he, Tim Rostokin, snogging Her Majesty the heiress of Rodion Furtzev's media empire, the coveted, the untouchable. She pulled away, and shook her head in approval.

"I'll call you." She sank into the cab's seat. "G'night."

Tim followed the departing cab with his eyes, and pulled his shirt lower. Being sixteen and in love had certain inconveniences.

***

Tim returned home past midnight. He wheeled his bicycle through the garden gate and left it next to the compost shed, then walked along the wet stone path, careful not to step on the slugs that came out for their usual night rendezvous. He opened the sliding ground-floor door with a flat metal key that often attracted surprised looks from those not familiar with their family's lifestyle, and turned on the lights in the living room. Nobody. They must have all gone upstairs.

Tim hesitated for a moment then walked back to the wooden terrace. He sat down on a damp step next to an iron rack with dusty ecoplastic bottles of artesian water.

The air was moist and tepid. Tim unbuttoned the collar and sleeves of his formal black silk shirt and pulled the sleeves up his arms, already touched with early summer tan. He then put his index finger and thumb inside the shirt's chest pocket and found a small, long object. It had fallen out of his wardrobe that morning, when Tim turned it upside down in search of suitable attire: nothing too dorky, but still classy and respectable enough to sit next to the most well-dressed girl in Academia. Tim had put it in his pocket without looking; he knew what it was and he didn't want his mum to find it.

He took out the cigarette from inside the thin, protective, waterproof shell and rolled it between his fingers: A souvenir from Universum.

He had found it last summer. Stan used it as a bookmark in a yellowed leather-bound Shakespeare volume on his desk. It fell out when Tim picked up the book, surprised to see it there, and opened the bookmarked page.

Stars, hide your fires;

Let not light see my black and deep desires

The eye wink at the hand; yet let that be

Tim cracked the shell in half, the way he had seen Stan do it, and took out a bendy stick. He put it in his mouth and sharply inhaled twice. The tip of the stick lit up. His mouth filled with pungent smoke that brought his throat to a spasm. Tim coughed and blew it out. *Bloody hell… Why does he do that?*

He twitched the smoldering cigarette in his fingers, like an incense stick, watching the silvery smoke curl and rise, tickling his nostrils. Then he heard approaching steps behind him. He hastily dropped the cigarette onto the ground and stomped on it with his foot.

"How did it go?" His mother came out to the garden and sat next to him. "Did you like the play?"

The image of the disappearing man once again flashed in Tim's mind. "Masha said the one last year was better."

Irina nodded and looked down. Faint smoke still curled from under Tim's sole. She didn't say anything.

"I've spoken to Jem," she finally said. "He's okay with not going to Universum."

Tim moved his foot. The cigarette lay on the ground, now all flat and soggy, like a squashed bug.

"Then I guess I'm okay too." He looked up; the sky was clearing out after a short summer rain. The clouds glowed with a mulberry hue. Irina took Tim's hand and squeezed his fingers.

"Stan was in love with this girl's mother. Always."

Tim pulled his hand out. "I will call Stan tomorrow." He looked at the squashed cigarette butt that at last stopped smoking. "Tell him we won't be coming."

"Thanks." Irina put her hand on his shoulder and held it there for a minute, not saying anything else then stood up. "I'm going to bed. Don't stay up late."

On her way out, Irina turned off the ground-floor lights. The garden lit up with a scattered array of solar spotlights that attracted a few curious moths, encouraged by the glow.

17

Stan expected another sleepless night, but the pressure of the past week finally helped him crash. He slept through his alarm clock – something that he hadn't done in many months – and woke up with a jolt, realising it must be very late. The mountain ranges in the VR windows, synchronised with July in New Zealand, were brimming with morning sunshine. Harvie was already up; he could hear the hushed humming of a news channel. Stan jumped in and out of the shower and pulled on the shirt and trousers without waiting for the water to dry off properly.

He found Harvie in the living room, sitting cross-legged on the sofa with a glass of orange juice in her hand. She was wearing the same manga T-shirt, but now with a pair of loose white shorts. She must have got them in the city centre yesterday, along with a pair of red trainers he noticed sitting in the hallway. The post-surgery scars were still visible on her legs and arms, but he could see that she'd run some concealing spray over them.

The media centre was tuned to OrbiNews, with a dozen or so additional screens flickering on the side without sound.

"Anything exciting?" He tried to sound casual. "Is the

world still there?"

"Ophelia bid went through. Leggies got it."

"F—" Stan bit his tongue. "I mean, that's a shame."

"I know what you mean, Captain." Harvie stood up and turned the centre off. "I figured out how to work your delivery service," she said. "You should really pick another one, this juice sucks." She put the glass on a low wooden table Stan had bought from a local antiques dealer. "Thanks for the money, by the way. I found some clothes that fit."

"Good. I don't know what you normally wear. If you need something else, I can take you to the mall later today."

"You don't need to. What I've got is fine." Harvie walked up to the full-length mirror next to the bookcase, took a black hairband off her wrist and pulled her hair up into a ponytail.

"How did it go with Sharon?"

"Okay." She shrugged and carried on staring into space. "We went shopping."

"Nice. Did your cash account work?"

"Yes."

"I've uploaded you 150; let me know if you need more."

"That's plenty, thanks."

Stan brushed his lap. He'd have to bring up this question at some point, why not now? "Kato said he wants us to let you use some of your insurance fund money."

"Some?" Harvie let go of her hair and turned her head.

"I'd gladly let you use all of it, but you might get some ideas and there are plenty of people out there willing to help out, if they know the sum in question." Stan remembered well how easily he and Rod had acquired and refitted *The Ranger*. As if they'd gone shopping for a hoverbike.

"Even I don't know the sum in question."

Stan rolled an imaginary cigarette and wondered if he had any left hidden in his bedroom. "Let's put it this way: you have worked hard. Very hard."

"Glad to hear that." Harvie's voice expressed no joy.

"You'll get all of it when you're twenty-one. And if I were you, I'd seriously consider an early retirement."

"I may start practising right now then, if you don't mind." She sat down and demonstratively closed her eyes. Stan took the hint and stood up.

"I'll be having breakfast. Join whenever you're ready." Stan walked down into the kitchen and found coffee cups and plates already neatly arranged on the table. He turned background music on and selected an ambient jazz channel.

Harvie walked in with the glass in her hand, sat down, picked a piece of toast and sank her teeth into it a bit too vigorously. Stan sat next to her and grabbed another one.

"It's not about the money, Harvie." Strangely enough, he now felt the urge to defend Takura. "You know better than me that Kato would never put a price cap on your life."

"That's what I thought too." She looked into her orange juice. "And here I am. Drinking this shit in your kitchen."

"You don't have to if you don't want to. It's not the Confed prison."

Harvie took a large gulp and put the glass down. "Doesn't matter."

"So now you sit here planning how to kick the Legion out of Ophelia and make them pay for Gulescu, right? Is that what you want your money for?"

"You may think whatever you want, but I do believe in payback." Harvie put the half-eaten toast back on her plate. "You're the one who just lets things go. Until there's nothing left to let go of and you're stuck alone in your show home with fake sunsets and plastic food! Does your son come here on court orders too?"

Below the belt.

"Look, Harvie. Last year my team closed a number of projects that almost halved Legion's sphere of influence in Nearspace. All this without firing a single shot. You can finish your dad's job. There is another way, the one your father never saw…" He cut the sentence but Harvie's face had already grown cold. Stan cursed himself for bringing Rod into the discussion. He rushed to change the subject.

"I need to clean your bedroom out; there is a lot of stuff in there you don't need." He stood up, leaving his coffee unfinished. "You'll have more room for yourself."

"I thought it's your son's bedroom?" Harvie frowned. "Are you kicking him out of there? Where is he going to stay?"

Stan felt a sharp pinch and next, a hot wave of shame. "Tim only stays here for a few weeks every year. He won't make a big deal out of it. I'll set something up for him and Jem in my bedroom."

Stan went upstairs and opened the door to a small room with an en-suite shower that he had once outfitted especially for Tim. His son's face looked at him from a blow-up sepia photo-studio portrait. He had convinced Tim to have it done last year, and after they opened the package, Tim decided it didn't turn out too bad and let Stan hang it on the faux brick wall, above a taupe settee with scattered fabric cushions in earthy colours. The photographer made Tim look as if he'd just stepped out of the rain, his hair wet and spiky, a few strands hanging across his forehead. But what Stan loved about the photo wasn't the 'Krot-boy' effect. It was the look in Tim's eyes: dreamy, yet focused, as if beholding something only he could see. His drawing look.

Stan opened the wardrobe and took out a neat stack of T-shirts and jeans. Tim always travelled light, and Stan kept a set of clothes for him at home. That was probably all there was; the boy never left much of his personal stuff in the room when he wasn't here. Stan double-checked the drawers of a small writing desk, just in case, and took the pile of clothes to his bedroom.

Stan put the clothes on his bed and looked around. Some work had to be done here before the boys could move in. The moment Jem set foot inside, he'd get nosy, and there might be things not intended for his eyes. First, the cigarettes; Stan had promised Tim last year that he would have quit smoking by the time the boys came to visit again. He almost had.

Almost.

Stan took the 'emergency pack' out of the drawer, checked the insides, thumbed out the last remaining cigarette and put it in his shirt pocket, then looked around. There was another thing Stan positively couldn't let Tim see, and he had to find it.

Where could it be? He pulled out drawer after drawer, going through some old scratchpads, a few antique books Kato Takura had given him when they were still on speaking terms, a binder with Tim's drawings the boy had made for Stan when he was ten or eleven, and other assorted keepsakes. Had he lost it?

Stan tried to calm down and think. It had to be filed somewhere safe; he wouldn't have just left it lying around. He bent down and pulled from under his desk his last hope, a heavy plastic box with old-fashioned paper appointment diaries, about a dozen in total. He took one, a navy-blue Moleskine, and opened the back cover.

It was a wonder how these things stayed in vogue, even a century and a half after the world had gone digital. He and Irina had kept up with the trend, duly presenting each other a new year's one for Christmas, even though the last one hardly had any pages used. As if they wanted to mark a turning point, a year of new possibilities in the way that something as mundane as a calendar app couldn't quite replicate.

This one was the diary for 2102. The year the Separation War had concluded with a shaky truce, with the Confederation retaining about a quarter of their former Nearspace territories, and the rest forming a corporation-state called Unia or going independent; Bel Dubois had been resting in her family burial grounds near Bordeaux for over a year; the Rangers had split up, going to whichever side offered a better deal. Rod Flemming had crammed the last remaining crew of his loyals onto the same ship they had started with, and disappeared, hunted by the Legion on the Confed's warrant; Tim had started bringing home from nursery school his first hand-drawn pictures, and Irina had left Stan for good.

It was there, just as he expected. A thin sheet of writing paper, folded in four, tucked into the scrap notes pocket at the back. Stan wanted to put the diary back into the box and take the whole thing down to the den, but once again couldn't resist opening the letter, even though he knew that the hasty lines of words in neat flying cursive would hit him like a sledgehammer.

I'm losing you, I know I am, or have already lost. I wake up and you are not there. There is a shell, a dummy of a man that looks like you, talks like you, but he isn't you. I don't know where you are. I hate to think that you are with her, in your thoughts and in your dreams. Maybe I'm wrong, but I want the man I used to have by my side, and he's not there.

So I release you, go, you are free, go back to your – whatever!

Just let us be and I'll let you be and that's about it. Go where it has gone, whatever it used to be inside that shell. It scares me when I come home to ghosts, and I don't want Tim to grow up around these ghosts either. They are in every room.

I want you to go and take them with you, where they belong, to those stinky, rusty rat cages you call home. Because I can't be there any longer. It's madness. Our parents were mad, and I've had enough. My child won't grow there. If you don't understand why, may peace be with you, but I've made my choice. I need sun; I need air, real air, that doesn't smell of that green octalon shit. Even thinking of it makes me want to throw up.

I thought time would change you, if not for us, then for our son. But I feel like I'm losing and I have no more will to fight.

Tell your buddy Rod that he has won. He always wins.

Go. I've had enough ghosts in this house. I want to be with the living.

Irina.

He'd never let Tim see this letter. Enough spite. Stan fumbled through his trouser pocket for a lighter, one of the few useless gadgets he carried around for no reason since he had long ago switched to self-lighting cigarettes. Burn it, now. It had been sitting in this house for long enough. Time to let it go.

You have a habit of abandoning people.

Stan remembered the way Harvie had looked at him in the cab and hesitated. Perhaps he should still keep it; the last and only evidence that he wasn't the one who'd left.

He put the folded letter on top of the diaries, threw the empty cigarette pack in the bin, and picked the box up. Time to take it where it belonged; with the rest of his sentimental shit.

Stan exited his bedroom and descended the spiral staircase all the way to the kitchen landing on the bottom floor. He pinched a code on the keypad lock and opened the door to a crummy, un-fitted room with bare mesh walls and an unmade bunk bed. Stan set the box next to a pile of similar looking dusty storage containers in the corner, mostly filled with broken appliances and old clothes. Some marked with 'Danger. Keep out!' stickers held his old guns with disabled chargers. The place looked exactly like a crew compartment on *The Ranger*, the effect amplified by Stan's Ranger uniform on a hanger right next to an emergency oxygen kit and a pressurised spacesuit, a legally required must-have in every Confederal Nearspace household.

Pointless nostalgia. Stan touched the rough fabric of his uniform jacket and cringed. All he'd ever be: a collection of old memories locked away from prying eyes. *This* was Stanko.

An alarm on Stan's watch buzzed. He looked at his wrist and saw an incoming call from Irina. Stan forwarded it to the 3Dcom in his bedroom and rushed upstairs.

***

The call answered into Tim's bedroom. The boy sat at his desk in a rolling chair, arms folded on his chest. Behind him, Jem shoved his head through the door and looked around, as if searching for something in Tim's room, his look vacant. "Where is she? The space gang girl? Is she coming here?"

Stan looked up in surprise then realised Jem was looking at the projection of his bedroom, expecting to see Harvie. "She's downstairs, in the kitchen. 'Space gang girl?'"

"That's what Mum said!"

"That's not what she said," Tim interrupted.

Jem made a face that typically meant 'Squirrel knows when the big ones are trying to dupe him.'

"Squirrel? Can I talk to Uncle Stan alone?" Tim gently pushed his brother towards the bedroom door. Jem pushed him back and huffed, but left.

"'*Space gang girl*'…" Stan smirked. "What else has your mother told you?"

Tim's face tensed up. "Shouldn't it be *you* breaking the news to me in the first place?"

Stan stayed silent for a minute, rubbing his fingers as if rolling a cigarette between them. "I don't know whether I have much to add to what I've already told her. The girl is my friend's daughter. Her parents died. She has nowhere else to go."

Tim looked around as if in search of the right word. "Did *you* have to take her in?"

"Look…"

"She was beautiful, was she? Her mother?" Tim's chin went up. He looked defiant, ready to challenge.

"This is truly none of your mum's business!" Stan snapped and instantly bit his tongue.

"See? I think she's right."

Stan shook his head. *Damn, Irina, why wouldn't you just let it go?*

"Right about what?" Stan's throat went dry. He should have burnt the damn letter before reading; one less memory. '*I hate to think that you are with her, in your thoughts and in your dreams.*' Bel's dead, Irina, and I let her rest in peace. Why can't you? "There was nothing between us, not even a kiss, and if your mother told you otherwise, she lied." He looked Tim in the eye. "Nothing. Never."

"She didn't, but it doesn't matter. I'm not an idiot. That girl—" Tim pointed in the direction of the stairway in Stan's flat. "She's the kid you always wanted. Now you've got what you wished for. Mum is right."

"Is that what she said?" Stan clenched his fists. "Can I please talk to her? Now?"

"She didn't have to say anything. It's obvious." Tim shook his head, clearly not intending to move.

"It's not true, Tim, you know that!"

"Know what?"

That I love you, Stan wanted to say. The spasm in his throat grew stronger. "We'll talk when you come here."

"I will not be going there, Stan. Not this summer, not the next one." Tim leaned forward and put his elbows on his lap. "This is my decision, not Mum's. She had nothing to do with it. Please, do me a favour; don't try to fight this in court." The picture blinked, as if the connection was about to break off, but then restored. "You have plenty on your plate anyway, like that Laika girl to care for and—"

Laika girl. Did Tim even know what it meant? The way the boy spat out his mother's words was beyond ironic.

"Your mother is a Laika, has she already forgotten that?" Unlike Earth-born Stan, Irina took her first breath in Esperanza, one of the few permanent space towns.

"I don't think it's something she's very proud of," Tim said, with a slightly sarcastic grin.

Stinky, rusty rat cages you call home...

"Fine." Stan took the last remaining cigarette out of his shirt pocket and put it in his mouth. "You are a grown-up now, and Jem is not my child. If this is your choice, so be it."

The screen went dead. Stan took the unlit cigarette out and threw it in the bin. *So be it.*

He went down to the kitchen. Perhaps he should take

Harvie out to see the city. Maybe even go to the movies together. He wondered what the girls her age were into these days. He'd have to check with a few colleagues who had teenage daughters.

Harvie was not where he'd left her. The abandoned toast still waited on the plate for her return. She must have gone upstairs to watch the news again. Or to her bedroom, perhaps.

"Harvie?" The living room was empty too. Stan shrugged his shoulders and checked the top floor. Nobody. Where had she gone? There weren't too many places to hide there, except the one he hadn't yet checked. Could she have…?

He hurried downstairs again.

The door to his den was locked. Stan couldn't remember whether he'd done that when he went to pick up the call. He opened it and looked around.

She'd been in here; there was no mistake about why. Stan's uniform had been moved off its usual place, now hanging in front of the dusty spacesuit. All the boxes were still closed, except the one he had brought in. He looked inside and his heart sank. Irina's letter lay face down on the top, unfolded, with a few pencil lines on its reverse written in square, block letters that he'd never seen before. It was weighted down by the UID token bracelet he had given to Harvie yesterday.

I've used 57.50 for shoes and some clothes. Ask Takura to charge it to my insurance fund.

You did all you could have, but I can't stay.

You need your son here, not me.

ごめんなさい, *HF*

Stan stared for a moment at the row of hiragana characters next to the initials. *Gomennasai* - I'm sorry. Then he sank onto the bed and rubbed his face with his palms.

"Stupid, stupid little girl… Why?"

18

Harvie waited for a patrol pebble to pass over her head, pushed the heavy manhole cover aside, and looked around. A man-made dawn tinted the high street buildings in orange shades; they barely cast any shadows in the even light of the overhead plane. In Stem 18, like in many less affluent settlements, the virtual ambience didn't extend as far as the simulation of weather or seasons. Even the night was nominal: a perpetual dusk that never quite got dark, like one of those summer polar nights she had seen in documentaries. The street looked deserted. Harvie pushed onto her stomach, crawled out of the hole, put the cover back, and waited a minute to make sure no one had seen her climbing out of the manhole. Then she pulled the hem of her T-shirt down, brushed off her shorts and bare legs, and moved towards a narrow passageway between two shops with shuttered front windows.

Another pebble swooshed in the distance; she ducked behind a chest-high tube of the distribution pipeline and ran, keeping low to the ground. The pipeline was already busy with its dispatch of morning deliveries, and the rhythmic clang of passing containers blocked other street sounds. During short, silent intervals she raised her head and listened for the sounds of any approaching police patrols. Nothing so far. Good.

At this hour the shopping street clientele consisted mostly of crew handlers and a few off-duty Confed police officers hanging around in small groups around cylindrical media screens tuned to sport news channels. A few men and women in civilian clothes skulked about, looking in a hurry to finish their errands and get back into the safety of their homes.

Harvie skimmed the shop signs, and picked the one that read 'VR-gemu paroru' in katakana. She bent her head lower and sneaked inside the game parlour. It was deserted, save for a twenty-something male in khaki stretch trousers, a pair of boots cut off an old spacesuit, and a light grey knitted sleeveless sweater with a stretched collar that revealed a woven leather neckband. His long dark-brown hair, brightened with blonde highlights, curled all the way down to his bare, bronze shoulders. The guy slept in a wheelchair blocking the way to the VR game stations, his face covered with a paper book that had a missing cover. Harvie took a sneak peek at the title page. *The Principles of Cartesian Philosophy*, it read.

"An odd choice of a tranquilliser," she said out loud.

The guy lifted the book off his face, looked at her and put it back.

"We're closed," he said.

"I need to cash a kilo of Kamakura-sekai tokens. Three to one."

The guy stirred and put the book on his lap. "Five to one."

Harvie whistled. "A little knowledge is a dangerous thing. It definitely messed up your head."

"You won't cash a thousand platinum-level tokens without a background check, not anywhere on this tin can anyway." He rolled aside in his chair. "Four to one and a snog in the back room. You look tense."

"Four to one and a kick in your balls. That will make me relax."

The guy sneered and pointed at one of the terminals. "Use this one, the rest are crap."

Harvie sat down and powered up the station. A varistate dome covered her and drowned everything in bright turquoise light. She squinted and waited through the ad clips that even the platinum players had to suffer. Finally the glow dimmed and she found herself inside a VR locale that look like a 1930s jazz cafe. She logged in as 'Mowgli', a gaming alias set up for her by USF. She hoped the Takuras hadn't disabled it. The surrounding interior changed to the one of her VR homeroom.

She'd modelled this VR locale after Kato Takura's private cabinet, just to mock him. Now she regretted that; the sight of familiar redwood bookshelves and antique furniture made her flinch. She touched the back spine of one of the volumes on the shelf. It floated out, opened and hung at chest level. She scrolled to the page with a manga picture of a purple fox with anthropomorphic features and white hair styled in three braids: a long one at the back, two shorter ones in the middle. Harvie waited for a copper taste on her tongue to pass.

"A message from Mowgli to Lady Murasaki," she said.

A scroll of parchment paper appeared in front of her.

Murasaki-sensei, she started. A line of kanji appeared on the scroll. Harvie hesitated.

They will detain you and ship you back to us.

"Delete," Harvie said. The scroll disappeared with a puff of smoke.

She didn't need Jen Takura. She needed her insurance fund money. All of it.

Harvie flipped the book pages till she found a picture of a spectacled raccoon in a green Stetson hat. She had never used him before, but he'd know what to do with a message that came though this channel.

"English," she said. "Mowgli to Desert Cowboy."

Another scroll appeared.

The party is a blast. Everyone is having the holiday of a lifetime. Wish you were here. Talk to you soon. She paused. "Send."

That should be enough. The Cowboy would track the location of the terminal it came from.

She waited. The seconds dragged. If nothing happened within the next few minutes, she would have to log off and come back again.

Another scroll appeared with a message. *So jealous,* it read. *A local friend wants to join you. Will you show him round?*

Where and when? She replied. "Send."

The next scroll came almost instantly. *Need a few hours to prep the costumes. Can you come back at 4 a.m.?*

I'll be there, she replied.

Enjoy the party, the last scroll said.

She opened a virtual drawer and took out a bag with coins. She put it in a carved wooden box at the top of a mahogany reading table to her left.

"My gratitude to my hosts can't be expressed in words," she said.

Your 1000-token deposit is transferred, the caption on the top of the box said. She logged out and turned the VR dome off.

The guy with the book was already behind the counter. He passed her a cash chip. "Two hundred and fifty, as agreed." The guy wheeled his chair to the door and held it open for her. "Get moving before the boss comes. He doesn't like your kind here."

"What kind?" Harvie frowned. "I'm a trainee electrician at the docks."

"I can smell a duct rat from a mile away."

"With such a sensitive nose, you should bathe more often." Harvie put the cash chip in her shorts pocket.

"Only with you in the bath." The guy bent over the counter and put a little black box in her hand. "Network jammer. Might be handy in the tunnels."

"Sorry, can't take it." Harvie handed it back. She couldn't risk taking along a potentially bugged device.

"It's clean. I've put it together myself. Consider it a promo gift. I could use more customers."

She hesitated. If the guy wanted to set the Confed police on her, he would just call the patrol from the street.

"I'll spread the word," she said.

The guy smiled. "Stay safe. My name is Arren, by the way."

Harvie took the jammer and said nothing.

"Howdy, boss." Arren nodded towards a stout black man with pink dreadlocks, who had just entered the parlour and headed straight to the adjacent room labelled 'Staff'. "Make yourself scarce, now," he whispered to Harvie and wheeled away. "Good hunting, packsta."

Before she could bolt, the parlour owner stepped out of his office. "May I have a word with you, young lady?" He scanned her head to toe with his eyes.

"Yes?" A sinking feeling crept into her stomach. Something told her he didn't intend to offer her a part-time job at the parlour.

"In private." The man pointed towards his office door.

Harvie complied.

"It's the first time I've seen you here." The man closed the door behind him. "And I strongly advise you it should be the last." He gripped her shoulder and moved his face close to hers. "We don't need your kind here. Understand?"

"What kind?" Harvie tried to fake surprise.

"Don't take me for an idiot, you Litter scum." He pushed her away, and grabbed her wrist. "That kind." He turned her palm to the light. Three faint, barely visible scars ran across. "Pretty old, huh? What were you? Eight? Seven?" He let go of her hand. "You duct rats are so funny. You take your 'blood oath' and think it's some kind of a game. Let me tell you: we don't play that kind of game here. Get out."

Harvie panted. How had he known? The scars were almost impossible to see; it must have been something else.

The man grabbed her shoulders and led her to the door. "I'd advise you to put as much space as you can between you and this place." He shoved Harvie forward and closed the door behind her.

Harvie stood there for a moment, her heart racing, and then headed down the street.

****

We don't need your kind here.

An hour later, the words still burned in Harvie's ears. Well, she didn't plan to stay here much longer anyway. She would hang around till the man the Desert Cowboy had promised to send came to meet her, and would pay him to arrange a secure passage from Universum to one of the indep stations; Saudade, perhaps.

That would be a good place, Harvie thought, if it lived up to its name, 'a memory of something with a desire for it' in Portuguese.

Tenho saudades de você, Growler used to say. He talked to himself often, sometimes for hours, especially when drunk. But every packsta knew who their pack leader was really talking to: Anjia, his dead girlfriend. *I miss you.*

If Growler had lived, he'd be twenty now. Could even buy his own 'grown-up liquids'. And he would probably look a lot like Arren, with long, dark, curly hair, bright hazel eyes shining with mischief and naturally bronze skin. Only the Litter never grew up.

Harvie sped up, her feet marching to a rhythm.

Litter is one, Litter is all

Litter is young, Litter is old

Litter is big, Litter is small

Packsta is part, Litter is whole

Harvie put her hand in her shorts pocket and took out the network jammer. Sweet. Yes, these things did come in handy in the tunnels. She stroked it with her thumb as she walked past the opening shops. About time she had some brunch.

Something kept bugging her, some small thought, as if she still had some unfinished business. She fumbled through her pockets and realised: the cash token. It wasn't there.

She was certain she'd put it in her pocket before she left. She racked her brain, trying to remember everything that had happened. She was talking to Arren about his boss; then his boss was yelling at her and pushing her out of the shop and…

She gulped.

The click. The soft sound of plastic hitting the tiled floor. Now Harvie clearly heard it in her head. The chip must have fallen out at the door and she hadn't noticed; too busy swallowing insults from the parlour owner.

She had to go back. There was nothing for it. The man the Desert Cowboy was going to send would demand an up-front cash payment before even sitting down to talk to her. She turned around and ran back to the parlour.

It took her almost half an hour. She didn't realise she had wandered that far from the place. She hoped that the owner would still be in his office, and she could quickly locate the lost token and go. Harvie put her hand on the glass door and listened. Nothing. She pushed it a notch and saw a squished cigar butt on the floor. She bent down and picked it up. It was cold and soggy. Could have been there for days. The parlour wasn't a smoke-free establishment, after all.

Harvie stopped and drew the air into her nostrils. A faint, almost indiscernible smell of fresh cigar smoke made her stomach churn.

She should go back in. Now. Get the token and run.

Harvie tried to open the door, but it stuck. She put some force to it, and it gave way, tearing off a few pages of a coverless paper book wedged underneath.

"Arren?" she called, hating to say that name out loud. "Are you there, dude?"

Arren's wheelchair lay on its side, with one of its wheels bent as if an elephant had accidentally stepped on it. Bits of broken glass and plastic littered the floor amidst upturned furniture. She had either missed a wild party or – Harvie lifted her head. The body of the parlour owner hung from the ceiling, spinning slowly on a bright yellow rope tied to a grid in a ventilation pipe, his hands behind his back. The man's head was tilting to the side, and pink dreadlocks only partially covered his face. He was grinning.

Harvie exhaled and closed her eyes. The man was right. She should have never come here. It was she who had killed him, as surely as if she'd tied the rope around his neck with her own hands.

"What did *he* do to you bastards?" Harvie shook her head. *Wrong question,* she thought. What had *she* done to him, she should have asked. She should have told him to run, hide, get as much berth as possible between him and the place where their paths had crossed.

And what about Arren?

Harvie rushed to the parlour staffroom. Empty. She looked around, scanning the parlour for the places he could have hidden, and froze. A distinct shuffle of feet came from outside, a group of four people approaching.

Harvie looked around, searching for an intact VR station. A few consoles were broken, but the one she'd used last time seemed all right. She powered it on, but instead of launching the varistate dome, she minimised the portal to a sphere the size of a football and waited.

The steps drew nearer. The door squeaked and opened.

"Shall we take the scum down?" a male voice said.

"Nah, let him hang," Marko chuckled and walked in. "I like the way he makes the place look. Gothic."

A bout of laughter echoed through the empty street.

She touched the console and zoomed the projection to the maximum. "Showroom," she whispered. "Combat skins." The parlour's floor filled with salivating alien monsters, medieval soldiers in combat gear, busty women in catsuits brandishing guns with muzzles the size of a fire hose coupling, all shaking their weapons, making aggressive passes, as if ready to fight.

More importantly, to an untrained eye they all looked real.

"What the…?" Marko pushed one of the goons aside and took out a gun. "Who turned the bloody thing on?"

Harvie made a semicircle, hiding behind the back of a droid who spun and waved his six arms in an uncoordinated fashion. The leg of the hanged man brushed against her shoulder. She turned around and saw Arren.

"Go," he said and pulled her hand. He limped towards the back door of the parlour, and shouldered it open.

"You can run?" Harvie breathed out.

"Yes," he said. "But I prefer driving."

Harvie followed him into the dimly lit service tunnel, instantly reassured by the familiar sights and smells. The wall glistened with condensation running down to the puddles that splashed under their feet. It felt almost like a sim, with only one small difference: the warm, sweating hand that held hers was real.

They reached the end of the tunnel that opened into a manhole with a ladder. Harvie climbed first, helping Arren up. She could now see that one of his legs was shorter and turned inward. Arren must have noticed her looking.

"Don't worry, I've been getting along with it for a while," he said. "I only used the chair so that Gus didn't push me around too much. The fat man just had it coming…"

They now were well above the street level, moving towards the stem's rotating axis, their best chance to get a skeeler, the small but fast quad bike used by tunnel maintenance crews. Arren seemed to have the same idea in his head. He moved without saying a word, without asking questions. Like Growler.

By the time they reached the axis, they were both soaked and sweaty and breathless. The time Harvie had spent without training was starting to take its toll. She stopped for a moment to catch her breath and looked around.

Arren pointed at the vehicle parked in the charging alcove. "Do you still have the jammer?"

Harvie nodded. They ran up to the skeeler and climbed on top, Harvie in front, Arren behind her, clutching her waist. Harvie took the jammer out of her pocket and put it on the dashboard. The box blinked at the rim and buzzed. The skeeler's dashboard screen lit up. Harvie made sure that all security locks were disabled and set the driving mode to 'manual'.

"Do you know how to drive?" Arren asked, clearly fascinated.

"With my eyes closed." Harvie kicked the engine on. "Where to?"

"Let's go to the sixteenth," Arren said. "I know a place where we can lay low for a while. And…" Arren bent down and pressed his lips to hers. "Thanks for saving my ass."

"*De nada.*" Harvie leaned forward and pushed the throttle. Her face was burning.

***

"Why is it so cold in here?" Harvie blew on her hands, trying to return the feeling to her numb fingers.

"They're rebuilding the air conditioning in the whole stem." Arren rubbed his bare shoulders and shuddered. "We've always had a problem with condensation here, but now they've reduced the ambient heating as well." He pointed at the status display with the current time and temperature on the skeeler's dashboard: 13:46, 9°C, high condensation. "Will be at least another three weeks like this, I've heard. Can you believe that shit?"

Harvie shook her head, trying to remember if she had ever

been outside of a standard 22.5°C ambiance. The tunnels were often even hotter than that because of the heat emission from all the machinery, but cold at the street level? The feeling was new.

"*We?*" She turned the skeeler's ignition off. "Do you actually live here?"

"Yes, born and bred Lower Croydoner." This was the first time Arren had referred to the place as anything other than 'Stem 16'. "Let's go up, I'll show you the place." He stepped off the skeeler. "But don't get your hopes too high. It doesn't actually look that much different at the street level."

They climbed up through the access well that Arren had located behind a thick bundle of pipes and cables without looking, as if he knew where to find it. He pushed aside the street-level door — not locked, Harvie noted — and helped her out.

The sky over Lower Croydon was milky white, a steady glow like a blank screen.

"They turned all the ambience visuals off too," Arren explained. "It's like that or black, no other choice."

The zerograv train platform glistened with water, reflecting the metal rods of a surrounding see-through fence.

"Told ya." Arren rubbed his hands. "Total shit. Might even snow today."

Harvie bit her lip, trying to take her mind off the chilling wind that pierced through her T-shirt.

"There is a place here where you can crash; it's a bit warmer. Not much though." Arren pointed at a gutted seven-storey building at the end of the platform. It looked like a giant concrete sewage grid cover turned on its side. "At least there's no wind."

They climbed over the fence and walked to the edge of a slippery concrete surface adjacent to the building.

"You'll have to jump." Arren pointed at a two-metre-wide gap between the concrete platform and the floor of the semi-demolished building.

"Not a problem." Harvie frowned at him. "What about you?"

"I'm not going there." Arren shook his head. "I need to see someone. Maybe get us something to eat."

Only now did Harvie realise how hungry she was. The cold had driven all other sensations out of her body for a while, but now she could feel a steady rumble and pangs in her stomach.

"Yeah, that would be good." She ran, leaped over the gap and grabbed a thick electric cable hanging from the ceiling. It too felt freezing in her hand. A sharp burst of tiny icicles blew into her face. Snow.

"Stay warm, packsta." Arren turned around and limped along the platform.

Harvie walked inside a concrete cubicle that must've once been a stairwell. A large white sack with demolition rubbish sat next to the doorway. Harvie grabbed it and dragged it to the corner, away from the draught, and sat on top, feeling strangely at home. She pushed her hands deeper into the pockets of her shorts and curled into a ball, trying to picture herself into warmth.

The Litter hideouts had mostly been derelict buildings like this one, empty and hollow, where the sound of their feet carried through long murky corridors, shooing away any ghosts that could have taken up residence there.

Shadows come at night...

The pack would set out the night watch and cram into one room to stay close. Stolen food would be shared, stories would be told, chants would be sung, until the little ones would start dropping off in exhaustion, and then Growler would order everyone to arrange the beds out of fireproof blankets pinched from maintenance lockers and call it a night.

He'd often be the last to fall asleep, sitting alone at the side, staring into darkness.

Air howls…

Harvie closed her eyes, singing the chant in her head.

Anywhere, nowhere, all in one, one in all.

19

"Six-hundred-and-seventy-five thousand and not a dime less."

Stan fidgeted inside his oversized school jumper and tried not to blink.

"Holy crap," Rod said and whistled.

Zhao Li, the used-cargo ships dealer, lifted his bespectacled head and looked at Rod with suspicion. "What did you say you need this ship for, boy?"

He hadn't said. It was Stan who had made the initial call to the dealer. Before Flemming could open his mouth, Stan jumped in. "As I've told you, me and my friend want to start a delivery service. You see, I lost my parents in the Celesta accident and…"

The dealer frowned. "Celesta? I've heard they closed it for good."

"Yep." Stan nodded. "That's why we are here. All survivors were rehoused to Saudade."

Zhao Li sighed and flipped through his catalogue, zooming up and closing image after image of chunky spacecrafts, except the last one, a boxy cargo carrier with four large loading gates, two at each side. "That's the only one I can offer you, kids. The rest are way out of your price range. How much did you get from the insurers anyway?"

"About 250K each," Stan lied. The figure was closer to 350, but he needed to bring the dealer's price down, or they wouldn't have anything left for the outfitting.

"Let's go and have a look." Zhao Li stood up and waved for Rod and Stan to follow him.

"How old are you, again?" He looked Stan up and down as they walked to the docks. The dealer, a short, slender man with wrinkled willowy arms and a melon-like head that had patches of grey hair, was a good inch taller.

"Nineteen." That one Stan had already rehearsed a few times. "We have all the IDs and stuff."

The dealer nodded. "Here she is."

It was hard to see the ship in the murky dock, yet Stan could tell it was in a far worse shape than the picture in Zhao Li's catalogue. He checked the registration number. 7773-6328-8865-5532. Nope, it matched. The catalogue photographer must have done a hell of a job to put it in such a good light.

"Gee," Rod said, tracing the etched numbers with his fingers, "three sevens, three eights, three fives, that's our lucky ship! Hey, Stanko, don't you just love this beauty? Let's take her."

Stan grabbed his friend's sleeve and pulled him aside.

"Flemming, you're mad," he whispered through his teeth into Rod's ear. "This 'beauty' needs three new thrusters and a whole new gravi-engine. You can't pick the ship by just its number."

"C'mon, Stanko, don't be such a douche." Rod elbowed him lightly in the ribs. "You'll remember this number to the grave."

"Listen, Rod, if you want a ship, let me do the talking, okay?" Stan looked up at Rod's bright face and shiny eyes hovering above his. Sometimes he wished their height difference wasn't so striking. "If we have nothing left for a pair of decent side guns, we'll end up in a grave before we ever get a chance to punch this number into a docking comm."

"Don't you worry about the guns." Rod smiled his usual secretive smile and brushed back a flock of blonde wavy hair. "I'll have that part covered."

***

7773-6328-8865-5532.

Stan punched the number into the code lock of his den. The door beeped and sealed. He gave a denim jacket that he had retrieved from one of the storage boxes a good shake, and turned to the light to inspect it.

Should still fit. It used to be loose and Stan hadn't put on too much weight over the years. This jacket, a pair of expensive loafers from the wardrobe upstairs and purposefully understated faded black jeans from a designer label would complete the look. In the place Stan intended to head, keeping up appearances meant keeping all your body parts in one place. You either belonged, or—

He checked the time. Harvie must have gone downlevel; there was no doubt about it. But she would resurface, sooner or later. And there would be only one place in Universum where she would eventually end up, if she wanted to get out of the city undetected. Harvie had no intention of staying in the tunnels forever, he was sure. She would try to board a ship. Hence, she would seek someone to help her get on board unnoticed.

Stan walked upstairs, found the shoes and the jeans, barely worn and still retaining a new-garment smell. He changed his clothes, sending his khaki slacks to the laundry, added to the look a thin black T-shirt with a printed head of a snarling mole wearing a bandana and pair of large black sunglasses, then put on the jacket. It sat a bit tight in the shoulders, but didn't restrict Stan's movements too much. Finally, he grabbed a bottle of hair gel from the drawer and carefully worked it into his hair. Not too smooth, a bit ruffled and spiky. And definitely not looking like he had put any effort into it. Stan put the bottle back and turned to face the mirror.

"Hello Stanko," he said and winked. "What are you up to these days, man?" Stan smirked at his own reflection. Looking good.

He descended the stairs to the lobby and threw one last, parting look at his flat, mentally running through a 'good to go' list: Keys; Comms; Cash. Stan checked his pockets. All in place. He locked his apartment door and headed towards the commuter train station to catch the zerograv to Lower Croydon.

Stan's block of flats lay right above the station; the location he had chosen on purpose to shorten his work commute. A varistate lift spat him out directly onto the train platform. Stan scanned his UID and stepped through the gates. The incoming zerograv train whooshed and slowed, then swayed side to side and came to a halt. The walls perforated, letting out the incoming passengers.

At this hour most travellers were suburban dwellers and tourists heading to the city centre for weekend shopping and fun. Stan stepped inside the emptied carriage. Not many seemed to have the desire to include Lower Croydon on their sightseeing route plans.

Stan chose a window seat, sat down and closed his eyes. The trip would take about an hour, plenty of time to have some rest and get his head together; to dig himself out of the avalanche of this morning's events. He thought of Harvie and her terse note, signed only with her initials. How typical. Just like Rod.

When did it start going wrong between him and Rod Flemming? Stan wondered. Was it when he married Irina?

Stan had managed to hide his feelings for Bel well, sometimes even to the point of risking alienating her or getting a stern look from Rod for being mean to his wife. Both hardly suspected anything, too enamoured with each other to notice an absent look on Rod's quiet sidekick's face. The status quo lasted for a good couple of years, until on the day of his twenty-first birthday Stan Kozerski fell in love.

He met Irina in a small town-hall building on Saudade, where Stan had gone to collect the portion of his trust fund money sitting in a locked account until his coming of age. He was about to leave the building and, shortly after, the town for good, when he saw his ex-classmate walk in. Stan assumed she had come here for the same reason – Irina too was one of 'Celesta's orphans' – and asked her out to celebrate the inheritance.

Maybe it was their mutual loneliness in that place of sad memories, or maybe Stan was just relieved to be with someone who knew things about him that he didn't talk about much, but somehow it all felt natural. Like destiny.

A week later, they were married.

When Stan had returned to *The Ranger* with Irina, Rod didn't look too happy. He didn't say anything but his sense of discontent permeated their every conversation whenever Irina was present. Even though Stan's wife had quickly learned the ropes and even got a pilot's licence, she had never quite become a part of the crew.

"Rod Flemming doesn't want me here," she said one day. "He thinks I'm breaking you two up."

"That's nonsense." Stan shrugged. "It will take more than that."

But he too had noticed the cracks that had started to appear in their once unbreakable bond.

They argued more and more over every tactical decision, and Stan found it next to impossible to hold his tongue whenever Rod came up with yet another reckless plan bordering on madness. It would be fine if these plans had worked, as they once did, pulling Rod's reputation as a charismatic visionary to exorbitant heights. But now the Rangers started to lose on occasion, and they couldn't afford too many mistakes.

Rod wanted the Rangers to become more aggressive in pushing the Confeds out of Nearspace; his vision was always the total and complete independence of all space colonies. To Stan, that once inspirational, noble pursuit now more and more seemed like a plain old hubris.

"You can't drag mankind into your brand of happiness with an iron hand," Stan tried to reason with his friend. "Not every station wants to break up with the Confederation."

"They don't know what they want till they have it," Rod snapped. Irina, who sat in the meeting as the second pilot, stood up and turned to leave.

"I didn't dismiss you." Rod Flemming frowned.

"I have a medical emergency, Commander." Irina tried to square her shoulders but she still looked downtrodden. "Your wife will explain it to you later."

When Irina returned, she called Stan to the side and asked

if they could talk in private.

"I want to go to the mainland. To Earth," Irina said. "I'm pregnant."

Stan took it all in one long, silent minute. "You'll go to Universum," he said. "It's almost like Earth. You guys will be safe there and I can come when I can."

"When you can…" Irina put a hand on her belly and didn't say anything else. A week later, Stan put her on the shuttle to Universum and told her to take good care of the baby while he still remained at Rod's side.

Until the day when the Rangers wiped out the town of Saudade.

***

"You should learn from my friend Stanko, Chris. You break a man's arm, you go to jail for six years; he kills 20,000 people, he gets promoted." Vassilis Kolopoulos, a fat balding Greek man with arms that could probably strangle a medium-sized boa, flipped hot pitta bread on the grill and squirted a bit of oil and lemon juice over it. "What are you now, Stanko? A captain?"

Stan had made it to Lower Croydon by lunchtime, and the smell of roasting meat sent his stomach into painful spasms. He eyed the pitta with longing, watching Vassilis put a generous helping of chopped vegetables on top. "Yep, a captain."

Vassilis laughed and poked his helper, a tall and muscular Latino guy with elaborately tattooed arms and back, and a shock of dark dreadlocks with blonde highlights. "See? Told ya." He arranged the pitta on a paper plate and put it in front of Stan. "They should have hanged you in the market square with your pal Flemming."

"They thought about it." Stan carefully bent the hot sides of the bread, lifted it to his mouth and took a bite. "But then decided it would be too lenient."

"So they gave you a job instead." Vassilis leered. "Man…" He took a three-quarter-full ouzo bottle from the shelf above the grill, then procured three small glasses from under the counter and sat next to Stan. "Come, Chris. Take a break. It's slow today."

The tattooed man joined them at the table and stared Stan in the eye, stroking his goatee beard, also of an unnaturally light colour, given the tone of his skin. "Are you a cop?"

"Sort of." Stan shrugged and took another bite. "Confederal Nearspace Security."

The man pulled back. "What the f— ? Vassilis?"

The Greek put his hand the size of a baseball glove on Chris's shoulder. "Chill out Camargo. I said he's my *friend*." He opened the bottle and filled the glasses. The smell of black liquorice tickled Stan's nostrils.

"Have you been back to the town at all?" Vassilis put a glass in front of Stan. "You should. Nice place. They've rebuilt it from the ground up. Cheers."

The Greek clinked his glass against Stan's and drank it up. Stan followed suit. A bold, fiery anise taste burned his throat.

"Remember Zhao Li, the Chinese who sold you your tin bucket?" Vassilis took a cucumber stick and put it in his mouth. "His family owns pretty much the whole place."

"I don't think he'd be happy to see me there." Stan shook his head. "His grandchildren…" He choked and put his glass down. A girl, five; a boy, three and a half; their mother; just one family out of the scores that didn't evacuate in time. "That's some strong shit you have here." He cupped his glass. "I think I'll pass the next round."

Vassilis shrugged and refilled his own and Chris's glasses. "Don't worry, the old fox is long dead; of a ripe old age. And about his grandchildren—" He lifted his glass and emptied it in one gulp. "He said, 'karma.'"

'Shikata ga nakatta,' Kato Takura had said. It couldn't be helped.

Vassilis sighed and put the glasses away. "So what brings you here, Stanko?"

Stan, who had long since lost his appetite, scooped up the remains of his meal and sent them into the bin crammed into the corner between the counter and the table.

"I'm looking for a girl."

"Here?" Vassilis laughed. "You've come to the wrong street, man. All the chicks are in Upper Croydon nowadays. More traffic."

"Not that kind of girl." Stan realised how ambiguous he had sounded and rushed to explain. "A friend's daughter; she ran away." That was the absolute maximum he could let Vassilis know. "I need to find her before the police gets involved."

"Doing a bit of work on the side, huh?" Vassilis winked approvingly. "I've always said Stanko'd make a great private eye. You have your ways with people." He threw a quick glance at Chris, who now had returned to the grill. "How much are you paying?"

"Depends on what I'll be getting." Stan didn't want to be the first to offer a figure. "I need to hear about any girl that matches her description that would try to arrange an illicit passage out of Universum."

"That's simple enough. Five hundred for each match, ten times that if it's a bingo."

Stan estimated the potential number of blonde teen girls seeking better prospects in Lower Croydon and squirmed. "That's a bit above my budget." In fact, he had no budget at all. All the savings Stan had made, he'd put directly into Tim's college fund that he didn't plan to touch until his son graduated from the academy. Well, he'd sort something out later.

He made a counter offer: "Four hundred and fifty for a match, and yes, 5,000 if it's her."

"Deal." Vassilis stood up. "Where can I find you if I hear something?"

"Here. I like your place." Stan leaned back in his chair. "And I'll book something overnight if it's taking longer than ten hours."

Vassilis shook his head. "If you want the results that fast, you need someone who knows the place inside out." He turned to the man at the grill.

"Chris? When is your brother back?"

"He's coming now." Camargo bent down and pulled a box of frozen meat from under the counter. "I can hear him in the backstore."

"Speak of the devil." Vassilis went to unlock the back door of the pitta joint.

Stan too heard the rushed steps approaching.

"Here he is." Vassilis pushed the door open.

Stan lifted his head and saw a sixteen-year-old Rod Flemming standing in the doorway.

"This is Arren, my cook's brother," Vassilis said.

The illusion was gone. Now Stan could see clearly that the boy didn't have even a family resemblance to Rod. In fact, Arren indeed looked like a younger copy of Chris Camargo:

flocks of highlighted curly hair, dark skin, hazel eyes. It was the eyes that had confused Stan. They had Rod's stare. The intense yet carefree, shiny gaze of infinite possibilities only granted to those who considered themselves immortal.

"Hey, kid, have you eaten something?" Vassilis grabbed a stack of pitta breads and put them into a cardboard takeaway box. "Come. Sit with us for a minute. My friend here might have a job for you."

The boy sat down at the table, facing Stan, and stretched his hand for a handshake.

"I'm Arren Camargo."

20

A touch of a soft, warm hand on her shoulder made Harvie jump. Arren was standing next to her, with a small cardboard box in his hands.

"Here. I've brought us some food." He opened the box. The sharp smell of sour dough sent Harvie's stomach into painful spasms. She gulped and touched the bread with the tips of her fingers. It was still warm.

"My brother works at a Greek joint here at the station." Arren squatted and put the box on the floor, then took the pitta on top, tore it in two and handed half to Harvie. "He lets me eat there for free."

Harvie shoved the bread into her mouth. The dough tasted spicy and bitter on her tongue, sharp and unfamiliar. She swallowed it all down and rubbed her lips.

"Thanks, I was starving." Harvie looked around for something to wipe her oily fingers.

"I thought as much. With all that running." Arren handed her a napkin from the box. "Here."

He took Harvie's hand and began wiping it with the tissue, finger by finger. Harvie didn't move. Strange, unfamiliar spasms once again clutched her belly, only this time not the stomach. Lower.

She pulled her hand out of his. "I need to find another VR place around here. I'm supposed to meet someone."

Arren shoved the empty box into the rubbish sack and stood up.

"Let's go," he said. "I'll take you to the library."

Harvie followed him out of the stairwell cubicle and gasped. The bright sunshine lit up the sky, basking Lower Croydon district in a warm glow that made every building of the station complex shine anew, even the crumbling concrete carcass they stood in.

"Wow," Arren said. "It sure looks better after the upgrade."

The sky burst with deep cyan colour, so bright it hurt Harvie's eyes and made her squint. The rays of sun cast deep shadows across the platform that now was drying up in front of their eyes.

Arren reached the edge of the concrete floor and hesitated.

"Are you sure you can do it?" Harvie looked down at the ten-metre-deep drop under their feet. Getting back to the station square platform would require another jump that even she found quite a challenge.

"I came up here; sure I can make it back." He laughed and walked into the corner of the floor where the building came in touch with the platform, separated only by a newly erected glass barrier. Harvie squirmed. There was nowhere to set a foot on this side of the barrier, so she didn't see how Arren could make it unless he had a set of wings under his vest.

"Watch this." Arren grabbed the side pipe of the scaffolding that supported the outer wall to prevent it from collapsing. He then put the weight on his arms and extended his good leg over the glass barrier that separated the open platform from the construction site, but then he got stuck. "Erm, I think I could use a hand."

Harvie grabbed Arren's arm, waiting for him to move his body over the barrier, then grabbed the pipe and vaulted over in one swing, feeling his eyes on her. Arren had caught her mid-air, grabbing her waist as she landed, and gently put her on the ground. "I wish I could move like that," he said. "Looks like you've had a lot of practice. Where are you from?"

"New Alb," she said, worried that if she named any other place, Arren might start asking questions she wouldn't be able to answer. At least she had some insider knowledge of life at New Albion.

"No shit!" Arren's eyes widened. "That's, like, sixteen hours' space flight! How did you get here?"

"Walked." Harvie looked down at her shoes. "Shall we go?"

They crossed the platform towards an irregular shaped two-pronged tower, whose glass facade now reflected bright sunbeams. "I think they are still adjusting the filters." Arren shielded his eyes. "Anyway, better than before."

They went through a revolving door into a large hall. The seventh floor of the library building ran across the perimeter, leaving an airy well in the middle. "I've heard they have some dissolving doors and stuff in other stems, but not here." Arren looked at Harvie. "What about New Alb?"

"Yep," Harvie nodded. "It's pretty big on varistate." Arren's nosiness was starting to worry her. She looked around, scanning the place for potential escape routes. A large floor chessboard made of marble tiles caught her attention. "Does anyone actually play this?"

"Me and Chris did when we were kids. Not anymore." Arren walked over to the board and moved a black pawn from E7 to E5. "He hasn't been as much fun since he got out."

"Out?"

"Of jail. Armed robbery, cop assault, that kind of thing." He dragged the figure back. "I think he was framed."

I know the feeling, Harvie wanted to say. "I guess that would put anyone off chess for a while."

Arren shrugged. "The portals are on the second floor. Free of charge. I don't think a vacant station should be a problem. It's a *library*."

They went through a couple of floors before Harvie settled on a discreet cubicle overlooking the entrances to both the library and the station. "Can you leave me here for a while?" she asked Arren. "I need to talk to someone in New Alb."

"A boyfriend?" Arren winked.

"No." Harvie shook her head. "I don't have boyfriends."

"Really?" Arren squinted and stared at her, and again she felt a spasm in her lower body. "Why?"

"It's..." Harvie powered up a VR station, "complicated."

She selected the Monkey Zero Universe game and logged in. Arren looked over her shoulder and must have caught a glimpse of a red fox with a pearl necklace, twirling a large orange paper umbrella in her paws.

"Is it a girlfriend, then?"

"Get lost." Harvie flipped on private mode and went in.

✳✳✳

"What has got into your head, Mowgli?" The *kitsune* folded her umbrella and rose onto her back paws, a bamboo forest swaying behind her in the wind. The umbrella turned into a long, thin bamboo stick blackened at one end.

Murasaki-sensei— Harvie's typing hand froze. The kitsune lifted her stick and slammed it against the bauble of hiragana characters hanging in mid-air. They scattered onto the ground and splat into black ink puddles.

"I did ask you a question." Lady Murasaki stepped forward, her fox face morphing into a white and red mask with glowing yellow eyes. The hem of her purple robe tossed in the wind. "But I don't expect an answer."

How did she find out? Harvie thought in despair. Jen Takura's virtual persona tended to be even more intimidating than her real one, and her online scolding bordered on a lashing with a cat-o'-nine-tails.

申し訳ございませんでした。Harvie pressed the dot key and jerked her hand again, away from the swing of the bamboo stick. Way too real.

"I didn't ask for an apology either." The stick in the kitsune's paws sprouted long, edgy leaves.

"And I didn't ask to be sold to Krots." Harvie switched to English. "But since you've done just that, I want my share." Her heart thumped.

"Why?"

"Mowgli wants to go back to her pack." In tough conversations with Jen Takura blunt honesty always worked best.

"It's about time." The stick once again turned into a paper umbrella. The fox opened it and twirled. "Summer is in the air."

"Then let me have my money," Harvie typed. "So I can go."

The fox spun round and spread out nine fluffy tails, one by one. "Tanuki the Cowboy will come to see you. You'll get what you wish."

Is it a trap? Harvie never expected it to be so easy.

The kitsune lifted her tails into a peacock-like fan. "Tanuki doesn't play games." Her orange umbrella whirled in the air and closed. The kitsune was gone. A short, chubby raccoon in a Stetson hat sat in her place. He lifted his hat off and smiled.

"I want what is in my insurance fund at USF. I've earned it," Harvie typed.

The raccoon shook his head. "You won't cash that kind of money out of *Kamakura-sekai*, Mowgli." He was right. Harvie needed something she could use straight away and without middlemen. "I'll come to you and I'll bring the guild cash chip with me." The raccoon put his hat back on. "Stay where you are. It won't be long."

"How…?"

Your Monkey Zero account has been disabled. Please contact Kamakura-sekai administrators for any questions or assistance.

Harvie let out a short English expletive and turned the portal off.

Arren waited for her outside the library, a can of beer in his hand. The sun was off, the wind picked up again and the first snow particles drifted in the air.

"Well, it was good while it lasted." He smirked. "Did you talk to your friend?"

"Yes." Harvie sat down onto the wet bench next to him. "She'll be sending someone with a bit of money for me."

"That's good. We need some cash to get by. Chris can get us a takeaway or two, but not much beyond that. We may need to rent a room." He handed her the can. "Want a drink?"

Harvie took a sip out of his can. The beer tasted flat and stale. She handed the can back to Arren and shook her head. "I need to get out of Universum."

Arren took a few long sips. "I don't know. It will cost a fortune to get to New Alb from here." He put it down and Harvie noticed another empty one, lying on its side under the bench.

"I'm not going to New Alb." She sniffed, feeling the wind once again pierce through her clothes. "I want to go to a place where they trade used spaceships. Like Saudade. Do you think someone can get me there?"

"You want to buy a spaceship?" Arren laughed and threw his arm over her shoulders. "Girl, you're so funny."

"What's funny about that?" Harvie wriggled out of his hold.

"Are you serious?" Arren sobered up. "Do you actually have enough money for a spaceship?"

Harvie made some mental calculations. A standard payout for a successful mission of the Ophelia project complexity would be around 100,000, doubled in case of the loss of the mission partner. Plus bonus, another 100,000, perhaps? Didn't add up to much, but a small two-pilot shuttle wouldn't cost a lot either, especially if it needed maintenance. "Not a very large one, but…"

Arren put his can down and looked at her. Then he leaned forward and covered her lips with his. The dull pangs in Harvie's stomach burst with a liquid fire.

"I'm going with you," Arren said, finally letting some air into her lungs. "You know that, don't you? I'm so getting out of here."

He found her lips again and this time she was ready. She focused fully on each and every one of the new sensations and her body responses, savouring them all. Yes, she did know that.

"Wait." Arren stopped. "I have an idea. Come." He grabbed her arm and pulled her with him.

"Where are we going?"

"I said, wait. You'll love this." Arren led her across the station square towards the roof of the building, adjacent to the platform. He vaulted the metal fence with ease then helped her over. They splashed across the puddles towards a metal stairway at the end of the roof and went one flight down. Arren pushed open a small door leading into an unlit parking lot with a few empty pebbles beside charging bays.

"This place is dead," he said. "It's perfect."

Perfect for what? Harvie looked around. It smelled of decomposing food leftovers and soggy cigarette stubs. In fact, there was a whole school of them, swimming in the puddle next to her feet.

Arren dashed to the side and returned with a short, thick metal bar that he swung like a nunchuck. "Like this one?" He put his hand on a neon green pebble with pink flowers at the bottom.

"Arren?" Before Harvie said anything else, he smashed the bar through the pebble's window.

"Get inside."

Harvie swore and grabbed his hand. "Listen, these types of pebbles are…"

She didn't finish. Arren opened the door.

"You idiot!" Harvie grabbed Arren's arm and pulled him away from the pebble. The shriek of the anti-vandal alarm had drowned her voice. A man dressed in a police uniform flipped open the gate at the opposite end of the parking lot.

"Run," she said. "I'll hold him."

She didn't have any plan in her head, but she knew that

Arren stood no chance of out-chasing the cop, unless she could gain him a bit of a handicap. He must have figured that out too. "I'll get Chris," he said. "We'll come for you."

"You, don't move!" The officer shouted, but Arren had already dashed through the door.

The officer flipped out a pair of handcuffs. "You stay here, young lady, I'll go and get your boyfriend." He dragged her outside and upstairs, towards the fence that surrounded the parking lot's roof. Harvie didn't resist. She could easily knock the man down, but then she'd have to go on the run again. And she needed to meet the Desert Cowboy and get her money. She'd talk herself out of it. Couple of teen joyriders, a few drinks… couldn't be that bad.

The cop locked one ring of the handcuffs around her right wrist and attached another one to the fence railing. "Be good. I won't be long."

He turned and gasped as Arren slammed the iron bar into his stomach, bending him in half. Arren hit him again, this time over the head, and the cop collapsed face down into the puddle. Harvie felt a handful of crystal salt in her mouth. "Arren."

The siren silenced, and the parking lot went dead quiet once again. Harvie could hear her own heart thumping. Arren came to her and pecked her on her cheek. "Did you get scared?"

Harvie didn't answer. "I think you killed him." She looked up at the boy. "Why?"

"He had it coming." Arren bent down and searched through the man's pockets until he found the handcuff release key. "Let's go." He returned to Harvie and stroked her hand.

"Open it," she said.

"Wait." Arren stepped back and laughed. "You know what?

It's just perfect."

"Just let me go already." Harvie jerked her hand. Perhaps the police officer wasn't dead yet, just unconscious. She should check that out.

"It's just perfect," Arren said again and pressed her into the rail. Harvie felt the button on her shorts loosen and a warm, dry hand slide between her legs.

Without thinking, Harvie slammed her elbow into his stomach. Arren gasped and let go of her, looking surprised. Harvie bent down and drove the heel of her shoe into his face.

***

Growler is wobbly again and smells of liquor.

'Tenho saudades de você,' Growler says. He talks to himself often, sometimes for hours, especially when drunk. But every packsta knows who their pack leader is really talking to: Anjia, his dead girlfriend.

I miss you; that's what he says.

He stumbles through the floor of the empty warehouse where the Litter crashed overnight. All packstas are now asleep in the small side room; Harvie is alone on watch.

The place smells of dampness and fear. Ghosts lurk in every corner, but Harvie isn't worried. "Come out, play," she whispers. "I'll make you some tea."

"Who are you talking to?" Growler says.

"No one." Harvie sits on the floor, cross-legged, the cold metal side of her gun pressed to her cheek.

Growler bends down and takes it out of her hand. "You go to sleep. I'll watch."

Harvie shakes her head. She knows Growler had too many

grown-up drinks tonight and might fall asleep on the watch. It's happened before, and the packstas are starting to rumble about their pack leader 'losing it'.

"Stay then," he says and sits next to her.

Bone to bone...

"I need a new girl," Growler says all of a sudden, "now An-jia is gone."

Harvie looks at him and realises what he means. She pulls back and tries to put some distance between them, but Growler grabs her shirt and pulls her forward. "You'll be perfect, Packsta."

He's strong, forceful, no match for an eleven-year-old. Harvie wants to scream, but she knows that the sounds will carry far in this place, giving away the Litter's hideout.

A thin, bright blade slides under Growler's chin. He lets Harvie go, and she sees Min Li standing behind him, a knife in her hand.

"If you as much as put a finger on her," Min Li's eyes are narrow slots, "I'll cut your throat in your sleep."

Harvie knows that she means it.

"Whoa, whoa, what's going on here?"

Harvie lifted her head, and saw another Arren, aged at least ten years older, standing in the parking lot gate, dressed in black slacks and a sleeveless denim vest over wide, tattooed shoulders.

"Chris?" Arren wiped the blood off his face, "You're bang on time, bro. We've got a situation." He came up to Harvie and hastily unlocked the handcuffs. "Sorry."

"Did he do that to you?" Chris looked at the dead cop and then at Arren's swollen, bloodied face. "Who would have thought?"

"Yeah," Arren shrugged. "Mean bastard."

Chris took a comms pod out of his pocket. "We need to take some pictures; can claim it as self-defence if you get caught."

"I'm not getting caught."

"That's what I said once." Chris snapped a few pictures and tucked the pod back into his pocket. "Let's get out of here."

They followed Chris to the parking area two levels below and then to a run-down turquoise pebble covered with Greek art motives.

"I can't take you to the shop." Chris opened the trunk, took an ice pack out of a crate of soft drinks, and handed it to Arren. "That CNS cop is still there; helping Vassilis in the kitchen now. They seem to have some kind of past together."

A Confed? Here? Harvie stopped breathing. Had Stan already ratted her out to Amina? That would suit him well. Double-faced Krot… A *moru*.

Harvie turned to Chris. "I need to meet someone at the high street. He will get us a bit of money. Should be enough for a ride out of here."

"Us?" Chris frowned. "That's new, bro. I don't think you've introduced me to your girlfriend."

"Denise." Harvie stretched out her hand. "I'm new here."

"Then you sure move fast." Chris didn't shake hers. "Get in."

Harvie sat in the front seat, next to Chris. Arren curled up in the back, clutching the ice pack. She caught his glance in the rear-view mirror and shook her head.

She looked at Chris. "Do you know anyone at the port? The traffickers?"

He scratched his beard. "You mean you want to get a *space* ride?"

"I don't think it's safe for us to stay in the city. The Confed police will issue a Universum-wide search warrant. So we'd better move." She looked at the rear-view display once again. "Unless your brother has any more 'ideas.'"

"I've said I'm sorry. I was drunk." Arren licked his broken lip. "It won't happen again. I promise."

"I just wasn't ready." Harvie looked through the pebble windshield. Water streaks raced down from the top, bending and curling around dirt spots. "I can't do it like that."

"I promise," Arren repeated.

Chris looked at them both, in turn. "It would cost you about ten grand to leave this tin can. You really think you can get that?"

Harvie looked at Arren, who still sat with an ice pack pressed to his cheek. "I think so."

Chris started the pebble's engine, and drove off.

"Is there a Japanese place around here?" Harvie zoomed up the navigation map.

Chris glanced at her sideways and shrugged his shoulders. "Could be. Why?"

"A good one?"

"Are you asking me?" Chris laughed. "Do I look like a sushi eater?"

"You never know." Harvie checked the time on the pebble's dashboard. 16:10. Chances were Desert Cowboy would already be waiting inside. They hadn't agreed on a place or time, so that would be her best guess. A default option.

Chris checked the map. "Kintama Restaurant, four stars or something. Good enough for you, Your Majesty?"

Kintama. Golden Eggs.

"Yep." Harvie nodded. "Sounds right."

The drive to Kintama Restaurant took about ten minutes. Chris parked downlevel and let Harvie out.

"You two stay here." She looked at Arren. "I won't be long."

"Is your girlfriend always that bossy?" Chris squirmed. "Where did you guys meet?"

"In the library," Harvie said. "We played chess." She closed the door and headed upstairs to the restaurant.

The place looked huge in its emptiness at this hour, with lunchtime over and dinnertime not yet close. A kimono-clad hostess bowed to her and pointed to a massive wooden stairway with a black metal railing. Harvie followed her without asking questions. She *was* expected.

Huge bell-shaped paper lanterns hung from the ceiling at the right-hand side of the stairway; white, orange and yellow, they indeed resembled giant scrotums, another meaning of *kintama*.

"Miss Flemming?" Another hostess came out of a private room on the upper floor and held the sliding screen door open for Harvie. "Mr Kato Takura is here to meet you."

The name crashed on her like a paratrooper on a picnic.

'Tanuki doesn't play games.' Damn you, kitsune.

Harvie kicked her shoes off and stepped up on a black podium with low tables. She had walked into this trap; she'd walk out of it. With her money.

Kato Takura was sitting at the far end of the table, a coffee pot with two empty cups and two plates of coloured rice balls on sticks in front of him. He wore a civilian formal suit with a dark-blue tie. Not the best choice, Harvie thought. The grey suit highlighted similar tones in Takura's wavy hair, making him look older.

Harvie sat on the red cushion opposite the general and bowed.

"*Hanami-dango, kudasai.*" Takura moved the plate towards her. "*Oishiidesu, ne?*"

"*Dessert* Cowboy." Harvie chuckled. "A fat tanuki. I should have known." She picked up a stick and put a pink rice ball into her mouth. She loved these, that was true, and so did he. "You've been here the whole time, haven't you? Since you came to see me in the Confed prison?"

"What makes you think so?" Takura took a dango stick from his plate and finished all three sweets on it in one go. "You called me. I came."

"No chance you could have made it all the way from New

Alb to here in that time, even if you left straightaway. It's been less than eight hours."

"You can do your maths, can't you?" Takura took another stick. "I must have taught you well."

"You handed me over to Krots, but you didn't leave. Why?" Harvie finished two other rice balls and twirled the sharp stick in her fingers.

"Maybe because I know you a little better than they do, Mowgli."

"Don't call me Mowgli. We are not in Monkey Zero anymore. You've disabled my account."

"*Sumimasen, Harubi-sama.*" Takura opened his left palm and showed a polished transparent crystal disk with a hole in the middle. "I brought you the money."

"How much?"

"Everything." Takura fumbled through his pocket and took out a black silk string. He made it into a loop, and put it through the hole in the disk, then pulled one end of the loop though the other and tightened. The disk hung on the rope. "All yours." He handed it to Harvie. "Four and a half million."

Harvie felt the taste of a cold steel spoon on her tongue.

"It can't be."

"Two-fifty is your standard payout for the Ophelia project. The rest is a bonus from the board."

Harvie's legs turned to cotton wool.

"I'll have my two-fifty. Take back the rest." She handed the disk back to Takura. "Or better yet, give it to Captain Kozerski. He may want to contemplate an early retirement."

Takura shook his head. "Don't worry about Stan. He will work something out. He's good at that."

"I don't need it either." Harvie took the disk and snapped it in half. She cut her thumb with a splinter but said nothing.

"You've earned this money, Harvie." Takura scooped up the pieces and put them on top of a black paper napkin.

"Whatever." Harvie sucked the cut on her thumb. "I only want what's mine."

"Fine." Takura reached into the inside pocket of his jacket and got out another disk, this time a blue one with uneven white stripes, with a string already attached. "I thought you might say that."

Harvie made the loose ends of the string into a knot and put it over her neck.

"The rest will be waiting for you if you change your mind."

"I won't." Harvie stood up, put her shoes on and bowed. *"Sayonara, Takura-sensei."*

He bowed in return. "Good hunting, Mowgli."

Harvie went downstairs without looking back and headed downlevel. The parking lot was empty, save for a couple of posh-looking vehicles in private bays. The Greek joint pebble was still there, but Chris and Arren had disappeared.

Harvie looked around, trying to figure out where they'd gone. They couldn't have left without her. After all, Arren needed her help more than she needed his. But she still hoped to use Chris to make contact with the traffickers. It would take longer without him, and cost more.

The Lower Croydon ambiance maintenance seemed to have made another go at testing the sunshine simulation. This time the light was softer, more subdued. Sun rays cut through the wall grids and criss-crossed the parking lot floor. It looked almost friendly.

She was certain Arren and Chris couldn't have got out through the restaurant. Definitely not past the needle-eyed hostess at the entrance. But there was a small yellow door that led to another part of the building, perhaps to street level.

She pulled the yellow door open and bumped into Stan.

"You," Harvie said and stepped back. "That was quick."

"Did you enjoy your meal?" Stan looked at her as if nothing had happened in the past ten hours. "You should have waited for me; I'd take you out."

"He ratted me out to you, didn't he?" Harvie realised. "Just like he promised."

"Who promised?" Stan's surprise looked almost convincing. "The boy? Do you know him?"

"I thought General Takura would have the decency not to tell you or Amina that he'd seen me," Harvie snapped. "My bad."

"Is Kato here?" Stan grabbed her arm. "Upstairs, in the restaurant?"

"Was. I don't think he stayed."

"Did you talk to him?" Stan frowned. The clutch of his fingers grew stronger.

"Yes." Harvie pulled her arm out of his grip. "He gave me what I asked for and left."

"You know that Amina—"

"Screw Amina." Harvie stepped back. "I'm not going to your place again." She tried to push past him.

"Where are you going then?" Stan blocked the doorway with his body.

"None of your business." She tried to duck between his legs, but Stan dropped to one knee and blocked her again. Harvie backed off; Stan followed.

"He paid you, didn't he?" He clenched his fist as if ready to hit someone, but he wasn't looking at Harvie. "*Baka*. Idiot."

"I only took what's mine."

"Harvie, do you realise what that kind of money can do to your head? Even if that was less than four million."

"Did he just say 'four million'?" someone said.

Harvie turned around and saw Chris and Arren walking towards them from a large black pebble parked next to the vehicle exit. They must have found the trafficker and come back with him. She tried to make out the silhouette of the man in the pebble, but the windows were tinted.

"Yes, Chris." Stan put his hand on Harvie's shoulder. "That's what I said. Is there any kind of a problem?"

Harvie looked at Chris and Arren, then to Stan and then back to Arren again. A taste of a hairbrush's bristles mixed with chewed cardboard made her want to spit.

"You scum." She wiped her mouth with the back of her palm. "Orbital rubbish. All of you."

"Chris?" Arren looked at his brother. "How did *he* get here?"

"You called me." Stan shrugged his shoulders. "I came."

Arren shook his head. "I didn't call him, packsta! I swear!"

"You didn't tell us about the four million." Chris looked at Harvie with interest. "This kinda changes the whole deal."

"What deal?" Arren stepped away from his brother. "That man—" He looked at the black pebble. "He said he'll get us out of Universum for twelve grand; that was the deal."

"What I'm saying is he's getting *you* out of Universum. As for her," Chris pointed at Harvie. "She goes back to her daddy, whoever he is, and takes that Confed scum with her; unless she can up his offer, of course." He moved closer. "How about we go fifty-fifty, Denise?"

"I don't have four million." Harvie shook her head. "Never did. It wasn't mine." She pushed Stan's hand off her shoulder.

"Let me talk to the man." She headed towards the black pebble.

"Whoa!" Chris blocked her way. "How about *I* do the talking here?"

"I suggest you listen to her, Chris." Harvie heard Stan's voice behind her back. "If you do want to ship your brother out. And you are right. She's going with me."

"Says who?" Arren stepped forward and trained the muzzle of a gun over Harvie's head.

Alymov-23zx, she thought mechanically, octalon charge, semi-automatic, trigger-to-fire delay 0.146s.

"You've done enough killing for today." She pulled the gun out of Arren's hands. It discharged to the ceiling. An overhead light burst with a handful of sparkles and went off. She reloaded the gun and pointed it at Stan. "Go home."

Stan didn't move. "Over my dead body."

"That can be arranged," Harvie said.

They eyed each other in silence for a few seconds then Harvie heard the engine of the pebble starting.

"He's going!" Arren shouted. "The trafficker, he won't wait. You've gotta come now!" He pulled Harvie's arm and she felt her finger slip down the trigger.

Stan looked at her with surprise. "Really?" Then he glanced down at a small hole in his shirt, right in the middle of the printed mole's left sunglass, and collapsed to the floor. A police siren blared in the distance.

"Fuck," Chris said. "You deal with this situation on your own, bro. Get your girl and get out, now." He dashed to his pebble and disappeared inside.

"Let's go." Arren pulled her arm. "The police are coming."

Harvie shook her head and sat down onto the floor next to Stan.

"Whatever." Arren shrugged and dashed to the black pebble. The door opened and a leather-clad arm dragged him inside. The pebble turned around, then reversed full-speed and stopped by Harvie's side. A tinted window rolled down and a half-finished cigar stub flew out.

"I'll come back for you, girl," Harvie heard through the heavy pounding of blood in her ears. The voice wasn't Arren's.

***

Shadows come to steal your heart
Your head, your teeth, your eyes, your fingers
Carry your body on their dark wings
To the land of the shadows

Harvie sits on the floor, cross-legged, the cold metal side of her gun pressed to her cheek. Blue mist curls up, turning the rays of light coming from the metal grid above the ducts into a semi-transparent web. Somehow this gives her an illusory feeling of safety, as if these lines are solid.

Packsta stays to keep watch over his little brood.
All-eyes, all-ears, all-nose, all-skin
He will know the shadows are coming

Harvie moves the power slider on the side of her gun into the 'max' position. If the Litter has to kill, it kills.

He will feel the wind from their wings
The smell of their breath

She inhales air into her nostrils and listens. Sounds travel far in this empty space. Some are natural: the whirling of water in the pipes, the whooshing of air in the ducts, the beeps and crackles of the switchboards. Some aren't. Like this long, dull sound of a copper gong. It resonates for a good half a minute, filling every corner, before fading away.

The ruckus, the rattle, the rumble of the wall
He'll know when it comes all the way
From the land of the shadows

Harvie stands up and walks in the direction the sound is coming from. It changes; no longer a gong, it sings a hollow song the way glasses do when you rub your finger against the rim in a circular motion.

Your eyes, your ears, your nose, your skin
Must too know the way of the shadows

A girl of about twelve sits squatted in the corner, mixing tea leaves into the pot. In the blue light coming from the grids her hair is almost white. The girl turns her head, and Harvie sees her own face.

Silent they come, but they make noise
Hidden they are, but they leave trail

Harvie points her gun into the girl's chest and shoots. They both scream. And scream. And scream. The scream bounces of the walls and ceiling and deafens Harvie. She can no longer hear.

The girl falls on the ground, her raven-black hair spread like a halo. Packstas run to her, and surround her in a circle edging Harvie away. Growler steps forward and bends down, touching the girl's chest?

"Min Li?"

He then stands up and shakes his head, not looking at Harvie.

Bone to bone.

Harvie pushes the packstas aside, and runs over to her friend, trying to wake her up. But Min Li's face is calm and peaceful, and only her lips are spread apart a notch, as if smiling.

Know it, and you will never have to go again
To the land of the shadows

22

Stan was falling through a funnel made of rustling paper in all possible shades of blue, from indigo to arctic sky, spinning on his way down. He wished he could stop spinning: it made his stomach wretch. He heard voices in the distance, loud and clear, but he couldn't make out what they were saying. All the words in the sentences seemed out of place. Finally he figured out one word. Someone called his name in a soft, low, unfamiliar voice.

The funnel started to dissolve, transforming into a spinning mosaic of coloured spots. He tried to focus on the largest of them, the one that seemed the most stable. Slowly it flew into focus. A face.

"Hey, Stanko," Rod said. "I knew you'd come back."

The spinning stopped. The voices had disappeared too; all that remained was a long monotone single-pitched beep.

"And you and me are gone again." Rod smiled with his signature carefree sixteen-year-old smile. "You're still looking good, Stanko."

"Not as good as you." Stan tried to take his mind off the distracting sound. "You haven't changed a bit."

"Being dead has its advantages." Rod's face sobered up; his cheeks fell in and the fluff-like stubble on his chin disappeared. Now he looked exactly the way Stan had remembered him last. "Did you miss me?"

"Occasionally." If Stan was going to be stuck with his old friend for the rest of eternity, he had to start this conversation on a right note. "You were kind of a son of a bitch, but the right kind."

"What about your wife? She never liked me."

"I think it was mutual." Stan smirked. "She's gone. We had a son together, but then she left."

"And you let her?" Rod shook his head. "That doesn't sound like you at all."

"You let Bel leave you. You and your daughter."

Rod's eyes chilled. "That was you who wanted her to leave. She *stayed*."

"I wanted her to *live*."

"You loved her, didn't you?" The strands of blonde hair fell across Rod's face. "All this time."

"No, not all this time. Not after I had my own child. You know how it changes things."

"No, I don't. It didn't change anything for *me*." Rod's face became unfamiliar; softer, more thoughtful. Stan didn't remember him like that. "Anyway, it's over now."

That Stan had already figured out. The beeping sound had disappeared and no other noises reached his ears, apart from Rod's ironic voice. "You know we had it coming."

"We did," Stan agreed.

"You know what's funny, Stanko?" Rod squinted. "It was

you who opened fire. But it was me who ended up the villain."

"What are you talking about, Flemming?" Stan shrugged. "You're a cult revolutionary out there. Short of having your face printed on T-shirts."

"Really?" Rod chuckled. "What we've become."

So this is what Hell is, Stan thought. *Being stuck face-to-face with your worst memory. Forever.*

"You know what Kato would have said?" Rod rubbed his chin. "*Shikata ga nai.*"

"Kato wasn't there," Stan squeezed through his teeth. "He doesn't have 20,000 ghosts visit him every night."

"You won't, either." Rod looked over Stan's head into the distance. "This too shall pass."

Indeed Stan felt sudden lightness, even joy, running through what once used to be his body. The weightlessness he hadn't felt in years, perhaps since the day he and Rod had closed the deal on *The Ranger*.

"That's the biggest perk of this place," Rod grinned. "You don't *remember.*"

But I don't want to forget them, Stan thought. *It's not fair.*

A small orange ball of fire burst in his chest, then the glow intensified, grew bigger, devouring him from inside. Rod moved a few steps back.

"I have to go. Someone else is here to see you." He stepped aside, letting forward a small woman with long blonde hair, all dressed in white. "Stan is here, Bel."

Stan felt his heart skip. Then again. As the figure in white drew closer, the skipping changed into a fast, steady thumping. Bel Dubois looked at him with a mix of sadness and surprise. The ball of fire in Stan's chest had gone and instead he felt like he was being wrapped, cocooned, absorbed and basked in a warm yellow glow.

Bel stretched her hand. Stan grabbed her fingers; they seemed smaller, almost a child's. "I'm sorry, Stan," she said and squeezed his hand. Stan looked into her eyes.

They were grey.

"I'm sorry," Harvie said again and wiped her nose with the sleeve of a white hospital gown.

"Hello, heartache," Stan whispered through a spasm in his throat. "What's new?"

***

"You are a very lucky man, Captain." The medic rubbed his tired eyes and adjusted a few settings on a sixteen-legged black metal spider, busy with boring its scalpels through Stan's chest. "Extremely lucky."

"I've been told that," Stan grunted. "Many times."

"Is that your daughter?" The medic pointed at Harvie, who sat motionless in a white mesh chair, nursing a glass of tepid water in her hands.

"Yes," Harvie said. Stan scanned the room for any sight of Arren, just in case. Nope. She was on her own and not intending to move. This was new.

"She looks like you." The medic nodded.

"Can't be," Stan looked at the clinking and whizzing spider with disgust and sighed. "I'm her foster parent."

"Well, she has your guts, that's for sure." The man bent down to check the stitches the mechanical beast had sewed in Stan's skin. "Did you know that the guys who attacked you had already murdered another cop earlier today?"

Stan squirmed and looked at Harvie. "Do you know anything about that?"

Harvie shook her head. "I didn't do it."

"Of course not." The doctor laughed and looked Harvie's small body frame up and down. "He had his skull crashed with a metal pipe. It would take a guy of your dad's size."

"Oh." Stan squinted and looked at Harvie with suspicion.

She shrugged. "He said *your* size."

"I have an alibi, just in case, you know." Stan grimaced as the spider pulled and tightened the web of blood-stained silver threads. "The owner of the Greek restaurant."

Harvie shut her eyes and exhaled.

"No worries, guys." The doctor laughed again. "The police already found the assault weapon. Fingerprints matched." He took the spider off Stan's chest and put a few strips of mediskin bandages over the wound in the centre, slightly to the left.

She had aimed for his heart, Stan thought. Right through, and she wouldn't have missed. Perhaps Arren had moved her hand just a tiny notch.

"Are you sure you don't want to stay at the hospital, Captain?" The doctor handed Stan his clothes, freshly washed, ironed and folded. "We could put you on a list for a regen treatment within twenty-four hours."

"No." Stan stood up and put his T-shirt on, noticing that the hole in the mole's left eyeglass had been neatly patched from inside with matching fabric. "I'll see a CNS medic on Monday. They have better equipment."

"Sure, Cap." The doctor nodded. "Our funding sucks. And now with all that ambient refurb I'm not sure we'll be getting anything more from the district. I shouldn't really discharge you that soon, after a cardiac arrest and everything, but…"

"I'll be fine." Stan rubbed his bandaged chest. "Still have about four or five lives left, I reckon." He looked at Harvie. "I'll settle the bill privately. Will sort it out with CNS later."

He let the doctor scan his UID and whispered into Harvie's ear. "I'm so getting this out of your pocket money, young lady." She twirled a crystal pendant hanging from her neck on a black string and grinned. Stan hadn't known she was into that kind of jewellery.

They went out of the hospital building and strolled towards the zerograv station along the street lit with bright night-time spotlights. The skylight was completely off and every highlighted building stood in sharp contrast against the black void.

"You aren't going to see a doctor at CNS, are you?" Harvie said.

Stan smirked. "Nope."

"It's going to hurt like shit, you know." Harvie looked at the white stripes of bandage under Stan's shirt. "Without the regen."

"Well, if this is what being a father means, it's worth it." Stan again rubbed the left side of his chest and squinted. "Anyway, it's over now."

The zerograv train whooshed and stopped at the edge of the platform. Stan got inside and headed to the seat in the corner, reluctant to cross glances with any of the passengers in the carriage. They sat down and he stared at the projection screens broadcasting the latest news. Arren's mugshot filled the screen. Stan focused on the running news ticker.

…18-year-old Arren Camargo charged with a lethal assault on a police officer. The suspect was found dead with a gunshot wound in the back of his head. The investigation continues.

"Shit," Stan said. "I'd say he had it coming, but…" He shook his head and grimaced again. "Way too young."

"Uh-huh." Harvie bit her lip and turned to the window.

"How did you meet that guy, anyway?" Stan leaned back in the seat and stretched his legs.

Harvie looked out of the train window at the silhouettes of Lower Croydon disappearing in a white milky mist.

"We played chess," she said and curled into a ball.

* * *

Harvie had fallen asleep on the train shortly before they arrived at the station. Stan wanted to wake her up, but changed his mind. He would only need to carry her across the platform to the lift, not a big deal. He had chosen his apartment with greater foresight than he had imagined, it seemed.

Stan turned his back to Harvie, put her arms on top of his shoulders and scooped up her legs. Harvie clutched his collar and dropped her head over, deep in sleep.

Stan stood up and groaned. She couldn't weigh more than fifty kilos, but still— Tiny red speckles were slipping through the bandage. Not good.

It will heal soon, he told himself. It all heals.

Stan managed to keep his steps steady all the way through the station to the lift, and almost to his floor. Then he stumbled through the doorway, unlocked the door without looking, and dropped Harvie on the floor in the lobby.

"We are home."

Harvie opened her eyes and looked around. "You shouldn't have—"

"That was small trouble; compared to everything else." He bent down and released her shoe straps, then slowly took them off. Harvie pulled her feet out as if the insoles were burning.

"What happened to your shoes?" Stan picked up the pair, stained and smeared all over with blots of dried-up blood, and shook his head.

"Nothing." Harvie's eyebrow bent in a defiant arch. Had she actually just given him sass?

"Looks like you've stepped into every puddle of muck in this city," Stan chuckled. "I'll get you Tim's old ones. He outgrew them years ago. He's a careful guy, so they are almost brand new."

Harvie rubbed her feet. "I kinda like mine, though. They fit well."

Stan put Harvie's shoes down. "I'll send these to get cleaned. Will be like new tomorrow." He helped Harvie stand up. "Let's get you settled."

Upstairs he handed Harvie a set of fresh bedding from the wardrobe and a bathroom kit. "Get some snooze." He leaned to the wall and grimaced. "Damn. This thing is really playing up."

"Stan, I…" Harvie hesitated.

"We'll talk tomorrow." Stan grabbed the stairway railing; the floor swayed under his feet. "I'll take some painkillers, should be in my drawer."

Stan waited for Harvie to close the door behind her and carefully stumbled to his bedroom, like a heavy drunk in the wee hours of the morning, then crashed onto his bed and closed his eyes.

So. Damn. Tired.

Something kept bothering him, as if he had left some unfinished business in Lower Croydon. He thought hard about what that could be. Vassilis? No, the Greek had long ago got used to Stan's sudden comings and goings without saying a word. 'As long as you remember to invite me to your funeral,' he used to say.

Stan squirmed, seeking a more comfortable posture on the bed. Once again it seemed that the wake had been postponed.

And then Stan realised: he still wished he'd seen Bel. Even for a fleeting moment, even if she was just an illusion of a distressed brain and no longer existed; not in any universe, not in any form.

He had lied to Rod, of course. Stan never stopped loving her. Not after he fell madly in love with Irina, like a schoolboy who'd lost all his gears after running into a specimen of the opposite gender. Not after he took Tim in his arms for the first time, breathing in the soft milky smell of a newborn boy. He could still sense this smell every time he occasionally stumbled over a box with Tim's old trinkets and toys and would blink hard.

Who said men don't cry? You just can't see their tears.

And not even after they walked with Rod through the streets of a dead city, and Stan felt his insides bleed every time he caught sight of a white body bag. The clean-up crew combed the station for the desiccated bodies before the flagship cruiser arrived, and put them into neat stacks of white bags. Rows and rows of white bags.

Whatever Stan had in his heart capable of feeling had died that day. Or so he hoped, until one night he had woken up in a room full of ghosts.

But he still loved Bel. Was it wrong to have so much love in one man's heart?

Stan checked the time. 3:58 a.m. He sat up and commanded the blinds open. He had chosen this apartment carefully, one of a precious few that had a balcony with a view to a real outside. The swollen disc of the Earth hung in the horizon, a mix of cobalt and cerulean blues, with long white smudges over the masses of green and orange; a torn pancake of Australia, a curly, broken banana of New Zealand. Stan turned the globe in his head to see the shapes of the Old World, not visible from geostationary Universum.

"I think Tim should see that letter," he heard Harvie say from the doorway.

Stan sighed, stood up and opened the drawer, looking for the blister with the painkillers.

"Here." Harvie handed him the pack she held in her hand. "They were in the bathroom. I took a couple last night, but there are still a few left."

"Thanks." Stan popped out two white pills, then added another one, to be sure, and gulped them down.

"I'll call him tomorrow," he said. "It's late there now."

"Only one hour ahead." Harvie took a comms pod from Stan's desk and handed it to him. "Do it. I'll talk."

Tim showed no signs of being woken up. He sat in his rocking chair with a sketch pad in his lap, biting the dull end of a pencil. He looked at Harvie with surprise and said nothing, only took the pencil out of his mouth and clutched both ends.

"Can you come here?" Harvie said.

"Why?" Tim leaned back, and squinted, as if measuring her up for a drawing.

"Your father needs you."

Stan tried to suppress a sudden burst of cough that felt like an alien beast trying to dig its way out of his chest cavity.

"What happened?" Tim tilted his head so he could see Stan, lurking at the edge of the transmission capture zone. "Is he sick?"

"He got shot," Harvie looked Stan straight in the eye, "because of me."

"Harvie, that's—" The beast spat another portion of acid and dug its claws into the goo that had once been Stan's lungs. Stan reached for the pill box and opened the last blister.

"Stan, I said I'll talk." Harvie sat down on the edge of the bed and continued. "I'd got into a situation, and your father saved me."

"Then it looks like he's doing just fine." Tim drummed a beat with the pencil against his left index finger. "Why do you want me to come?"

"I need a friend," Harvie said. "I don't want to get into any more trouble here. It's like another planet to me."

Tim twirled the pencil again then put it in front of his eyes, like a little boy playing on an imaginary spaceship. He dropped it onto his lap.

"Your father and mine once destroyed a civilian town," he said. "Did you know that?" He looked straight at Harvie. "They sieged it and threatened to blow up the main oxygen supply reactor if the council didn't open the docking gates within twenty-four hours. When the deadline passed, they didn't change their minds." Tim caught his breath and continued. "The governor had ordered to open the gates but it was too late. Only about five thousand people managed to evacuate, out of twenty-five."

"Yes, I've read about it," Harvie said. "The town of Saudade."

Every kid knows the word nowadays, Stan thought. Hardly a name out there more appropriate for what had become the largest one-time civilian loss in the whole history of the Separation War.

Saudade: a longing for the people and places that are lost and will never return.

"And you're cool with it, are you?" Tim squinted. "Well, I'm not."

Harvie pulled her legs to her chest and put her chin on top.

"I don't know how my father would feel about it right now," she said. "He's not here to tell me. But yours is."

"I know how he feels about it," snapped Tim. The pencil rolled down from his lap onto the floor. "What I don't know is why he never talks to me about it."

"Maybe you should give him another chance." Harvie put her legs down.

"I gave him plenty of chances. I stayed at his place for four weeks every year and all we talked about were school grades and sport." Tim bent over the pad, picked the pencil up and put it between the pages. "Whatever he feels about his past, I'm apparently not worthy of him sharing it with."

Stan had kept silent long enough. He pressed his right arm to his chest to keep the beast inside and moved into the transmission zone, checking in a side screen that Tim could clearly see his face.

"You want to know how I feel?"

Tim's face was calm, not confrontational. "Yes."

"If I could bring back just a single person out of those 20,000, even if it would cost me my own life, I'd do it right here and now. But I can't."

The beast, finished with Stan's lungs, went on crushing his ribcage. He should lie down, Stan thought.

"I can't bring my friends back either." Stan had to wrench each word out of the beast's claws. "And I can't stop missing them."

"You mean missing her mother." Tim pointed the pencil at Harvie.

"Yes, I loved her mother. But I loved yours too." Stan edged back on the bed and leaned against the wall. Harvie moved the pod closer to him so he still stayed within the catch zone.

"I've seen Mum's letter," Tim said. "Long ago. I should have told you about it."

"No," Stan shook his head. "I should have told you something long ago." He studied Tim's face with a sudden chilling realisation of how much the boy had grown. How had he not noticed this? "In my whole life I've had only one true love, the kind that makes you want to change the world to make sure that your loved one is safe and happy. And that's *you*."

The pencil once again rolled onto the floor but this time it didn't look accidental. Tim bent down, trying to fetch it.

"Tim? Why are you crying?" Jem's head appeared in the foreground. "What happened, Uncle Stan? Why is he crying?"

"It's nothing, Jem." Stan heard Tim sniff. "Why are you up so early? It's Sunday." Stan realised that the time had already flown past what could have been considered a late night.

"I want to talk to the space girl!" Jem waved his hand and froze. "Hi. I'm down here."

"And I'm up here," Harvie replied.

"Cool." Jem made a quick succession of finger figures and stopped.

"Sixty-one," Harvie said. "The next prime, descending order."

"Is that some kind of code?" Stan looked at both of them in turn. Both shook their heads and shrugged.

"I'm going up there," Jem said. Like a done deal.

Tim sighed. "Okay, Jem. I'll talk to Mum." He flipped his sketch-pad pages and Stan caught a glimpse of a few phantasmagoric floating cities, suspended in mid-air.

"What if she says no?" Without much ado Jem opened the sketch pad. "I like this one!"

"Then I'll get Dad on my side, as always." Tim took the pad

from Jem's hands and tucked it between heavy volumes of old art books. "Stan? If we book the tickets for Monday, will you meet us at the port?"

Stan nodded. "As always."

"That's it." Harvie hung up and put the pod down. "You'll have your son back here. If this is what you really want."

Maybe the fourth pill finally worked, or maybe the beast had decided to call it a day and retreated back to its nest in Stan's abdominal cavity, but the chest pain was finally almost tolerable. Stan thought that he might even face some breakfast downstairs in the kitchen. He stood up and put his arm around Harvie's shoulders.

"No, what I want most of all is for Rod and Bel to be here now. To see what you've become. I'm sure they'd be proud."

Or maybe they are here, Stan thought, *who knows?* One day he would know for sure, but not today. Not yet.

Harvie sniffed and looked up. "I—" She sniffed again. *"Gomennasai,"* she whispered. *I'm sorry.*

Stan put his palms on her shoulders and looked into the girl's face. Yes, they were both there: Rod, Bel. And they would always be, as long as their stubborn girl lived.

"C'mon." Stan pressed his thumb to her cheek and wiped off a faint streak of moisture. "You're the Commander's daughter, Harvie. You can't be crying."

The End

COLIN MOERDYKE

BOOK TWO

HARVIE

THE HOLIDAY OF A LIFETIME

The Holiday of a Lifetime
By Colin Moerdyke

Universum Publishing

"DON'T TAKE ME FOR A FOOL!
SHE'S THE KID YOU ALWAYS WANTED."
STAN & TIM

Sunday morning in the Rostokin-Nielsen family didn't go as planned. It started out just fine, the smell of ground coffee and fresh pastry mixing with the usual family chit-chat and banter that drowned out the hushed humming of the news channel. A monotone voice of a vidcast lecturer delivered advanced mathematical insights on a screen that hovered above the head of a toy tortoise occupying the spot at the middle of the breakfast table. But it soon ended, as it often did, with the two adults getting into an argument, while their sons, Tim Rostokin and Jem Nielsen, nibbled on their cereal and milk, pretending to be numb, deaf, and blind.

"What are you so fussy about?" Ian Nielsen, Tim's stepfather, pushed his glasses up to the top of his long, slender nose. They slid right back down. "Stan is a very reasonable man. Aren't you rushing to conclusions?" He patted his wife's shaking hand. "Look, we planned it all six months ago; I've already arranged the funding, the team! If we don't do the field research this summer, we may just as well leave the village underground for another

4,000 years. Do you want me to tell Santiago: 'No, Bill, we are not going because Irina is having a riff-ruff with her ex?'"

"It's not a riff-ruff and we still can go." Tim's mother, Irina's, face looked drained, with dark circles over her eyes. She had aged a couple of years overnight, Tim thought. "Gran can take the kids for a few weeks."

"We are supposed to leave tomorrow. My mother lives in Mexico." Ian pulled a fresh set of plates out of the dishwasher and began to arrange them on a round wooden table. "And you're dumping this all on me today."

"We can get a childminder," Irina sighed. "Anything."

"Anything but Stan, who, by the way, still has partial custody over Tim and pays both boys' school fees."

"We can manage without his money." Irina looked at her husband. "Can't we?"

"How? Go back to octalon trade?" Ian smirked and took four tea mugs out of the cupboard. "We're blessed with two bright boys who unfortunately or fortunately have very expensive academic inclinations. I can't quite turn to Stan and say, 'Thanks for your check, pal, shame you can't see the kids!'"

"I know." Irina 's voice verged on tears. "I can't let them go. Not while she's there."

"What do you have against that girl?" Ian ran his fingers through his thinning red hair.

"Everything! Her father ran away from home when he was sixteen and took Stan with him to start a space gang. She grew up on a battleship, and then God knows what happened, and now Stan is fostering her as an alternative to jail. Is that not enough?"

Tim and Jem exchanged glances. The younger boy's eyes shone with excitement.

"Boys," Ian said, looking at Jem. "Would you go to your rooms, please?"

"No." Jem made circles in his bowl with a spoon, sending the soggy cornflakes spinning. "Andy has not finished his breakfast yet." The tortoise nodded, as if in agreement, and changed the lecture subject to particle physics.

"Andy can eat upstairs," Ian persisted. "Tim?"

That's it, Tim thought with a sinking feeling. Now or never.

"I promised Stan that we'd come tomorrow," he said, avoiding his mother's eyes. "Sorry, Mom."

"You didn't." Irina exhaled. "You said you didn't want to go. Not this year, not ever. What happened?"

"I thought about it more and changed my mind." Tim looked around, hoping to come up with a plausible lie. "I think Dad is right. It wouldn't be fair to Stan. I still have another year left at the Academy—"

"You're getting a scholarship for your last year. Your mentor confirmed it two days ago. I didn't tell you because we wanted to make it a surprise." Irina shook her head. "Your father just ruins everything."

"A scholarship?" Jem left the cornflakes in peace for a second. "Wow."

Tim felt the ground under his feet tilt as if he were already on a spaceship. That explained everything: Augusta's call to his mom, her words that Tim's work "is not competitive enough," her constant nitpicking on him in the past semester. Just twenty-four hours ago this news would've meant everything to Tim. The world. The Universe.

But it didn't any more. Not after what Stan had said to him when they talked last night.

In my whole life I only had one and only true love, the kind that makes you want to change the world... you.

"He's still my father," Tim said, standing up. "Squirrel?" He pulled Jem's sleeve. "Let's take Andy upstairs, I've got a new code patch for him from Marat, he says you'll love it."

Jem didn't move. "I want to go to Universum."

"We can go another time, honey," Irina said. "We don't have to stay at Uncle Stan's.

"But I want to see the Space Girl!" Jem finally lifted his gaze off Andy's screen. "Dad?"

"I'll talk to Mom, Squirrel." Ian took his glasses off and rubbed them with a paper napkin, leaving them even more smudged. "Can you go to your room now?"

"Only if she says 'yes.'" Jem shrugged and rubbed Andy's head, launching another screen with a string of code.

"C'mon, Irina." Ian tried to force a smile. That was another thing Tim and his step-father shared, apart from the love of old books: they both sucked at pretending. "When was the last time Jem was interested in another human being?"

"I'm not sure Harvie Flemming is human," Irina snapped.

"Honey." Ian lowered his voice. "I'm sure she's a perfectly ordinary teenager."

"I've said 'no' and that is final." Irina clenched her fist. "Call Santiago, tell him I'm opting out this year. He has plenty of grad students to do this job."

The adventure continues with *The Holiday of A Lifetime.*

www.ingramcontent.com/pod-product-compliance
Lightning Source LLC
Chambersburg PA
CBHW032000050726
47590CB00006B/1991